Beyond the Arc

THE STARTING LINEUP SERIES

MONET SIMONE

Table of Contents

Chapter One

INDIRA

The stench of old drywall and decades-old sweat hit me the moment I stepped inside. The front door barely stayed on its hinges, the living room ceiling had water damage, and the kitchen cabinets looked like they hadn't seen a sponge since Bush was in office—the first Bush. But to me? It was beautiful.

My general contractor, Asim Draper, shook his head as he stepped into the foyer, boots squishing against the waterlogged floorboards. He eyed the ceiling and scratched at his beard. "You really think you can flip this in eight weeks?"

"If the city doesn't drag its feet with permits."

He snorted. "They will. Historic district? That means two rounds of approvals and some bitter-ass inspector looking for a reason to shut you down."

I didn't slow down. Just stepped over the mess and opened the dining room window to let the funk out.

"You knew that and didn't say anything?"

"I didn't know until yesterday. They just added the zone last quarter. Slid it into a memo like we read those things for fun."

I exhaled through my nose. "Then we go around them."

He arched a brow. "Meaning?"

"Meaning I'll make the calls. Find someone who knows someone. We're not stalling."

"Hope that someone fixes this foundation, too. You're looking at a money pit."

I turned toward him. "Then I'll fill it. Brick by brick if I have to."

He chuckled under his breath. "You don't pay me enough to lose sleep over your ambition, Indy."

"That's why I don't ask you to."

His words were a reminder that when shit went sideways, I was the one who had to hold the line.

I nodded anyway. "Get the demo crew lined up. We're not stalling. Not yet."

As he walked off, I stood in the middle of the busted living room, phone already in my hand, scrolling through contacts.

I wasn't panicked. Yet.

But my chest was already squeezing with that familiar tightness. Once again, I was on my own, solving life's problems.

Another fight I hadn't planned. Another battle I'd have to win alone.

I inhaled deeply, trying to control my excitement. This long-awaited day had finally arrived. The crew had sailed through repairs, demo, and rehab. The punch list and inspection were done yesterday. There was just landscaping and a final cleaning left. Then I'd head to the open house to showcase this spectacular property. I was more than prepared to reap my profits with a quick sale.

I couldn't have been prouder of this accomplishment. The naysayers insisted it would take me four months to flip, but my team had pulled it off in less than ninety days. Given that this was only my third house flip, I'd say three months with minimal cost overruns and few surprises was an A+ effort. I only hoped the purchase offers would come in just as fast and furious.

I pulled my Ford Flex in front of the four-bedroom cul-de-sac home. I couldn't help but frown when I spotted a caravan of SUVs parked along the tree-lined perimeter. The only truck I expected to see belonged to Asim. He should've been here awaiting his final payment; maybe the cleaning crew was still on-site. Instead, I recognized a fleet of vehicles from the landscaping company—including a dump truck.

I slid out from behind the steering wheel, eager to see the ornamental grasses and shrubs. With a bounce, I passed the trucks, and the front yard came into view. Suddenly, my feet froze mid-stride. For a second, I thought I was dreaming. Nope. The bewildering scene was real.

Instead of vibrant green grass, the yard oozed brown marsh. My eyes darted in disbelief. A lone pallet of sod sat at the top of the driveway like an apology.

"What in the entire fuck!"

"I know. I know! Indy, please don't panic." Asim appeared, jogging toward me. "Let me explain."

"It's Ms. James to you," I snapped, struggling to stay calm.

I scanned the mess, frustration bubbling. On any other day, I might've taken a moment to admire his thick frame and jackhammer arms. Not today.

"Ace, this better be good."

"The sprinkler system kicked on some time last night," he explained, hands up like I was about to throw a punch.

"What sprinkler system?"

"Hidden under the overgrowth. The new crew didn't know it was there."

"So, they didn't till or lay topsoil like we agreed?"

"They did. Just a different crew, no communication. By the time we showed up this morning, it was too late."

I exhaled slowly. "So now what?"

"Trenching, topsoil, sod. They're on it. We'll fix it."

"Before tomorrow?"

"Yes. My word is bond."

"Then I'll hold onto your check until I see the results."

He nodded. "Fair."

"Anything else I should know before I walk inside?"

"Everything else is good. Trust me."

Trust? Nah. I could count on one hand the people I trusted, and none of them were on my payroll.

I had to admit, flipping a house in three months while juggling my full-time real estate hustle was ambitious as hell—maybe even reckless. I'd done renovations before, but the market had allowed more wiggle room. Not this time.

I had to move fast. Even if the market were slower, I still would've pushed hard. That's just how I'm wired. Hustle. Grind. Repeat.

TWO DAYS EARLIER

"I need you to meet me at the house."

"Right now? I'm on the other side of town," I said, frowning.

"How fast can you get there then? I'll wait." My sister-friend Cairo Clayton sounded frantic.

"I just had a showing and have another client in two hours. Is everything okay?"

"Not really," she admitted.

"Alright then, CeeCee," I said, referring to her by her nickname. "I was going to grab lunch in between, but I'll starve for you, big head."

"Ma'Dear has something on the stove you can eat. Push your other client back and meet me in thirty."

I can never repay the debt I owe Ma'Dear — whose government name is Ida Mae — and her sister Mildred for taking me under their wing after Granny passed. The Sisters, as we affectionately called them, took me in shortly after Cairo came to live with them. I was

4

fourteen, lonely as hell, and they never made me feel like I didn't belong. For that reason alone, I'd do anything they asked.

I had barely trudged up the walkway when Cairo started her mess.

"Damn, girl, that purse is bigger than you!"

"CeeCee, don't you talk about my Neverfull! I worked hard to earn this bag."

"Yeah, well, I don't think Louis Vuitton designed it for people small enough to climb inside."

"Shut yo' ass up! You got me out here fooling with you, and I'm losing money. What in the world is so urgent that I had to piss off my client?"

"I have to go up against The Sisters, and I need moral support."

Annoyed, I slung my bag over my shoulder. "For what?"

"Our plan for Zahara to go to FCD fell through."

I gasped. "Why? How? We've been planning for so long." Farmington Country Day wasn't just another prep school. The Sisters wanted her to have a strong academic foundation, and CeeCee and I knew the athletics program was top-notch.

"I know we have, but let's break the news before Zee gets home from school."

When she opened the front door, I brushed past CeeCee, making a beeline for the kitchen. Just as I expected, there was a large pot on the stove. To my delight, one of my favorite meals was simmering.

I wasted no time helping myself to a bowl, making sure not to skimp on the chicken, sausage, and seafood. Before heading upstairs, I dipped a spoon into the gumbo, blew on it, and sampled the savory stew. "Hot damn," I whispered, letting the flavors linger. This more than compensated for my missed lunch.

When I reached the upper level, I found everyone where I'd expected. Ma'Dear sat in her wheelchair by the window overlooking the backyard. Next to her was an end table with the remote control, a rotary phone, and a glass of her iced tea, brewed fresh in gallons every Saturday. Aunt Millie, in her La-Z-Boy, had her own side table

— orange juice (probably spiked with vodka, unbeknownst to Ma'Dear) and a Sudoku puzzle book she swore kept her mind sharp.

"Hey, baby. I see you got yourself some gumbo and cornbread."

"Yes, Ma'Dear. You all must have known I was coming."

"I got up early to make that just for you," Aunt Millie boasted.

"You put your foot in this. Mmm. So good," I said with a smack of my lips. "You haven't made it like this with crab claws and big fat shrimp in a minute. What's the special occasion?"

That got a chuckle out of Ma'Dear. "Girl, hush. Ain't no occasion, but I know you better take that bowl out o' here and act like I taught you some sense. Go on and eat at the table."

"That was the last spoonful," I whined, scraping the remnants clean.

"You're lucky," Ma'Dear snapped. "Now I'm surprised we're getting both of you at one time. Seems like we haven't been together as a family in a month of Sundays."

"Oh, leave 'em be, Ida. You know they're busy," Aunt Millie said, sipping her drink. "So, what brings you by together?"

CeeCee chewed her lip. "I have bad news, and I wanted to share it while Zahara's not here."

"What's wrong, Cee?" Aunt Millie asked, brow furrowed. "You okay? You're not sick, are you, Baby?"

"There you go, always thinking the worst. Let the girl talk," Ma'Dear scolded, nodding at CeeCee to go on.

"Zahara won't be able to go to Farmington Country Day in the fall."

"Why not?" The Sisters exclaimed in unison.

"It comes down to money. She got a partial athletic scholarship, but that's it."

"I thought she wouldn't have to pay if you worked there," Aunt Millie said.

"I thought so, too, Auntie," CeeCee replied, explaining the tuition policy change. "We'll be short fifteen to twenty thousand."

"You've got to be shittin' me."

"Millie!" Ma'Dear shot her sister a sharp look.

"What, Ida? That's a lot of money. We don't have that lying around."

"No one's asking you to pay it," I said quickly.

"So, there's nothing else we can do?" Aunt Millie pressed.

CeeCee shook her head. "Not before the deadline. And if we miss that, we lose her spot."

I didn't say anything more, but I already knew what I was going to do. As soon as I got my next commission check, I'd cover at least the first semester. Family — the real kind — didn't let each other's dreams fall through.

By the time I left The Sisters' house, the gumbo had settled into a warm weight in my belly, but my mind was restless. I still had another showing before the day was done, and there was no telling what fresh chaos my clients might bring.

Chapter Two

MALIK

I stepped from my car into the dimly lit parking structure tucked beneath The Heights, the newest tower to dwarf Detroit's aged skyline. I'd been in the building numerous times, given that it also housed the offices of Blaise Harrington, my agent, and his brother, Bryce, my money manager. I couldn't think of a single visit when I was as tired as I was today.

As I made my way to the elevator bank, I glanced at my Patek Philippe. It was already after 11:00, which meant there was no way my fatigued ass would make it to bed before midnight. I dreaded admitting I was getting older, but it was true.

My career was taking its toll—the long days, travel, injuries, all of it. Once upon a time, my goal was to stay in the league for twenty years. I must have been smoking some good shit back then. This was year fifteen, and I didn't know if I had another season in me. I wasn't over the hill yet, but I was about to knock on thirty-five's door.

I entered the studio to the sounds of heavy bass and rhythmic beats. Immediately, I spotted my dog, Desmond Cole Montague (DC), bobbing his head to the music as he puffed on a stogie. I couldn't help but grin. He appeared relaxed and at ease. I was proud of him for launching such a successful podcast so soon after his NBA retirement.

Extending my hand, I greeted him Detroit style. "What up, doe, DC."

"What up, doe," he returned, bumping his fist against mine. "Grab a seat."

I dropped onto the leather sectional across from him and glanced around. Sports memorabilia lined the walls, most of it repping Detroit basketball. All the greats were featured, including the OGs from the Bad Boys era, like Isiah Thomas and Dennis Rodman, and other Hall of Famers like Ben Wallace and Grant Hill. It didn't matter that Desmond's later years in the league were spent playing for the Virginia Victors. My dude knew his roots.

"Nice studio," I remarked. "I can see you're legit. Congratulations."

"Much love, Malik. And it means a lot to me that you came through tonight. I know you're ready to hit the sheets."

"Hell yeah," I chuckled. "You remember how it was. Trying to ensure you get at least eight hours so your body recuperates to do it all over again."

"I sure do," DC nodded emphatically. "That's why my ass is retired now."

We laughed in unison before it dawned on me that it was just us. "What? No co-host tonight?"

"Nah, your boy Diesel had another commitment. Besides, I don't need help kicking it with my day one." DC explained. "You ready to get started?"

I glanced at my watch and knew that was a rhetorical question. I was more than ready. "Do your thang."

Desmond exchanged a few words with the producers before launching into his routine. "Welcome back to your favorite basketball show, *Moneyball*, and I'm your host, DC Montague. We have a close friend and a future Hall-of-Famer in the house. You don't want to miss this. And you want to tune in tomorrow, too, when we'll cele-brate our hundredth live episode."

With excitement, I chimed in. "Shout out to the Moneyball Mob?"

Desmond chuckled. "Malik, man, let me finish with my sweet introduction."

"Bet," I raised my hands in surrender as DC commenced.

"He's the two-time champion and three-time All-Star. I also can't forget that he's the reigning NBA MVP, and some say he's poised to receive the prestigious honor again. He's also a two-time Olympic winner. The resume is crazy! Malik Latimer, aka L-Train, is in the building, y'all!"

Humbled, I pounded my chest. "I appreciate you for having me. I'm honored."

"Man, the pleasure is all mine. Thanks for fitting me in. I know you're a busy man," DC quipped.

"Shiiit. It's a long season, man, but I can't lay down yet. I have to get this ring. But before we get into it, I must give you *your* flowers. You clinched your MVP and Olympic titles and got *three* rings. Yo, I'm just trying to level up."

Desmond shook his head, amused. "But I'm living that retired life. I'm chilling, but you still have a few games before the Playoffs start. How you feeling?"

I was relieved he started with an easy question, so I didn't hesi-tate to answer. "I'm feeling good. Really good. Our team is resilient. We're laser-focused on what we do well and play team basketball on both ends of the floor, so I think we're unstoppable."

"That's what's up. You know I'll be watching."

"I appreciate that," I replied sincerely. "I know you're always in my corner. Shout out to Malcolm, too." I replied, referencing my twin brother.

"You, Malc, and I go way back, since Hally Middle School."

"Shit, we been thick as thieves for more than twenty years. And we can't forget JB," I added, referring to Jarvis Bentley, our mutual friend and my current teammate.

For a few minutes, we chopped it up about the shenanigans the four of us—me, Malcolm, Desmond, and Jarvis—got into. We were inseparable, and if I'm being honest, mischievous as fuck. It was a miracle, really, that we all made it to the league. I mean, what were the odds?

Yeah, we started hooping while our bikes still had training wheels, but still…Only divine favor could explain our mutual success. A memory came to mind that I just had to share.

"DC, do you remember the time I got my hands on that smoke grenade and let it off in the house?"

"Do I?" Desmond howled with laughter and slapped the arm of his club chair. "Man, it took your sister Jackie like two hours to find you, and when she did, she beat your ass!"

"Sure did. I knew it was a wrap when she pulled me from behind Daddy's recliner! And you know, when my parents got home, Mama whooped me again!"

"Yeah, you were so bad; Malcolm took the rap half the time just to give your behind a break from Mrs. Latimer's leather belt."

"He did. That's my guy. My day one. And not just because we're twins. Malc has always had my back. Always wanted the best for me."

"Malik, speaking of Malcolm, I gotta ask—when are we gonna get him on here? The man stays grinding like we're still eighteen and broke."

I chuckled. "We both know that ain't true. He's an up-and-coming chef, pulling in more money than he'll admit. And he's allergic to the spotlight, which is fine by me—it means I can finally be the good-looking one in the family."

Desmond laughed. "Chef, huh? Guess Mama's proud of both her boys."

"Oh, definitely," Malik said. "But Marlane Latimer don't mince words when it's time to let her sons know what's what. Right now, she's on me about thinking beyond basketball."

Desmond leaned in. "Oh, yeah? You thinking coaching? Broadcasting? Opening a soul food joint?"

Malik smiled, but it didn't quite reach his eyes. "Let's just say I've been making some moves off the court. Basketball won't last forever, and I want to be ready for what's next. Something I can build on."

Desmond raised a brow. "You talking retirement?"

"I don't know about that, but Mama won't stop talking about grandkids." Malik said, shaking his head. "She wants 'em yesterday. Already told me I'm falling behind."

Desmond laughed. "So she's harassing both you and Malcolm equally?"

"Hell, yeah." I confirmed. "She's got a timeline and everything. I think she'd send out invitations if she could."

"Word. I know how that is. My mama is no different." We caught up for the next few minutes, checking in on our family before Desmond switched gears on me.

"So, we have our followers in the chat, who want me to ask you a question. But you might tell me to mind my business."

I snickered. "I might, but when I agreed to come on, I planned to keep it one hundred with you and your listeners. So go for it."

"A'ight. You mentioned that your mama is pushing you to think about life after the league. But inquiring minds want to know how you made it fifteen years in the NBA without wifing up or having kids?"

My eyes mushroomed. "Dog, are you kidding me? You managed to do the same thing? You can probably answer that question as well as me."

Desmond shook his head, smiling. "Yo, I know. We're both unicorns."

"Not really; it's a myth that everybody else is married with kids. Hell, less than half the players are married."

"Yeah, ML, but that includes all the rookies; some are barely nineteen. Let's be honest. Most old heads like us have settled by the time they're at the end of their career. I let one get away, and I'm still trying to figure out how to rein her in. But that's my story? I'm sure the ladies who listen want to know why you're still solo."

Here we go. Before any interview, I'm prepared for this question. In today's day and age of social media, everyone's life is under a microscope. And for us professional athletes, it's no different. Fans feel entitled to a sneak peek into our lives. It comes with the territory.

Let me get this over with.

"I don't know if there's a story, really. I had a girl, my college sweetheart, when I joined the league. I thought we would get married, but things didn't work out that way…"

"I can't imagine being in a serious relationship when I started my career. I can't lie. I was like a kid in a candy store," DC admitted, cracking a smile.

"Shiiit, but it's true I'm not married, no kids. I'm just focused on my career."

"I get that," DC related. "The question I always used to get was, 'Don't you get lonely?'"

"For sure. I've heard that a million times. And I ain't gon' lie. Sometimes, when you come off a long road trip, it would be nice to have someone waiting on you who's your ride or die. You know. To tell you that your game was trash, but still lick your wounds until you feel better."

"I can relate," DC cosigned. "You think you're ready to sign up for that?"

I shrugged. "I mean, I'm not going to go hunting for it, but if I walk into it or it falls in my lap, hell, I'll embrace it. A brother ain't getting no younger."

"That's what's up. If it happens, I'll have to have you back on the show."

"We can do that," I consent while resisting the urge to glance at the time.

"Alright, bruh, before I let you go, I see you rocking the new gear. Congratulations on joining forces with the Valet brand. You got the new collab with the *Malice* luxury streetwear."

"DC, man, I'm just walking in your footsteps. I know you signed with them recently, too. I'm just trying to be in good company."

"Thanks. Maybe we'll do a joint campaign. But for now, I'll let you go so you can catch those Z's and put on a great show for us tomorrow."

So, I didn't make it back home by midnight, but I climbed behind the steering wheel at 12:15, which was good enough. If I were going to show up in the morning for the team breakfast, I wouldn't quite get my eight hours, but I could always forfeit a few rounds of video games and nap later.

I cranked up my Dodge Charger Demon, ready to head to my condo, when the low fuel warning light flashed on the dashboard. *Shit.* I groaned and smacked the steering wheel.

How could I let my tank get to E? The last thing I wanted to do was stop in downtown Detroit for gas, especially without security. I wasn't trying to be anyone's target, so I made it a point to drive my low-key car instead of my Range Rover or Maybach. Irritated, I had no choice but to pull up to the nearby Speedway.

The station was well-lit, making it easy to scan the premises before I cut my engine. Fortunately, it was a weeknight, so there wasn't a bunch of riffraff out and about. Instantly, I spotted the infamous green light. Detroiters knew these flashing beacons were real-time surveillance cameras linked to the police department. But I also knew, just as well as the station's other patrons, they weren't necessarily a crime deterrent.

As I climbed from my ride, so did the driver in front of me. To my surprise, it was a curvy, petite woman in fitted blue jeans, a cropped hoodie, and Timberlands. She was a short distance away, but not so much that I couldn't make out her features.

Her hair was cut short and close in the back, but longer in the front, all soft and feathery. She didn't look like one of those women who hid behind long flowing hair. She was confident as hell, using her crown like a spotlight. Radiant pecan skin, almond eyes, and sky-high cheekbones came into view when her head swiveled to study her surroundings.

Smart lady, I thought. At least smart enough to have situational awareness, but...probably not smart enough to be out here alone. Before I could stop myself, I called out: "Should you be out here by yourself?"

Her neck whipped in my direction, and her eyes narrowed with reservation. "I'm fine," she returned and focused her attention on the gas pump.

"I can see you're fine, beautiful actually," I gestured toward her, "but there's plenty of lunatics that will take advantage of a woman out here alone."

She turned her full lips up at me, displaying her doubt. "Yeah, well, I got all the smoke if that's what they want." Without hesitation, she pulled a Springfield Hellcat from her waistband.

Shit. I didn't see that coming, but I should have. The number of women with concealed pistol licenses in Detroit was astronomical. "Okay, Shortie. I see you. But do you know how to use that?"

Her brows spiked high. "You want to fuck around and find out?"

I threw my hands up in self-defense. "Nah, I believe you. And if I might add, I'm impressed. Gotta be able to defend yourself against these fools."

She revealed a slight smile, pulling those gorgeous cheekbones even higher, before steeling her face again. "You damn right. For all I know, you're an axe murderer yourself."

"Who me?"

"Yeah, you. If not that, maybe you run a human trafficking ring. Hell, I don't know. But I do know that I don't make it a habit of talking to strangers." With that, she yanked the nozzle from her truck and returned it to the pump.

Was she serious? Did she really not know who I was? For a moment, I was speechless. I was accustomed to being recognized nearly everywhere I went, especially in Detroit. Maybe she didn't follow sports?

I was struggling through my wounded feelings and returning the nozzle to the gas dispenser when she called out. "I'm just shittin' you!"

My head swung in her direction. "What you say?"

"I know who you are. I think."

"You do?" My brows rose as she shrugged.

"You're friends with Desmond, right?"

"You know my dude DC?" Suddenly, my chest felt lighter.

"I do. He's close to Cairo, my sister. Well, she's not actually my sister —"

"Wait. Have we met before? I think I would definitely remember you if we had."

She wrinkled her button nose and pursed her perfectly symmetrical lips. She was so damn cute, I had to pull my eyes from her mouth.

"We haven't been formally introduced, no. But I think we've been at some of the same functions, like parties."

"So, then you know I'm not an axe murderer?"

"The jury is still out on that." She smiled at me, and my heart damn near turned to pudding.

"Dang, girl." I crossed my arms. "You know how to kill an ego."

"My bad," she thrust her hand my way. "I'm Indira James. I go by Indy."

"Pleased to officially meet you, Indy. I'm Malik Latimer."

"Malik Latimer?" She tilted her head to the side. "Sounds familiar. I don't know why."

"Are you pulling my leg again, or are you serious?"

Indy's eyes widened. "No, I'm serious. I recognize your face, but I wouldn't have connected your name. Should I have?"

I frowned. My ego felt like it had been in a fight with Floyd Mayweather. "Maybe. Did you ever attend any of DC's games?"

She nodded. "Cairo used to drag me to a few back when he played for Detroit."

"That could be where you heard my name. I was his teammate."

"Oh, word?" She flashed that pretty smile of hers. "Maybe that's it."

Maybe? Not to mention dozens of local commercials over the years. I kept that to myself. "I know my dude retired from the Victors, but I'm still with Detroit. You and Cairo should check us out. That is, if she doesn't have to drag you."

Now she was smiling even wider, and her lashes fluttered. *Sexy as hell.*

"Are you flirting with me, Malik Latimer?"

"Yeah, I guess you can say I'm trying to shoot my shot with your fine ass."

Her eyebrows flew up, and we locked gazes. I didn't dare back down either, even when she dropped her eyes to study her attire. "What? Indy, you know you look good. It doesn't matter what you're wearing."

"How can you possibly think jeans and Timbs are attractive?"

"Shiitt. Easy. I see that small waist, nice hips, and I bet if you turn around—"

"Hey!" She raised her hand in protest. "We just met. You can't be commenting on my assets. Not to my face anyway!"

"Okay, well, I'll just go home and dream about them. Is that better?" Seeing her scrunch her face, I revisited my earlier proposition. "So can I give you my number so I can arrange to get you some tickets?"

"I don't know about that."

"Why the hell not?" I snapped, feeling rejected.

"I don't do ballers," she shrugged.

"I didn't ask you to *do* me. Yet."

"I bet you think that's cute."

"I just asked you to come to a game. Maybe we can kick it after." Noting the cynicism in her pursed lips, I sighed. It was getting late, and I had an empty bed waiting for me, which was fine with me. I had never had to beg a woman for her attention, and I wasn't about to start. I made up my mind in that moment. The proverbial ball was in her court.

"I tell you what. Holler at DC about me. If you're interested, have him give you my digits."

Indy lifted her head in defiance. "I'll consider it."

I yanked my car door open and nodded in her direction. "You do that and be safe out here."

Chapter Three

After spending the entire day showing houses, I rushed home to shower and quickly get dressed before heading back out. I didn't bother calling Cairo to let her know I was on my way. That would give her time to make up some excuse —binge-watching Netflix or pretending she had to wash her hair. I was prepared not to take no for an answer, especially when attending Della Montague's engagement party, which had been her idea in the first place. And besides, chances to hang with Zahara were rare.

Zee, as we affectionately called her, was so much like Cairo; she always had a basketball in her hand. Ma'Dear wasn't too happy about her commitment to the game, but Zee's choice was fine by me. I admired the way she worked to perfect her craft, which she started when we took her to her first "lil' shooters" class at the age of five.

Still, even I could admit that at fourteen, Zahara needed a little fun off the court. So when she tilted her head and asked if she could tag along with me and Cairo—eyes wide with that hopeful glint—I couldn't help but smile.

The familiar sight of Cairo's sprawling ranch-style condo filled me with happiness. A few years ago, Cairo followed in my footsteps and decided to get her own place. We'd both been living with her grandmother, Ma'Dear, and Aunt Millie since we were barely teens. We escaped briefly to attend college back home in Georgia, but the magnetic pull of being in the city had us heading right back to Detroit to start our adult careers.

When I stepped out of the car, I was greeted by the distant hum of music. With anticipation bubbling in my chest, I grabbed my purse and makeup case. I made my way to the front door, where the sound of an energetic beat grew louder with each step. I rang the bell twice before using my key to enter. I swung the door open and found Zahara making a TikTok video while dancing at the mirror over the console.

She turned toward me, wide-eyed as if she'd been caught. "Indy!" She sputtered. "Bruh, you scared me."

"I'm not your 'bruh', Zahara Clayton." I chirped. "And you don't look a bit ready. How come you're still wearing your bonnet and your robe?"

"I just got out of the shower," she shrugged. "I was just killing time 'til you got here."

"Why?" I frowned. "You need me to put your clothes on for you?"

"No. But I do need you to do my makeup and help take out my flexi rods." Zee pouted, batting her lashes like she was auditioning for a soap opera.

"You ain't gotta do all that. You know I'm going to hook you up. Where's CeeCee?"

Zee squealed with delight and took off while yelling over her shoulder, "I think she's in her room."

"I'm right here!" Cairo called out, prompting me to head in her direction.

I entered her ordinarily neat bedroom and found clothing strewn across her bed, dresser, and storage ottoman. An assortment of shoes sat in a heap outside her closet, just beside a pile of handbags. I glanced around, trying to make sense of the chaos, before asking, "What the hell happened in here? And you're not dressed either?"

"No," she whined. "I need your help."

"Clearly. I guess I made it just in time. What do you need me to do?"

Cairo plopped on the edge of her bed, surrounded by an array of dresses in every shade. She furrowed her brow in concentration as she grabbed a garment and held it up to her. "I had settled on this dress, but I need your opinion. By the way, you look fabulous, but I'm shocked you're not wearing white."

"Trust me, I wanted to, but that wouldn't have been proper etiquette given the occasion, so I settled for this." I flourished my hand over the dusty rose body-con mermaid dress that had a flouncy finish at my knees. I paired it with scrappy rose gold shoes and a coordinating clutch.

"That color looks good on you."

"Thank you," I returned with a curtsy.

"What do you think about *my* dress?" Cairo asked, turning to me with a hint of uncertainty in her voice.

"Put it on and I'll tell you."

She quickly removed her robe and slid into the black lace, form-fitting sheath. I zipped up the back, and she did a 360-degree turn. "So? Does this work?"

"If I'm being sincere, when I first saw it, I was going to say that it was giving funeral…"

Cairo's shoulders slumped as she studied her image in the full-length mirror attached to the closet door. "Fine, I'll find something else."

"Would you let me finish?"

"I thought you were," she sassed.

"I was just going to add that now that I see you in it, the dress slays, girl!"

"Really?" Cairo's face brightened.

"Yes, really, that booty is thangin' and those legs are stretching for miles. Now what shoes are we wearing, 'cause by the time I'm finished with you, you're going to look like a runway model!"

"And let's be honest—tonight isn't just about Della. You want Desmond to see you as more than his bestie."

Cairo's eyes rolled dramatically. "Shut up, Indy."

"Why? You know I'm right! That's why you wanted to go to his sister's engagement party in the first place. So he can see you strut in there with this move-something dress."

"He won't even be there. Isn't it just women?"

"I doubt it. You said it's an engagement party, not a bachelorette party. You think I would have agreed to go to a party with no men in the building? Abso-fucking-lutely not! "

"I'm pretty sure Ma'Dear would wash your mouth out with soap if she heard what you just said."

I glanced over my shoulder at Zahara, who appeared wearing an A-line pleated chiffon mini dress in a peacock blue shade. "Zee, your dress is cute, but you need to stay out of grown folks' business."

She brushed past me like I hadn't just said a word, dropping into the seat. "All I need is hair and makeup. Can I go first?" One dramatic flutter of her lashes, and I was already giving in.

"Yes, I'll get started on you while Cairo finds her accessories."

Over the next hour, I carefully added the necessary finishing touches. I slayed their makeup and silk-pressed Cairo's hair. Zahara was restricted to a pouty lip and elongated eyeliner since she was only fourteen. But Cairo let me go full artist on her face, including false lashes, contouring, and highlighting. After a few spritzes of Burberry Body, we headed downtown Detroit to the museum district.

The venue was stunning. As we entered the rotunda of the Charles H. Wright Museum of African American History, we were greeted by the grandeur of architectural design. A stately glass dome stretched high above a terrazzo tile floor that would be perfect in a house I'd had my eye on for my next flip. Beneath the dome, nearly a hundred flags flew majestically, representing various African countries. If I were the bride-to-be, I would've felt like a queen in this royal chamber.

The opulent room buzzed with elegantly dressed guests sipping champagne and swapping stories. Cairo and Zahara moved a little stiffly, but I felt exhilarated—wealth practically shimmered in the air, and dollar signs danced in my eyes at the thought of potential clients.

Eventually, we were all comfortable enough to mingle, trying to blend in and make small talk. Not everyone was high society. Plenty were just down-to-earth family and friends swapping childhood stories about Della. Beneath all the glamour, they were regular people.

Of course, there was also a cluster of the ultra-polished, tossing out tales of Paris trips and designer finds. I mingled, curious, while Cairo looked bored and Zee scrolled her phone. By the time the dinner and toast wrapped up, I was itching to dance. "Let's go, Brat," I nudged Zee.

"Where?"

"On a mission," I said.

"And we never dropped the gifts off," Cairo added.

We cut across the rotunda to Beyoncé's "Before I Let Go," the place bouncing. Men in sharp suits caught my eye everywhere—it felt like a candy shop, and I was hungry.

At the gift table, a towering brass birdcage overflowed with cards, while packages in silver and gold gleamed on the table. Cairo and I played a quick guessing game—stemware, robes, maybe jewelry—before Zee squealed.

I covered my ear and fussed, "Don't get too excited, Brat! We can't take them with us."

"Duh. I meant him."

I turned, and my smile fell. Desmond Montague was striding toward us, sharp as sin in a tailored suit, pocket square perfect, Hublot flashing at his wrist.

And he wasn't alone. Beside him was someone taller, rugged—a dead ringer for Malik. His twin, Malcolm.

My chest tightened. I hadn't told Cairo about my run-in with Malik. I'd brushed him off with that "no ballers" line, but seeing Malcolm was a reminder. The resemblance was uncanny.

Cairo lit up. "Do I know you?" she teased Desmond.

"You know better," he grunted, kissing her cheek. "And you're being rude to Malcolm."

Introductions followed—handshakes, smiles. Malcolm was polite, quieter than his brother, though just as striking. Against my will, the gas station memory surged back.

"Ahem," Zee piped up, angling for attention. "So, Desmond, why'd you retire? Couldn't hang in one more year?"

"Zee, don't start," Cairo muttered.

"It's fine." Desmond chuckled. "Injuries. I wanted to go out on my terms."

"Interesting. Well, if you want to drop advice for the Victors..."

"Zee, hush," I warned.

She only grinned. "Anyway, good to see you, DC. Nice meeting you too, Mr. Malcolm." And with that, she was already walking off to find Della.

I followed, relieved to give Cairo and Desmond space. Malcolm fell in step beside me—polite, not pushy. Still, his resemblance to Malik gnawed at me, like fate wasn't done with that man in my story.

Chapter Four

MALIK

"I hate these types of parties," Jarvis grumbled, glancing at his watch for the third time.

"Not me," I said with a grin. "I already know I'm not leaving alone."

Then my phone buzzed. Of course it did—just a few Instagram baddies sliding into my DMs.

> Destiny: I could use some vitamin D.

> Misha: In Detroit. Just say the word and I can cum through.

> Jordyn: Lost my number. Can I have yours?

Decisions, decisions. Even if I struck out at this party, I had a whole starting five lined up.

Some of my teammates kept lists to track their conquests. Me? I wasn't that organized, and I didn't mind a surprise.

If I had a bad experience, I blocked her profile and kept it pushing.

Of today's trio, only Misha was familiar. We'd met in Atlanta, and she'd flown in a few times, sometimes on her own dime. I didn't mind reimbursing her. Talented tongue. Perfect.

Destiny? I'd been with a few of those, but the profile pic jogged my memory. Solid option. Jordyn? Pretty sure this was her first DM slide—she could wait.

"What are you doing?" Jarvis demanded.

"Checking my DMs," I shrugged.

"Exactly. You just proved my point. You can come and go as you please, collect phone numbers, and make hookup plans for later. Me? I have to battle my social anxiety for as long as Twinna wants to flit around, rubbing elbows with folks."

"Poor baby," I said, patting him on the shoulder. "You should be used to Mrs. Bentley and her highfalutin gigs."

"Whatever," Jarvis muttered. "I'm going to grab a drink."

I chuckled to myself, always amused by the antics between Jarvis and Twinna. She was a smart cookie. Snagged him as soon as we got to college —made herself his first serious girlfriend. While Malcolm, Desmond, and I were sowing our oats, he was sneaking off to her dorm. Every minute he wasn't in practice or class was spent at her side.

They married a year after he entered the league and two years after their son Jaeden was born. By the time Jarvis's rookie contract ended, he and Twinna had three children—and he was locked in. I missed most of their early years while he played out west, but once he came home to Detroit, I had a front-row seat.

He loved her, no doubt about it. But there weren't two ways around it —she was a snob and, usually, unbearable. We both knew it, but if he was happy, that was all I cared about. Lately, I wasn't sure that was enough.

Dragging my attention from the Bentley saga, I scanned the room. Dinner had ended, and several guests had vacated their seats for the dance floor or the bar, while others lingered at their tables. I spotted a few familiar faces, including the Montague clan.

Della was seated beside her fiancé, flanked by her parents at the head table. I started toward them to pay my respects when I caught sight of my brother in my peripheral vision.

And he wasn't alone.

I turned to give the scene my full attention and did a double-take. If I wasn't mistaken, the woman I'd met at the gas station was deep in conversation with Malcolm, Desmond, and another young lady. And for some reason, it rubbed me wrong—like he was standing where I should've been.

I headed toward the group, but just before I reached them, she slipped away with Malcolm trailing closely behind.

"Malcolm, hold up!" I called out.

His head swiveled, and he halted. By the time he realized who'd called him, Desmond and Cairo had turned their attention toward me, too. We all converged at the edge of the dance floor, where Malcolm dapped me up and pulled me in for a hug.

"What up, bruh? Y'all had to make a grand appearance, huh?"

"Malc, you know what they say," Jarvis piped up. "Better late than never."

"And if we're in town, we don't miss celebrations like this," I added, before dapping up my dude Desmond Cole. We exchanged our customized handshake—twenty years strong. I hugged and kissed Cairo on the cheek, and she introduced me to her sister, Zahara. After all the greetings, I focused on the woman before me.

The one with the beautiful fucking smile.

It was the first thing I noticed when DC initiated introductions. With one arm around his girl's waist, he pointed with the other toward her friend. "Malik, you remember Indira James? Indy, I think you've met my guy, Malik Latimer."

I was at least a foot taller than her, so when she tilted her head back to look at me, I wasn't surprised — but the way those chocolate eyes locked on mine made it feel like she saw straight through the jersey, the headlines, all of it, and into the man underneath. What caught me was the way her gaze traveled all over me—slow, deliberate, like she was taking my measure.

I was used to attention—lip licking, lash batting, chest thrusting, all par for the course when you were an NBA baller. Especially when you had All-Star status, MVP hardware, national endorsements... it came with the territory. But a woman who whistled her appreciation? That was new.

"Good to see you again, Indira," I said, catching the way her tone stayed even, but her eyes didn't flinch — like she was measuring me, deciding if I was worth more than a handshake.

I extended my hand and relished the feel of her soft skin. I squeezed gently and let my grip linger just long enough. When she looked up, I knew I'd caught her attention. I released her slowly, brushing my fingers against hers with intent.

Her mouth slid into a wicked grin—the kind that told me she was already setting the rules. "Same here."

"So you weren't gonna mention that we ran into each other?" I asked. So much for her telling DC to connect us about my game. I'd forgotten until that moment, but her silence stung a little.

Cairo's head snapped toward her friend. "Wait—what? You saw Malik?"

Indira shrugged. "It wasn't that deep."

"We had a moment," I added, smirking. "She pulled a piece on me."

"I did *not* pull a piece on you," she said, rolling her eyes. "I showed you I wasn't the one."

Cairo blinked. "Y'all are ridiculous."

I glanced at Desmond, who looked surprised enough that I had to explain. "She didn't tell you we ran into each other at the gas station *after* midnight?"

"Oooh, Indy, you ain't got no business pumping gas that late! At least you were strapped."

She cut her eyes at the teenager and snapped, "Zahara, how many times I gotta tell you to stay out of grown folks' business?"

While Indy was scolding, I couldn't help but check her out.
Again. She was a stunner—her petite frame only added to the allure.
Her makeup was on point, lashes long, and lips glossy with a bold
tint begging for attention. But what stood out most was the absence
of her freckles. I knew I hadn't imagined them. They were like the
final dot on an exclamation point that shouted, *I'm Indira.*

What were the odds I could ignore those DMs and win some of
Indy's attention tonight?

Before I could shoot my shot, Indira spoke. "For the record, we
did run into each other at the gas station," she said, emphasizing
each word. "I was leaving the property I flipped earlier this week.
Not that I have to explain myself, Missy." The last part was aimed at
Zahara.

"Yeah," I cut in. "I invited her to bring some friends to the game.
Tomorrow would be perfect. What you think?"

"We'd love to," Cairo nodded.

Hopeful, my eyes bounced to Indy, who rubbed the back of her
neck. "I don't know... I'm kinda busy after church."

"Busy doing what?" Zahara demanded. "It can't be better than
going to watch the current MVP."

"Little girl, hush," Indy warned, before turning her attention
back to me.

"Aww, come on, Indy. You gonna make a brother beg?" I
couldn't believe the words leaving my mouth, especially in front of
this audience. It was almost guaranteed one of my boys—
Malcolm, Jarvis, or Desmond— would be snatching my player card
soon.

I watched Indy's eyes slide over to Cairo and DC, searching for a
read. Cairo's mouth slid into a silly grin.

"Sorry, Malik," Indy said with a shrug—but her eyes stayed
locked on mine.

Sorry? Aww, hell nah.

"Indy, can I holler at you for a minute?"

She chewed her bottom lip like she was weighing the pros and cons. She didn't strike me as the type who second-guessed herself, so the hesitation caught me off guard. Finally, she stepped closer.

I moved far enough away from the group to give us a little privacy. Indira followed without a fuss.

"I just wanted to talk without spectators," I said.

"That's cool, I guess." She shrugged, working hard to sound casual, but I remembered the way she'd whistled at me earlier. She wasn't fooling me.

"Plus," I added, "I wanted to tell you that dress is doing something dangerous. I'm sure you've already heard it tonight, but I wanted you to hear it from me."

Her smile shifted, turning genuine. She tilted her head up, lashes fluttering. "Thank you. You clean up pretty good yourself. Is this a custom Versace tux?"

She reached for my lapel, fingers gliding over the fabric like she was checking the quality.

I frowned in amusement. "I thought you said you were in real estate. You moonlighting in fashion?"

"No, I am in real estate, but I know fashion—right down to your Patek Philippe wrist candy and your Santoni shoes."

Damn. Shortie knew her stuff.

"I'm impressed. And I'm pretty sure I didn't imagine that whistle earlier."

She smirked, unbothered. "Nah, you didn't. That was the real deal. You know you look good."

"You know what would make me look better?"

Her lips curved. "What's that?"

"A selfie with you, courtside tomorrow."

She bit her lip again, like she was really thinking it over. For a second, I thought I had her. Then those seconds turned to silence, and I felt the moment slipping away.

"I get it if you're not interested," I started, "but maybe we can—"

"Yoo-hoo. Look who I found, Malik!"

Chapter Five

MALIK

For a split second, I closed my eyes and inhaled, bracing myself. The voice belonged to Twinna Bentley, and when I turned, my gaze snagged on the woman beside her.

Briana Dillon.

Six feet three, poured into a red satin dress that flaunted every dangerous curve like she was hunting for her next payday. Her smile was practiced—perfect enough to fool a man who didn't know better—but to me it was a neon warning sign. I'd learned the hard way what hid behind it —lies, betrayal, and the kind of ambition that chewed up anything in its path.

My stomach tightened. For years, I'd kept her in my rearview, only crossing paths once—at our high school reunion. Even then, she'd left a bitter taste I couldn't wash away. Tonight, of all nights, she had to show up —when I was finally trying to lock in with Indira James.

"Yo, Malc. You seen that girl before?" My question fell on deaf ears as my twin brother crouched in a low athletic stance, pounding a basketball with his right hand before crossing over to his left. "Malc, I'm talking to you!" I approached, snatching the rock from his hands.

"What the fuck is wrong with you, bruh?" He yanked his head-phones from his ears and straightened, rubbing his one-inch height advantage in my face.

"Oh, I got your attention now, I see." I ripped the basketball out of his reach. Or so I thought. His arms were about two inches longer than mine, too.

"Give me my shit," he demanded and retrieved his Wilson. "What you yapping about, anyway?"

I pointed across the court, directing Malcolm's attention to a trio of girls turning heads in black spandex shorts. One in particular caught my eye. She wasn't the tallest in the group, but she was the most striking.

Her braids swung low over her shoulders, drawing my eyes to the perfect curve of her hips. The black booty shorts should have been banned for her; she'd steal focus from the whole volleyball match without even trying.

"You talking about Briana and her crew?" Jarvis asked.

I shrugged. "I don't know. Which one is Briana? I'm talking about ol' girl with the braids."

"Yeah, that's her," Jarvis confirmed, before hoisting his ball into the hoop. "She looks good, huh?"

"Hell, yeah! But I ain't never seen her before."

"She just transferred. Lauren told me a new girl joined the volley-ball team. I think that's her," Malcolm added, referencing his girlfriend.

"For real?" My forehead stretched as hope filled me. "You think she can introduce me?"

"Bruh, go introduce yourself." Jarvis challenged. "We ain't

supposed to be a stranger to nobody on this campus. This our house!"

"I know that's right!" Malcolm consented, egging me on. "Go give her a dose of that Latimer charm!"

"A'ight, then. Watch and learn, fellas!" I grabbed a towel from my gym bag and wiped the sweat from my face before heading out on my mission. With a confident stride, I crossed the outdoor basketball court and exited the opening in the chain-link fence.

Just a few feet away, Briana and her friends were parked on a bench, exchanging whispers with their hands cupped over their faces. I realized one of the girls was my boy Desmond's little sister Della.

As I drew nearer, I silently thanked my daddy for the acute hearing I'd inherited from him. "He is cute," the tallest one mentioned to Briana, who just giggled.

"Pshht, girl. That's just Malcolm," Della contradicted. "He ain't all that."

"Are you blind?" Tall Girl debated. "Him and Malcolm are the finest guys at FCD."

"Girl, don't let my brother hear you say that!" Della said, twisting her lips. "You know he thinks he owns that title, hands down."

"He may have a point," Briana tilted her head as she considered the claim.

Their conversation was amusing, but I wasn't threatened. In fact, I took it as a challenge. With just a few more strides, I closed the distance and stopped a couple of feet away, keeping my eyes glued on Briana. "Della, I can see you've been keeping secrets. You didn't tell me you had a new friend."

"Boy, ain't nobody gotta tell you nothing!" She sucked her teeth and glanced down at her nails as if she was bored.

"Fine, then." I extended my hand to Briana and took it upon myself to make introductions. "Hey, I'm Malik. You new around here?"

Briana dropped her hand from her face, and I'm sure I stopped breathing for a moment. She was more beautiful than I'd imagined from a distance. Her eyes were wide-set and naturally narrowed, fringed in thick lashes. Her irises carried a faint blue ring, something I'd never seen before —it caught me hard.

I didn't realize how long I'd been staring until her fingers slid against mine—slow, unhurried, like she meant for me to feel it. I looked down at our hands, then up at her, just as she caught my gaze and held it.

"Yeah. I just transferred," she said, her voice a little softer now, lashes fluttering like she knew exactly what she was doing. A sly smile tugged at her lips as color rose in her cheeks. "And don't listen to Della. You're way cuter than DC."

If only I could've known how much that smile would cost me.

PRESENT DAY

"Malik." I felt the tug at my hand, and it wasn't until then that I found my way back to the present. "I said it's good to see you. You look great."

Her voice was all sugar, her eyes skimming over me like she was checking my net worth. "It's been... what? Forever? You look great."

"Long enough," I said flatly, keeping my distance. I let my hands stay at my sides, not about to give her the satisfaction of thinking she still had pull.

Her gaze flicked to Indira, and her smile sharpened. "And you are?"

Indira's answering smile was sweet on the surface, sharp underneath. "The woman you're interrupting—and the one he was talking to before you wandered over."

Briana's laugh came a little too loud. "Oh, so you're the reason Malik's been dodging me all night."

Indira didn't miss a beat. "I'm the reason Malik doesn't even remember you're in the room."

The air between them tightened; it was quiet, but charged

enough that I felt it in my chest. If Briana wanted a scene, Indy was not the one to be fucked with.

Briana tilted her head, letting her gaze slide back to me. "Well, I guess I'll just have to steal you away later. For old times' sake." She laid a hand on my forearm, nails catching in the light. It was a move meant to claim space, and I knew it.

I stepped back, removing her touch. "Old times are exactly where you need to leave it."

Indira's phone buzzed in her hand, and she glanced at it like it had just given her a way out. "Excuse me," she said, her tone cool, "I see someone worth my time—and it's not standing here."

She turned on her heel, head high, the sway of her white dress pulling my eyes after her — daring me to follow. There was heat in her stride, the kind that made me think she was walking away proud —but maybe just pissed enough to make me work to get back in her good graces. She didn't look back once.

My jaw clenched. The second she disappeared into the crowd, I screwed my face and snapped my neck back toward Briana. "Enjoy the party, Briana," I muttered, already moving.

I took off in Indira's direction, certain I could catch her, my stride twice the length of hers. But requests for selfies and autographs slowed me down. I kept it polite—these were my people—but my eyes stayed locked on the door.

By the time I reached the museum steps, the night air hit me, and so did the reality: Indira was gone.

I shoved my hands into my pockets, scanning the grounds like she might reappear. She didn't.

For a second, I thought about checking my DMs. Misha. Jordyn. Easy options. Instead, I locked my phone, slid it away, and stood there in the quiet.

She had me chasing her. And I wasn't even mad about it.

Chapter Six

INDIRA

If Briana thought she could rattle me, she was in for a rude awakening. I don't do retreat, and I damn sure don't do backing down. She could be a foot taller and still get dog-walked if it came to it. Malik might've been caught off guard by her reappearance, but me? I clocked her the second she walked in, dripping in that red satin like a warning flare. The kind of woman who thrived on spectacle, always calculating her angle.

She had the gall to touch him while looking me dead in the face. A move straight out of the petty playbook. And Malik… He didn't shut it down as fast as I would've liked. Not because I needed him to —trust me, I could've handled her—but because I'd thought he was sharper than that. The whole exchange was short, but the stink of it followed me out the door.

I kicked off my heels the second I stepped inside, my feet practically moaning in relief. After tugging off my lashes and tossing my clutch onto the entry table, I poured a glass of wine and collapsed onto the couch like the day owed me reparations.

I wasn't looking for anything in particular. Just something to drown out my thoughts—and maybe silence that petty voice asking why Malik was still in my head. You'd think I'd shut the door on all that when I left, but no. He was still there, occupying more space than I wanted to admit.

One minute he was looking at me like I was the only woman in the room—and the next, his attention was on someone else. I didn't know who she was, and honestly, I didn't care. So yeah, I bolted. Before I made the mistake of thinking I mattered more than I did.

I sipped my red with one hand and pointed a remote at the TV with the other. I flipped through a dozen channels, and then suddenly, there he was.

Malik Latimer.

On screen in a pre-recorded interview. Sitting on a sleek black couch under studio lights, wearing a tailored charcoal suit and a smirk that probably had half the country's ovaries in a chokehold.

I sat up straighter.

"Pistons MVP Malik Latimer is joining us tonight after an incredible run this season," the host was saying. "Thirty-one points per game, a league-leading assist ratio, and let's not forget the nickname that has fans and media alike buzzing—'Malik the Freak.'"

Malik's smile didn't budge. Not even a twitch. But his hands lifted briefly, palms out, in a gesture of surrender. "Not touching that one. Y'all got it."

The host laughed like she'd won a prize. "Fair enough. Let's talk legacy. You've made it clear that basketball is your focus, but what about the next chapter? Family? Relationships?"

That's when I saw it—just the slightest flicker. A blink. A breath held too long. Then he reset.

He rubbed his palms together, then averted his eyes from the host. "The game's my priority. Always has been." His shoulders squared. "Everything else comes after."

I stared at the screen. That wasn't the same energy he had at the party. That night, he looked at me like he was committing me to memory. Tonight? This version of him was polished. Controlled. Practiced.

I remembered how he looked at me at the gas station. The way he insisted on making sure I got home safe. That version of him was real. This? This was the brand.

"You've never let the media in much," the host pressed. "But your good friend and former teammate Desmond Montague—DC—had some things to say about you on his Moneyball podcast. Said you were loyal. That you give until it hurts. That you've been burned."

Malik's jaw didn't move, but something behind his eyes did. His fingers tapped restlessly. "I appreciate DC. He's like a brother. But I'm not here to give the public a peek into my wounds. I'm here to win games."

There it was. The wall. Thick and high and polished like glass.

I sank deeper into the couch, swirling my wine. I wasn't mad at it. I had walls, too. But it was wild watching someone speak so carefully while everyone around him seemed to see straight through him.

I turned the volume down and just watched his face—the stillness in his shoulders, the way he kept his smile measured like it might crack if he wasn't careful.

Malik was tall, golden-brown, and looked like he was carved straight out of my fantasies. He looked damn near unreal on that screen. His shoulders were broad, his arms thick. His shirt sleeves that flexed every time he moved. The camera didn't even do him justice, but it caught the way his jaw tightened when he focused, the gleam of sweat clinging to his skin, the quiet intensity in his eyes. And those lips? Full, defined, and made for sin.

He was beautiful.

But there was something else under all that shine—a quiet, aching kind of solitude that didn't belong to a man like him. And I couldn't decide if that made him dangerous in a way that had nothing to do with his body. The kind of danger that could pull you close just to see if you'd survive it. And I wanted to know—no, needed to know—who he was when the lights went out, and the world stopped watching.

Chapter Seven

INDIRA

It took almost two weeks to close on the cul-de-sac house, a sprint compared to the usual six. Fortunately for me, the buyers had recently relocated to the Detroit area and were eager to stop living out of their suitcases at a nearby hotel. Armed with cash and skipping the appraisal, we signed on the dotted line.

Proud as hell and ready to celebrate, I pulled up at Cairo's place twenty minutes later. I'd cleared my calendar for two whole days—rare for me—and today I was ready to celebrate.

"Hey, girl, hey!" I blurted as soon as she cracked open the door. I took her long enough—I knew she'd been sleeping.

She loomed over me, arms crossed tight against her chest. "Do you know what time it is, Indy? It's too early for this. And you ditched me last night."

"Cairo Clayton, you ought to know by now that your bark doesn't faze me," I warned, following her into the kitchen. "I've been calling you, heifer. What? The Sisters been blowing up your phone? Your ringer off?"

Cairo sighed, shifting her weight. "Ain't nobody's ringer off."

"Whatever. I'm here now. You should've seen me-- painting ceilings, if you can believe that."

"Uh, no. You can barely reach the counter," Cairo snorted.

"Shut up, Jolly Green Giant. I ain't that short! And it turned out great. Anyway, I have news." I hopped on a bar stool, legs dangling in spiked heels.

"Whatever. I want to go back to bed."

"You do need your beauty rest, but it can wait. Why don't you just get dressed and come with me. I need a manicure," I waved my chipped nails in the air. "And then Somerset."

"Do you hear yourself, Indy?" CeeCee whined, leaning on the counter. "You didn't even ask how I'm doing."

"You're right. Hold that thought. Tell me on the way to the mall?"

"Really?" She glared. "How about I go cuddle up with my pillow?"

"Why you being so selfish, Sis? I need girl time."

"Fine," Cee groaned, "but I guess you can wait to hear who I ran into last night."

That stopped my legs mid-swing. "Ran into—or ran up in? Girl, stop playing."

Cairo sipped her coffee, hip cocked. "Do I ever play about men?"

"Hell nah," I snickered. "Basketball's your man."

"Usually. But this wasn't a first meeting."

"Then who?" My brows shot up. "Bitch, you holding out on me?"

"No. Desmond."

I frowned. "Girl, how is that news? You've probably seen him every day since he got back. Please tell me you finally shoved your tongue down his throat."

Cairo rolled her eyes, opening the fridge. "Hush, Indy. Bagel?"

"No, I'm watching carbs."

"Yeah, right. Nobody believes that. Anyway, he came out for a little while for my birthday."

"Define celebrate. Please tell me you finally let him hit." I pressed my hands together.

"No, silly. You know we don't get down like that."

"But you want to," I shot back. "Besides me, he's your closest friend. That should count."

Cairo stopped buttering her bagel, giving me a look. "I know, but that's how we'll keep it. Friendly. Besides, since you stood me up, I couldn't even count on you to stop me from making a fool of myself and confessing this attraction."

My thumb froze on my phone. "Trust, I wouldn't have stopped you. Your boy is so fine it makes no sense. Couldn't you let him know right then?"

"I told you, that's not going to happen."

"Damn shame," I scolded. "It's about time you let your guard down and get a little nasty."

Cairo frowned.

"What? I'm just saying. Dick does a body good."

For the next several hours, Cairo and I pampered ourselves and made the most of our free time. We strolled through the Somerset Collection Mall, drooling while we window-shopped in Prada, Hermès, and Balenciaga.

I'd earmarked part of my commission for Zahara's tuition at Farmington Country Day — but DC swooped in and covered it without a word to anyone. At first, I wanted to fuss at him for stepping on my plans, but truth be told, it freed me to repurpose the money for other things... like the retail therapy calling my name.

When we entered Neiman Marcus, I made a beeline for the shoe department. I'd had my eye on a pair of Valentino Garavani Rockstuds that I could no longer resist. Of course, my frugal friend thought I was insane. To stop her bitching, I copped her a pair of Off-White sneakers she'd been eyeing just as long.

Just before we reached our spending limit for the day, we

grabbed some gifts for the family. Ma'Dear would adore the sophisti-
cated white hat we snagged for first Sunday, and Aunt Millie would
enjoy her new bottle of Chanel N°5. Our trip wouldn't have been
complete without grabbing some expensive-ass leggings and
hoodies for the brat. If she didn't appreciate them, I damn sure
would.

We had just left the mall when an incoming call interrupted the
music we were blasting.

"It's Desmond," CeeCee squealed.

"Duh. I can see that!"

She mashed her finger against the phone to accept the call. "Girl,
hush."

"What up doe, Baby Girl."

"Hey, DC. You're on speaker."

"Word, what you getting into?"

Cairo quickly filled him in on our day, to which he responded,
"You should have told me. I would've thrown y'all a couple bands."

"We knew your pockets are deep," I chimed in. "But your girl
over here had her bag."

I caught a glimpse of Cairo rolling her eyes. "She just closed on a
house sale and couldn't wait to spend her money."

"Congratulations, that's what's up. I see you, Indy!"

I couldn't resist a proud grin. "Thanks, DC. And thanks again for
taking care of Zee's tuition — guess you're partly to blame for my
little spree today."

"A'ight then," he laughed. "I was calling to invite y'all out
tonight. You got room in your schedule?"

Cairo glanced at me with a hopeful expression. I'd already
decided I was planning to turn up, so I was down for whatever. "Say
less, DC. What you got in mind?"

"You still owe Cairo and me a raincheck to see my boy play. I got
tickets for Game 2 of the playoff series tonight."

"You know, I'm game," Cee answered before I could say a word.

I'd been so busy I'd forgotten about both my open invitation and my encounter with Malik, which was probably a good thing. I couldn't deny he was fine AF. Let me not lie. He *and* his brother were fine. But there was something about that Malik that screamed bad boy. I could definitely see myself falling into trouble with him, at least once or twice, until I moved on to different pastures.

I'd considered ditching my plans the Sunday after Della's engagement party to see his game. But when this tall, model-ass chick with perfect hair and legs for days strutted up to him like they had a scheduled appointment, I quickly canceled those thoughts.

The way she leaned in, staking her claim like she'd made a down payment on him, was all the confirmation I needed. Same high-gloss confidence, same vibe from the party that had me ready to grab my bag and walk. I didn't do sloppy seconds, even if I only planned a one-night stand with him.

Now that the opportunity had presented itself again, was I interested? "I don't know, DC. Last time I saw Malik, he looked like he had his hands full with Jarvis' wife and her friend."

"What you talking about? He just asked me about you earlier today when he arranged the tickets."

"She's talking about the woman Twinna approached him with at Della's party," Cairo explained, and the silence stretched before Desmond responded.

"You talking about his ex? Long legs, big—"

"Yes, DC, and you can spare us the description."

"Briana," he supplied, like it was no big deal. "They were together for years. That's over, but you know how some women like to test the boundaries."

The name landed like a pebble in my shoe—small but impossible to ignore. Briana. Even her name sounded pretty, the kind you could imagine etched across a perfume bottle. I hated that I could still see her in my head, gliding up to Malik as if she belonged there, owning the space in a way that made me want to grab my bag and head for the exit.

"Oh, trust me," DC continued, "you have no reason to be concerned about her. None. Nada. No cap."

I twisted my lips in doubt. "Are you sure? I mean, I'm not trying to encroach on anybody's territory. I am a savage, but not like that."

Cee shot me a side-eye at the shift in my tone. "Shut up, Indy. Do you want to go or not?" Before I could respond, she reached for the console and muted the call. "After all the shit you gave me earlier about 'letting your guard down and getting a little nasty,' you better be willing to hang."

"Sis, are you challenging me?"

"Yup." Cee nodded and lifted her chin.

"A'ight, challenge accepted." I said it with a grin, but when DC's laughter filled the car speakers, a shiver ran through me.

Because the truth was, I'd already seen enough to know Malik Latimer was dangerous—and not the kind you could walk away from after one night.

Chapter Eight

We were down by one with five seconds on the clock. I had the ball, wide open behind the arc. No one even bothered to close out … like I was just some washed-up vet, not a two-time All-Star with a jumper built for clutch moments.

I bent my knees, spread my fingers, snapped my wrist.

It felt perfect—until it wasn't.

As it sailed, I caught a flash of movement in my periphery—JT, cutting to the basket, wide open. No defenders. An easy two. The smarter play. And I'd missed it.

The ball hit the front of the rim like karma cashing in. JT's look afterward? I felt that shit.

I'd come into tonight's game ready to redeem myself. Locked in, grinding. But somewhere between trying to lead and prove myself, I lost the thread. Forced shots. Ignored better options. Played hero ball. Again.

I didn't need a damn highlight reel to see the mistakes. They were burning holes in the back of my skull. At halftime, we were up by five. But I couldn't admit that I still had one nagging distraction. I'd expected to see Indira courtside.

During warm-ups, I'd scanned the seats in the lower bowl near our bench and learned that neither she, Cairo, nor Desmond were in sight. I'd tried focusing, but I couldn't help searching for Indy's face among the sea of spectators during timeouts. I had to swallow my disappointment heading to the locker room at half time.

I had fifteen minutes to breathe, piss, and get my head right. I owned my mistakes and noted the coaches' adjustments before I jumped on the stationary bike to keep my muscles warm. Indira or not, I had to play team ball.

No more hero ball.

Fortunately, the second half was completely different. When I returned to the court, I couldn't help but check for Indira. And there she was —buried in the crowd, still fine enough to wreck my focus.

The fact that she was late didn't matter at all. Just knowing she was in the building was enough to elevate my game.

I wasn't the only one trying to turn up. Jarvis was a motherfucking highlight reel. He was aggressive in the third quarter, hitting multiple deep three-pointers and a couple of contested mid-range shots. Nasir closed the night by throwing down a reverse dunk that sent the crowd to its feet.

I would have preferred to be up 2-0, but with a 1-1 record, at least I knew the momentum had swung our way. My confidence was so high that I guaranteed a Game 3 win during the media session. Let the reporters spin it however they wanted—Game 3 was ours.

By the time I hit the VIP lot, I wasn't thinking about the win anymore. I was thinking about Indira—and when I finally laid eyes on her, it was worth the wait.

Her outfit hit different, not because it was blinged out. She wore a buttoned, single-breasted white blazer with nothing beneath it. Indira's bronze skin exposed to flash a tease of cleavage. Mission accomplished: equal parts edgy confidence and elegance. Paired with a white miniskirt and shiny crystal boots, her outfit radiated boss babe.

I knew my eyes must have lingered a little too long when she interjected, "You like what you see?"

"Hell, yeah," I admitted, returning my attention to her face, lightly accented in makeup just enough to let her freckles shine through. And those lips...glossed, full, pouty—dangerous.

Damn.

I had a major dilemma on my hands. She was giving me looks, but I resisted a leering grin. I'd already endured a thirty-minute lecture from Desmond when he shared that Indira was tagging along tonight.

He didn't trust me not to screw it up and land him in the doghouse with Cairo. With my rep, I couldn't blame him. He made it clear—no hands on her, or he'd rip my head off.

DC was a big man as well, with at least three inches on me. I wasn't scared, but still.

I understood that Indira was off-limits.

"You look good, Shortie, no doubt. But I'm ready to celebrate. You hangin' tonight?"

I flagged the attendant. "We're headed to Jazzmasters. You in?"

"Say less." ... I opened the door and offered a hand.

She hesitated and glanced down. "No running board?"

"Let me help you, Shortie." Her palm slid into mine—small and warm. The second our skin connected, every nerve lit up. Her scent followed—grown and expensive.

"Buckle up," I managed.

"It's a few blocks."

I glimpsed her way. "True, but why risk an accident with someone you just met?"

"Easy. You're not crazy—you won't kill me before you get the benefits."

My brow hiked. "Benefits?"

"Be patient. You'll see." She patted my thigh with assurance, and my dick leaped.

I opened my mouth to challenge her, then snapped it shut. Indira was a live one who liked to talk shit. I sure as hell wanted to know if she could back it up, but Desmond's warnings were ringing in my head like alarm bells.

I gripped the wheel, Indira's scent thick in my lungs. I lied to myself if I thought I could keep this night simple.

Jazzmasters was shoulder-to-shoulder with playoff buzz, live music, and double patios. DC had turned his spot into the hottest scene in Detroit.

Fans in Pistons gear mobbed the entrance. Slade was close, just in case, but I wanted him low-key. Tonight was about Indira.

Inside, the club was jammed as the crowd enjoyed an up-and-coming band. We were greeted by a hostess who directed us to a nook I knew wouldn't work.

I leaned toward Indira's ear and spoke over the crowd. You can't see a thing. Can you?"

"Nope," she frowned while shaking her head.

"That's what I figured." I would have been fine down by the stage, tossing her on my shoulders, but that would have earned me a firm reprimand from DC. Instead, I directed us to the upper VIP area with the balcony lounge.

We headed upstairs to the VIP balcony after taking a few selfies on the way. The band hit a new groove, and she started to sway. "Ayyy! This is my jam." Indira grinned.

I guided her to a plush semi-circular sofa. "Oh, yeah? You like that?"

"Yup. It goes hard." She swayed her curvy hips to the beat. "You want to dance, or you just plan to sign autographs all night?"

My neck snapped back. "What you trying to say?"

"I'm just saying," she shrugged, "you should pay a girl some attention."

"Oh, I plan to give you all the attention you want." I sat beside her and looped my arm over the back of the sofa. With her this close, I took a moment to study her features in more detail. Indira was naturally beautiful. Her makeup was light, revealing flawless skin and freckles dusting her cheeks.

I couldn't help trailing my fingers along her jaw. Her lush lips lured my attention, and all I could think about was tasting her.

Would she let me? Her lashes fluttered, and it looked like a yes. I licked my suddenly dry lips, deciding I would go for it. Before I could act on my impulse, a feminine voice interrupted. "Congratulations, Mr. MVP!"

Chapter Nine

INDIRA

Her timing sucked.

Malik was definitely about to kiss me when a VIP waitress in a painted-on mini showed up with an Ace of Spades, sparkler blazing like she'd won a reality show. I had the irrational urge to swat her tiara.

"Compliments of Mr. Montague," she sang as the lightbox lit our section.

Malik thanked her—of course—and peeled off a Benjamin. Over the top. Typical.

I clinked my flute to his water. "To getting to know each other."

"I can drink to that," he said.

The first sip fizzed bright and expensive. "Okay, that's… dangerous."

"DC's got taste," he said, eyes on my mouth. "Got a toast?"

I raised my glass. "May we kiss who we please—and please who we kiss."

His grin hit me square—double dimple on the left deeper than the right. "You trying to start something."

"I don't start what I can't finish."

"Duly noted." Heat flickered. "So—tell me about Indira."

"After I congratulate you."

"Did you enjoy the game?"

"You won, right?"

"Uhhh, yeah," he answered, stating the obvious. "Is that the only thing that stood out to you?"

There was plenty about Malik Latimer that caught my attention. But I knew this man was accustomed to women falling over their feet to get to him, so I resisted the urge to stroke his ego. I gnawed on my lip, pretending to ponder his question. "Would it be bad if I said yes?"

He clutched his chest. "Wow. I'm wounded. No highlights? My performance? Nothing?"

"Pass?" I said, sweet but merciless.

"You know anything about my record? Me?"

"Energy drink commercials. Right?"

He sipped, eyes narrow. "You know anything about basketball?"

"The truth?"

"I keep it one hund'ed."

"I don't know a damn thing about basketball."

He barked a laugh that cut through the music. "Thought so." Then he caught my chin and lifted it. "Then why come?"

"Duh—you're fine. And basketball can't be all you are."

"Facts. Other hobbies."

"Let me guess." I tipped my glass. "Comic books?"

"Nah."

"Poker?"

"Too complex."

"Fishing."

"Close." His mouth crooked. "When I'm not hooping, I'm out on my boat."

"Sea captain?"

"Yup. There's something about being out on the water that

brings me peace—tranquility. I have a small boat. I could take you—unless you're scared of water."

"Not many things scare me," I lied, finishing my flute.

"Is that right? I'll keep that in mind."

"You do that, Captain. You dancing, or I need to guard you from poachers?"

"You don't share, huh?"

"Not tonight."

We started with a two-step, but it was only a matter of time before we were grooving as if no one else existed. The bass threaded through him; he moved like it belonged to him. My gaze snagged on the stretch of his sweater, the heat of his hands at my waist.

A turn pulled me into his chest, hip brushing him—my brain short-circuited. I caught just enough of an outline to make my breath hitch. No way it was actually like that. Probably the angle. Probably.

"You having fun?" he asked, voice low enough to make my ribs vibrate.

"I am. You?"

"Yeah, Shortie." His arms dropped lower as the tempo cooled. His scent—warm, masculine—tilted my balance.

"I'm thirsty," he murmured. "Another?"

"I can't believe you lasted this long."

"You had me out here almost an hour."

His hand found the small of my back as we left the floor. I would've paid money for him to walk ahead so I could confirm my steel-glutes theory.

Upstairs, our balcony had been invaded—teammates, dates, laughter. Malik slid into host mode.

"Indira, my guy JB—Jarvis Bentley." If Malik was tall, JB was a skyline: broad shoulders, easy smile.

"Pleased to meet you," he said, with a gentle shake. "Known this knucklehead since middle school."

"Nice to meet you. JB or Jarvis?"

"JB, please. 'Jarvis' is when I'm in trouble."

"I'm Indy," I said.

"You didn't tell me that was your preference," Malik pouted.

"My bad. You can call me whatever you want." I pinched his cheek.

"A'ight, Indy—meet the rest." He pointed as we eased through the crush. "Nasir—and Mirabel." Nasir was a lamppost; Mirabel waved like we were already friends. "Jamel, Devarius, Maxwell." Surrounded by giants, I felt pocket-sized.

"Congrats on the win, everyone," I said.

Malik dropped onto a lounge sofa and tugged me into his lap like it was the most natural seat in the house. Heat climbed my spine.

"I owe you that drink," he said in my ear.

"I didn't forget."

"You still want it, or..." Malik glanced at his wrist where his watch was strapped.

"Or what?"

"You never answered my question from earlier. And it's too loud to talk. You wanna bounce?"

I kept my cool. "Uhm, sure." He must have signaled for his security while I was texting my departure plans to Cairo, because the moment I looked up, Slade materialized like a magic trick.

We slipped out. Malik's truck idled at the curb. Our fingers brushed at the door, and a current whipped through me. "I got it," he rasped.

Inside, my seatbelt clicked, but my focus sure didn't. His arm slid across my shoulders. Usually, I'm not a nervous girl. Tonight, I was.

I'd taken an instant liking to Malik. I didn't give a damn about his celebrity. It didn't hurt that he was fine as fuck, but he had a good vibe about him, too. He felt... fun.

As an extrovert, I thrived on the energy of others who loved to party. However, I sometimes overindulged, and I wasn't sure if Malik could handle that side of me. I guess I'd find out.

"Lean back," he said. "Let Slade get us home."

"Home?"

"Your place—unless you want somewhere else."

I went to protest—then his cologne hit. Clean. Seductive. The last ride was torture already: his thigh pressed to mine, all that manspread heat.

Now we were crammed together again, him smelling good as sin, me wound tight. If he kept tempting me, he could definitely get it, and if my neighbors heard, I wouldn't give a damn.

"Home works." I gave my address and settled into his warmth.

"You got a man?"

"Hell no. Why?"

"Wondered what he'd think."

"Then you can stop wondering."

He frowned, uncertain. "That's good... I'm just—"

"Just what?"

"Surprised. Fine as you are—and you've got good energy. What's the catch?"

I laughed. "You expect me to say I chew up boyfriends and spit them out?"

"I hope not."

"Truth? I haven't had time. And not many men can handle my hustle."

"People make time for what matters."

"When's your last relationship?"

"A real one? Rookie year."

"So, you are a fuckboy."

"Nah. I just hadn't met someone who could hold my interest long enough to settle down."

I let "until now" hang and ignored it.

"Tell me about your hustle."

"I'm flipping a whole block. Boarded windows, overgrown lots— the works. I want people to be proud to live there. Wealth. Legacy."

"Damn. That's big."

"It has to be. I didn't come from money, but I know how to make it. I'm not waiting on anyone."

He smirked. "So—no man, no distractions, no babies?"

"Mess up this figure? Hard pass." I grinned. "Cairo and I help with Zahara. She's enough."

"Facts. I'm not ready for kids either. Marlane—she hates that."

"Who's Marlane?"

"My mother. She and my dad want grandbabies. Me and my twin, Malcolm, aren't cooperating."

"Just you two?"

"Older sister, Jackie, from Mama's first marriage. We're close." He tipped his head. "You?"

"Only child. My grandma raised me; when she passed, I moved in with Cairo and The Sisters."

His fingertips skimmed my arm. "That must've been hard."

"It was. Leaving Georgia for Detroit was harder."

"Your mom?"

"She's alive."

"Why not live with her after your grandma passed?"

"That's a long story—for another day." The truck slowed.

"We're here," he said. "Let me walk you."

The night air was cooler than the club, still buzzing. He brushed my hand, then settled a palm at my waist. On the porch, I fumbled the keys; nerves prickled.

"So, Indy…" His dimples deepened.

"Yeah?"

"You inviting me in?"

"That depends." My voice wasn't steady. "You plan on being a gentleman?"

"That depends." His smile was pure trouble. "You plan on letting me?"

The line we'd been toeing all night disappeared.

Chapter Ten

I could see it in her eyes—the hesitation, the heat she was trying to hide. The porch light hit her just right, catching the copper in her skin and the gloss on her lips. I didn't need an invitation to know what I wanted, but I wanted her to say it.

When she finally whispered, "I want you to come in," it hit harder than any buzzer-beater I'd ever made.

She didn't flirt like the others. She didn't care about the bank account, the bodyguard, or the number stitched on my jersey. Hell, she barely blinked when I mentioned courtside seats. And somehow, that only made me want her more.

She was smaller than most of the women I'd dated—barely up to my shoulder in those boots. Her hair, cropped close and wild in front, framed a face that didn't need any extras. Soft, sharp, unforgettable.

If this had been any other woman, I'd already be planning the exit after the smash. Instead, I was trying to figure out how soon I could see her again.

My gaze crawled over her face. She was so damn pretty, and her offer was tempting as hell, but... "Nah, I can't."

She twisted her neck to look at me sideways. "Can't? Or won't?"

"Can't."

She stepped back from the doorway and bit her bottom lip. "And why is that?"

"I promised DC," I admitted quietly.

Her brows pulled together. "The fuck? Why?"

"He told me in no uncertain terms not to lay a hand on you." I shrugged. "And I ain't gonna lie. My fingers have been itching to grab your ass and more."

"Oh yeah? Good thing my fingers are itching, too." Catching me off guard, Indira stepped closer and boldly cupped me.

My dick was stiff as a brick, filling her palm and confirming the lust I'd already revealed. I blew out a hard breath, the urge to take her right there. My hesitation was different from how I usually moved with a woman. But this one I liked. She wasn't a fling; something about Indira made me want to delete all my DMs and put my energy into her.

When I felt her fingers moving, she snatched me out of my head. She caressed me generously for what seemed like an eternity while I gritted my teeth. If she didn't release me soon, I feared I'd embarrass myself, busting in my Tom Ford pants.

As if reading my mind, she unhanded me. "I see what you're working with. And for the record? Your friend needs to mind his damn business."

I dropped my head and exhaled.

"Why don't you come in, and I'll let you keep your promise?"

I looked her over, and damn—her jacket barely held what was underneath. One look at her, all that confidence and curve, and every bit of restraint I had went out the window.

"Come on, Malik. You know you want to."

Indira smirked and then unlocked the door, leaving me standing at the threshold as she entered her living room. I watched as she dropped her purse on her turquoise sofa and plopped down beside it.

When she leaned forward to tug at her boot, her blazer fell open, giving me a flash of soft skin and just enough to wreck my focus.

I couldn't look away if I wanted to. I'd pictured what they'd look like a hundred times tonight. Now I knew. Partially. My thoughts spiraled, imagining my lips latching onto those perky little berries while DC's warnings warred in my mind.

"I can't have you," I confessed from my post, "but I wish you knew how much I want you."

"Show me."

That was all it took for my resolve to break.

In a few short strides, I crossed the room. Restraint didn't stand a chance; every step stripped it away.

I finally reached the sofa and dropped down beside Indira. The sparks that had flickered between us all night suddenly burst into flames. I hesitated, tracing her lush lips and freckles, stalling past the inevitable. My hands moved to her face, cupping her cheeks as Indira drew in a breath. I leaned in to run my tongue across her lips, slowly swiping against their softness before dipping inside. Gentle, but holding back the urge clawing at me.

Indira responded instantly, her quiet whimpers an unmistakable pulse of pleasure as our tongues tangled. When her hands shifted from my chest to lock around my neck, my desire for her surged to new heights.

It took every ounce of control not to push her back, slide between her thighs, and give in. Instead, I reined in my wild passion and slowly retreated.

Indira was not pleased.

Through hooded eyes, she blinked in confusion. "Wait… why the hell did you stop?"

I inhaled deeply before letting out a deep sigh. "I told you. We can't do this."

Indira rolled her eyes and shoved me in my chest. "Tell me again about this promise?"

"I told DC I wouldn't touch you."

"That's what I thought." She slid her hand over the front of my jeans, bold and unbothered.

"How about you sit back and relax. I'll do all the touching."

I grew even harder beneath her touch. Suddenly, it was like she hit fast forward, fumbling at my button as if her patience had finally snapped.

"What are you doing?" I choked out, caught somewhere between surprise and pure need.

She answered boldly, "What do you think? I've been dying to do this all damn night." Her strength surprised me when she shoved me with all her might, and I collapsed against the sofa.

I snagged her gaze and found fierce determination mixed with raw lust. She had no intention of retreating, and frankly, at that point, I had lost the fight. When she pulled my underwear down, she gasped.

One look at my dick, and Indy's eyes went wide.

"I don't know what you were about to do, but you look like you're having second thoughts," I said.

"Shit, I am," she admitted, eyes wide. "Yeah, I saw the preview at the club. Thought I had you pegged. But the full-length feature? Whole different story."

I couldn't help but grin as I sat up, tucking myself back into my briefs. "You didn't think this through, did you?"

"Oh, don't get it twisted. I thought about it. A lot. I knew you were packing—but I didn't know it was going to be... like that." She gestured with both hands like she was measuring a fish she'd caught.

"I can't help it. I'm a grower."

She shook her head, laughing. "If you think that big ol' thing is fitting anywhere inside me, think again."

"This was your plan, not mine," I teased, tugging her hands until she was pressed beside me. "So, it's all good. But why don't you let me taste these lips again?" I paused just long enough to give her the chance to refuse before leaning in to capture her mouth.

Her lips were just as soft as the first time I sampled them. They were bare now—just her, no gloss, nothing but the real thing. I took my time sliding my tongue across the seam of her lips before pushing my way inside. Indy welcomed me, twirling her eager tongue greedily against mine.

Her body was as warm as her mouth, and I couldn't resist the urge to run my fingertips from her cheek down her neck before pushing open the lapels of her jacket. I continued my exploration, my fingers massaging a breast that filled my larger-than-average hands. Beneath my touch, Indira squirmed, and I smiled at the effect I was having on her. I lingered on her mouth until the pull dragged me lower.

I lowered my head and peppered the slope of her right breast with open-mouthed kisses. Her flesh was hot and supple, and before I knew it, I was sliding my lips across the surface until I found the chocolate tip I'd been seeking. I flicked it with my tongue repeatedly while palming her other breast with my free hand.

As I strummed her nipples, her quiet moans and the way she squirmed beneath my hand told me everything I needed to know. I loved seeing her like this—Indira always came off strong, in control. But right now, she was needy, breathless, and it threw me.

Her breath caught when I grazed her nipple with my teeth. My grip on her waist tightened—just slightly—as heat coiled low in my gut. Damn, I wanted her. Wanted to lose myself in the scent of her skin, to press deeper until nothing existed but this moment.

But the weight of my own conscience pressed heavier than her body against mine.

I froze, forehead resting against her chest, eyes shut tight. The tension in my shoulders wasn't lust—it was loyalty, desire in a war that had no clear winner. DC's face flashed in my mind. My day one. My brother. I'd promised him I'd tread carefully.

And here I was, standing on the edge of the line I swore I wouldn't cross.

I licked a path between her breasts and lifted my face toward hers. "Indy, look at me." She didn't respond at first, so I slid my mouth along the column of her neck. I grazed her ear lightly with my teeth, finally gaining her attention. "Indira. Look at me," I demanded, my tone more urgent. Her eyes fluttered open as her long lashes swept against her high cheekbones.

Her forehead creased, and her mouth fell open slightly as she inhaled deeply. "What? Why did you stop?"

Good question. I'd never pulled back unless protection was an issue —and I always came prepared. But with Indira, stopping felt damn near impossible, like throwing myself in front of a runaway train. "We have to stop, Indy. Please understand, but don't think for a minute it's because I don't want you."

"Then what's the problem?" Her face tightened in confusion.

I licked my lips, trying to get a grip on my racing pulse. "I gave my word to DC that I wouldn't...you know, try anything with you."

"Malik, I'm a grown-ass woman! I don't need DC's damn permission!"

Before I could respond, she shoved me in my chest and pulled at the lapels of her jacket. Those delicious tits were now hidden from my vision. Instantly, her mood shifted from hot and ready to cold and furious.

"I know you don't, but I do. I want to do this right and keep seeing you. Just let me talk to DC. Once he realizes I'm serious about pursuing something with you, it'll be all good."

She shook her head and shot to her feet. She narrowed her eyes and leaned over me, jabbing her finger toward my face. Her chest heaved as she fussed, and that shit turned me on even more.

"You are unbelievable, Malik! I know damn well you don't go around asking for approval for no pussy. And I damn sure ain't looking for authorization to get some dick."

"Indy, damn," I pleaded, feeling like a punk. "I'm just trying to do right by you. And you know DC doesn't want to make things difficult with CeeCee."

"Whatever," she waved her hand at me. "That's the stupidest shit I've ever heard. So, you, Malik Latimer, you need to go."

Really?

I stared at her in disbelief. Damn. Another first: Malik Latimer getting kicked out.

I was tight on time, but I agreed to meet Malcolm and Desmond at Sonny's before meeting the team. Once inside, the owner ushered me to our usual section, where I found them in a booth.

"What's up, bruh? It's about time you got here. Ms. Mavis had some pointers about your game yesterday."

"You talking trash again, Ms. Mavis?" I towered over her, but she didn't blink.

"Not trash, baby. Truth." She reached up and pinched my cheek. "Now scoot on in there so I can get some coffee in you quick."

I frowned while Desmond laughed at my expense. "Really, y'all? I just had an off night."

"Yes, brother, you did. You couldn't have hit that basket if it was three feet around."

"Malc, shut up. At least I played. And what about you, old man?"

"Yeah, aight. Tell that to your brother and Mavis. Bulls still ran y'all down, and you squeaked by."

"Sure did," Malcolm chimed in. "You can't let that game get that tight, especially if you're trying to get these back-to-back rings."

"Yeah, well, my performance was better than Game 1. And I plan to destroy them tomorrow, so stay tuned."

"Now that's what I'm talking about," Ms. Mavis added as she poured my coffee.

"At least somebody believes in me," I mumbled.

"Let me take your orders real quick, and then I'll leave you all to it."

After we placed our orders, Desmond offered, "I'll be watching from the comfort of my home. I invited some of the fellas to watch it at my place. Oh, and Cairo, too."

Desmond's mention of her name yanked me back to last night's shitty ending with Indira.

"Speaking of Cairo, I need to holler at you about that."

Desmond's face twisted like I had cursed his mama. "The fuck you say?"

"What?" I shrugged before I realized he misread my intention. "Nah, man, not about her, but her friend. You declaring Indira off-limits is a problem."

"Malik, you ain't gotta claim every woman that crosses your path, bruh."

"I didn't say I did, and I'm talking to DC, so stay out of it." I glared at Malcolm before turning to my friend. "What's the big problem? You and Cairo went and—"

Desmond's hand flew into the air to dead whatever he thought I would say. "Me and my girl don't have nothing to do with you."

My lips curled with doubt. "Oh, now she's your girl?"

"I'm working on it, but at least I have good intentions. I'm retired from the league, and I'm trying to retire my bachelorhood. You're trying to hang on to both."

Malcolm burst into laughter, and I wanted to knock both their heads together. "The fuck you trying to say, DC? I ain't got no game left in me?"

"Malik, I know you. You ain't trying to do both—stay in the game and settle down. You're not ready to quit partying, dating, and cycling through women. You enjoy your variety and freedom too much. Indira is a good woman, not the kind you just run through."

"That might be true, but I don't know if you know her as well as you think you do."

"What you trying to say?"

"I'm just saying she invited your boy back to her house last night." Before I could defend myself, Ms. Mavis was back with our food. I snagged a piece of turkey bacon from my plate before she set it on the table, and she swatted at me playfully.

As soon as she was out of hearing range, Malcolm scolded. "And? Malik, you know Latimers ain't the kiss-and-tell type. That shit ain't cool."

"I know that. I'm just saying ain't no way DC could know what she wants because she don't even know."

"How you figure that?" DC challenged.

"Oh, I don't know," I shot back. Like the way she invited me into her house *after* I told her I promised you I wouldn't touch her, and she still tried to get busy."

Malcolm twisted his lips. "You're lying."

"I'm not. On Bible. But you would be proud of your boy. I mean, don't get me wrong, I didn't turn down the opportunity to kiss her, but I did dead it from going anywhere. And that's only because you asked me to." I pointed angrily at Desmond.

"That's hard to believe." His lips curled in doubt. "What? You couldn't get it up or something?"

I sucked my teeth as my brother laughed at Desmond's insanity. "Miss me with that. My soldier functions just fine."

"So then what happened?" Desmond pressed me.

I finished chewing on my turkey bacon, reluctant to share. "She put me out."

"She did what?"

"Dog, you heard what I said. She kicked me out of her house."

"Why? I thought you said you stopped?"

"Exactly. I stopped, and she was pissed. I went home with blue balls, and she probably went to bed with the same problem."

Malcolm almost choked on his coffee before slapping the table. "You're fucking kidding me, right?"

"I wish I were," I quipped before biting into my avocado toast. "I was so damn frustrated by the time I made it home, I googled if women had an equivalent condition. I was happy as shit when I learned they do. I hope it kept her up all night."

I was practically pouting, just remembering how I had to take care of myself in the shower before I could sleep. Either way, Desmond needed to chill with his overprotective ass.

"So let's get this straight," Desmond clarified. "Indy put you out because she wanted sex, and you didn't."

"That's exactly what I'm telling you. She's cool people, and I'd love to kick it again, but..."

"But what? Sounds to me like you might be getting a taste of your own medicine. She might've wanted to hit and quit," Malcolm surmised.

"Wouldn't that be some shit," Desmond chuckled.

"That ain't funny, dog," I frowned. "Not at all."

"Yes, it is. Indira might have flipped the script on you. She might not need my interference, after all."

"Trust me, she doesn't. That girl is a boss. I'm pretty sure she gets what she wants and doesn't settle for less."

"So, what? You asking for my blessing or something?" Desmond smirked.

"You ain't her Daddy, and I ain't asking for her hand. But like you said, she don't need your interference."

"A'ight. But you fuck her over, and I'm coming for your ass."

"I hear you, man, and I'm up for the challenge." Despite my assurance, I had no idea what I was signing up for. I hadn't been in a relationship for years, but something about Indira James made me willing to give it a shot.

Chapter Eleven

INDIRA

I didn't do well with rejection. Correction—I wasn't familiar with it. I couldn't remember a single time in my life when a man had turned me down.

I'd learned early on what feminine power could do. Not because anyone taught me, but because I watched. Tamara—when she showed up— knew how to work a room. She didn't just wear pretty things; she armed herself with them. She knew which scents made men lean closer, which heels made her legs go on forever. To this day, the faintest whiff of Beautiful makes me think of her.

People say I'm her spitting image. Shorter, sharper, and less reckless —but still hers. Except for the freckles. She never had them. I used to wonder where they came from, but I stopped asking a long time ago.

Tamara used her looks to survive. I used mine because I could. Which is exactly why I had no problem making a move on Malik last night. It wasn't just the dry spell—I mean, yes, it's been six months and counting— but that man had me ready to risk it all.

I thought we were on the same page: bring him home, have my fun, knock the dust off, go to sleep satisfied. Instead, I ended up horny, confused, and offended. I practically threw my goodies at him, and he had the nerve to say no. Said he made a promise to Desmond. Like I needed a chaperone.

So, I did what any self-respecting, pissed-off woman would do—I put his fine ass out and finished the night with Rose.

The next morning, I woke up still salty about last night's turn of events. Just as I was recovering from round two with Duracell and zero shame, my phone lit up.

"Tell me you're not still in bed," Cairo said.

I groaned, dragging the sheet over my chest as I reached for the phone. "Good morning to you too, sunshine."

"You sound winded."

"I'm fine," I said, voice still rough with sleep. "What's up?"

"You remember that foundation DC set up for Zahara?"

"Yeah," I mumbled, shifting onto my side. "What about it?"

"He just texted me. Said the first semester funds cleared, and the scholarship account's officially live."

"Oh, that's good." I yawned. "So why do you sound like you're confessing a crime?"

Cairo sighed. "Because it still feels weird letting someone else handle it. I should be the one covering her tuition."

"You are—just not alone." I smiled into my pillow. "Take the win, Cee. You've been holding it down long enough."

She went quiet for a beat. "You always gotta make it sound so simple."

"Because it is," I said, sinking deeper into the sheets. "It's not charity —it's love. There's a difference."

"Uh-huh. Keep preaching, Reverend Indy."

I smirked, barely one eye open. "Amen. Now hang up before you ruin my post-Duracell bliss."

Cairo laughed under her breath. "You're ridiculous."

"Love you too," I murmured, ready to drop the phone and drift off again.

But before I could, Cairo's tone shifted. "Speaking of charity... I saw Malik on the news this morning."

My eyes cracked open. "He's always on the news."

"This was different. Something about grocery gift cards for two hundred families, donations to food banks. Apparently, he does it every year."

"Hmph. Good for him," I muttered. "But I don't have much to say to him right now."

"Why not? I thought y'all had a good time the other night."

I scoffed. "Tried to. Let's just say homeboy hit me with a plot twist. He resisted my advances. Said he promised DC he wouldn't touch me."

"Wait, seriously?"

"Dead ass. Who does that? Who tells a grown woman 'no' because their homeboy said so?"

"Well..." Cairo's voice softened. "DC might just be trying to look out for you, considering Malik's reputation."

"Whatever. I don't need protecting. If Tamara catches wind, she'll be in my texts asking for 'help' again." I rubbed my temple. "You think I should see him again?"

Cairo sighed. "I was going to say yes—at the risk of you biting my head off."

"Yeah—so I can check his ass. Him and DC. Since when do I need supervision?"

Cairo snorted. "You don't."

"Exactly."

I hesitated, then lowered my voice like I was confessing a sin. "Anyway... I finally wore his ass down. Thought I was gonna get mine and go to bed happy." I let it hang. "I found out he's packing."

Cairo groaned. "Indy."

"No, listen. I'm talking moose status. Not horse. Not bull. Moose." I spaced the words out for effect. "I saw it, and I panicked. Shut it all the way down."

"What?" Cairo cackled. "You? Scared of dick?"

"Girl, I'm not trying to die out here."

Her wheezing laugh nearly drowned me out.

"But don't get it twisted," I added. "Just because I had a moment of self-preservation doesn't mean I wanted him to get up, get dressed, and ask for permission. He said he had to talk to DC first. Can you believe that shit?"

"So you... what, kicked him out?"

"Damn right I did. Malik Latimer can kiss my entire Black ass. Got me out here feeling like I have to beg. Me. Indira Lynn J—"

"Girl, calm down," she cut in, breathless from laughing. "You're gonna wake the neighbors."

"I'm calm."

"You just said 'fuck Malik' two seconds ago."

"And I meant it."

"Famous last words," she sang, then hung up.

Silence filled the room, except for the low hum of Rose in the background. I stared at the ceiling, phone still warm in my hand.

"Famous last words," I muttered to myself, even though I knew damn well I'd see Malik again.

I stepped into the newly renovated gymnasium at Mount Moriah, taking in its familiar setup. It reminded me of the gym at Shady Grove, my home church, where Cairo and Desmond met at youth basketball. I'd been here for resource fairs before but today was different. Mount Moriah was hosting the One Roof Foundation for the first time.

I'd heard of them in passing—a nonprofit doing real work in housing across the city. That's why I bought a table for their brunch fundraiser. If their work matched the pitch, I'd consider getting involved—if I could find the time. Between teaching chair yoga at the nursing home and volunteering at the food pantry with Zee, my community service plate was already full.

Early on, I learned the importance of realtors building relationships, especially in the communities where we want to do business. This was the easiest way for me to gain insight into parents' top choices for school districts, local government happenings, and any other local services that were important to buyers, like grocery stores and salons. Armed with this information, I could share the key information my clients would need to make a well-informed decision about where they want to live.

One of the best ways to build these connections was through volunteering. Donating my time rooted me in the community—and it killed two birds with one stone. Stronger neighborhoods meant stronger property values, which meant higher commissions. A win all around.

I stepped deeper into the gym, immediately overwhelmed by the hum of conversation and the squeals of children darting between tables. Clearly, they weren't raised by Granny or The Sisters. One out-of-pocket move in church used to earn me a switch across the legs—and always in public.

Sunlight poured through the vaulted ceiling, casting a golden glow over the room. Tables were draped in crisp white linen and crowned with bouquets of crème roses, lilies, and eucalyptus. Banners with the foundation's mission—"Building Futures Together"—hung from the rafters.

At the far end, the stage was framed in white-and-gold curtains, a wooden podium at its center engraved with the church's logo. A hymn lifted from the youth choir as a slideshow flashed across a screen: smiling faces, rehabbed homes, clean stats. Then Malik Latimer's face filled the frame, surrounded by kids.

I froze.

I glanced around, wondering if this was a joke—if Malik had arranged it. Then I spotted him not ten feet away, back turned, chatting near the refreshment table.

Of course, he stood out. No one else here was a foot taller than the crowd. No one else could rock a Thom Browne suit like it was stitched to his body. And no one else could make my pulse stumble like Malik.

It didn't matter that our last encounter had gone sideways. The man had stoked a fire that hadn't burned out. But I had more than my libido to wrangle—I had a bruised ego. His rejection still stung, all in the name of Desmond.

I squared my shoulders and walked toward him. "Malik," I said through clenched teeth, low enough not to draw attention.

He turned quickly, chest rising with a breath he didn't finish. The flicker in his eyes vanished, replaced by control. "Indira."

"I didn't expect to see you here," I said, annoyance sharpening my tone.

"Of course I'd be here. I've invested a lot of time in One Roof." His smile was dazzling. My body betrayed me—just a little.

"I wish I'd known," I muttered, studying my shoes.

"And why's that? Would you have stayed home?" He stepped closer, tilting my chin up with one finger.

My eyes narrowed. My posture stiffened. "You can't scare me off, Malik. But I don't have much to say to you right now." I hadn't planned to approach him at all, but my ego had marched me across the gym before my common sense caught up.

"I know last night ended badly. I wish I could have a do-over."

"Is that so?" My voice was cool.

"Yes." His eyes softened. "If I'm honest, I've never been in that situation before."

"What situation?"

"I've never wanted someone who was off-limits."

"Really?" I shot back. "Because I've never been declared off-limits. That was new."

"Resistance isn't my strong suit. But since our gas station meetup, you've had me working harder than I ever have with anyone."

My eyes widened. I guess we were both in foreign territory. "I hadn't thought about it that way."

He nodded once. "I get it if you're still salty. But I hope we can talk when you're ready."

I glanced around the room, then back at him. "Maybe," I said, my tone softer. "Let me see what this One Roof Foundation is about."

Near the end of the program, Malik took the stage, commanding without even picking up the mic. The room hushed instantly. He didn't read notes or pace. Just stood there—palms open, voice steady.

"Three years ago, I met a twelve-year-old boy in one of my mentoring programs. Smart, funny—a natural leader. Then, one day, he stopped coming. Not because he lost interest, but because he was couch-surfing between friends' places.

"When we first talked, he said he wanted to be a doctor. He used to patch up his little brother with Band-Aids and pretend he was in the ER. But when I found him again, he told me, 'I can't plan for college when I don't even know where I'm sleeping next week.'"

Sympathy rippled through the crowd.

"That stuck with me. Because how do you tell a kid to dream big when their basic needs aren't met? That conversation planted the seed for One Roof. With the help of donors and partners, we've launched skills programs, funded housing stipends, and next summer, we'll break ground on our first supportive housing complex right here in the city."

Applause thundered.

And I was floored. It wasn't the money. It wasn't the scale. It was how effortlessly he let the work speak for itself. No ego. No show-boating. Just conviction.

And God help me, he looked good doing it. That suit was fighting for its life across his chest and shoulders. That toffee-colored skin, the neat goatee catching the light—he had presence, yes. But he also had body. Power and polish wrapped in one package. I blinked hard, trying to reset.

Across the room, I leaned into a conversation with a city council rep I recognized from another coalition. As we spoke a woman with a camera drifted over. "Mind if I grab a quick photo for the church newsletter?"

"No photos, please—work thing. Appreciate you." *Publicity has a way of making certain relatives think my wallet's open.*

She backed off. I returned to the councilman, exchanged cards, asked about zoning. Business, not flirtation.

Even so, I could feel Malik's gaze tracking me as I headed back to my table. I gathered my purse and scanned for Malik.

After the benediction, the crowd thinned. Gone. A pinch of disappointment tugged, but I brushed it off and headed out.

I had just eased the Flex into reverse when a knock on my window made me jump.

Malik grinned sheepishly.

I rolled it down. "Hey."

"I looked for you after, but…"

"Had to step out for a call," I lied.

"Did you enjoy yourself?"

"The food? Immaculate. The keynote?" I tilted my head. "Not bad."

He smirked. "I'll tell Malcolm about the food."

"You catered *and* gave a TED Talk? You're really trying to flex?"

"Just trying to stay in the running. Figured I'd bring my A-game."

I folded my arms, studying him. "You made quite an impression."

"Thank you."

"Why didn't you tell me about all this?"

"I don't do it for recognition. But you're right—I should've said something," he admitted, rubbing the back of his neck.

"You should be proud. Ma'Dear always says, 'To whom much is given—'"

"Much is required," he finished. "Luke 12:48. I know."

I raised a brow. "So you a church boy?"

"I've done my time on the pews." His eyes twinkled.

"Interesting."

"You got plans tomorrow?"

"Dinner with The Sisters. They've already given me a list of things to cook."

"We play Game 3 tomorrow, but I'll be free after. Maybe I can steal you away for dessert. Just us."

"As long as you're not still taking permission slips from DC."

"Nah." His hand rested on my door, leaning in just enough to shift the air between us. "I don't need permission for what I want."

I told myself not to read into it, but my pulse didn't get the memo. My eyes flicked to his hand, then to his mouth—then quickly away. "We'll see if you've earned it."

Chapter Twelve

MALIK

We stormed past the Bulls in Game 3—fast breaks, crisp passes, slam dunks. I dribbled through traffic like the hardwood was mine alone, threading assists and sinking jumpers with a calm I hadn't felt all season. I didn't just show up—I showed out. Years in the league, and this felt like a statement game.

After the final buzzer, cameras swarmed. Sweat clung to my brow as I grinned at the mic.

"What changed tonight?" the reporter asked.

I glanced at the lens, thinking of Indira. "Found a new good luck charm," I said, voice low but steady.

He blinked. "Care to elaborate?"

"Nah," I replied, smile lingering. "That's on a need-to-know basis."

Then I shifted. "But credit goes to the squad. We pushed the pace, took smart shots, locked down when it mattered."

It was nearly 8:00 before I made it to Jazzmasters. The whole city seemed to be celebrating the win. I stepped out of my truck and followed Slade through the building's rear entrance, straight into the private VIP lounge.

After a quick word with security, Slade vetted the room. I took in the space—plenty of square footage, soft lighting, and just enough soundproofing to make it feel like we'd left the chaos outside. Perfect for tonight. He gave me a nod, then took his post outside the door like a sentry, making sure my peace stayed intact.

I'd called ahead to the kitchen to have Malcolm's chocolate pecan pie ready. Mika was setting the plates and utensils when the door opened. Indira stepped in wearing a white dress that managed to be both simple and lethal. Strappy sandals with leather laces wrapped up her toned calves, stopping just below her knees. The lighting caught the smooth glow of her pecan-toned skin, making the faint dusting of freckles across her cheekbones look like they'd been painted on just to mess with me.

I'd noticed those freckles before—hell, I clocked them the first time I saw her at the gas station, rocking fitted blue jeans, a cropped hoodie, and Timberlands like she was born to ruin a man's focus. I spotted them again at Della Montague's engagement party in that white jumpsuit with DC hovering like he was ready to run inter-ference.

But this was different.

Here, it was just us. No crowd or distractions. Just me, close enough to count every single one.

"I couldn't forget these if I tried," I said, leaning forward and brushing a finger lightly over the bridge of her nose as she took her seat. Her breath hitched, and she shifted just slightly—enough for her knee to bump mine under the table. She didn't pull back. "But this is the first time I've had a chance to really take them in."

Her lips parted like she had a comeback, but nothing came out. She glanced at the dessert plates, then back at me. "So, do I get to try the famous pie you promised me, or was that just bait to get me here?"

I smirked. "I didn't have to bait you, Shortie. You were coming regardless."

"Confident, aren't you?" she said, arching one brow.

"Not confidence. Just facts." I slid a plate toward her and handed over a fork. "Malcolm's pie is dangerous, so pace yourself."

She took a bite, eyes closing briefly as she chewed. "Okay… you weren't lying. This is criminally good."

"Right? That pie has started fights in my family. One time, my pops didn't get a slice, and we all suffered for a week."

She laughed, low and warm, and the sound made something in my chest loosen. "If I had this whole pie, I wouldn't share either."

"Noted," I said, watching her take another bite. "Next time, I'll make sure you get one to yourself."

I let a grin tug at my mouth. "Though I gotta say—I looked for you in the stands tonight. Could've used that good luck charm in person."

Her fork paused mid-air, and she shot me a sideways glance. "Don't tell me you're superstitious now."

"Not superstitious," I said, leaning in just enough to brush her knee under the table. "Just observant."

Her eyes flicked up to mine, and for a beat, neither of us said anything. The pie was good, but she was the reason I wasn't hungry for anything else. She set her fork down slowly, her fingers brushing mine in the process—an accident that neither of us bothered to correct.

The air shifted. The music outside faded until all I could hear was her breathing and mine. Her fingers still brushed mine, light but deliberate. Every part of me wanted to close the gap, claim her right there. But I held back. I wanted her to lean in, to make the next move. If she chose me, I wanted it clear—no promises, no interference, just us.

Chapter Thirteen

INDIRA

My phone hadn't stopped buzzing in days—buyers, inspectors, unknown numbers. A voicemail preview flashed:

Indira, baby—saw you on church Facebook. Call me back. Mama just needs a little help 'til Friday.

Delete. Next.

By Wednesday, I swore it felt like there were billboards on the Lodge Freeway advertising my services. "Indira, did you get my email?" a voice chirped through my Bluetooth.

"Working on it now," I lied, dragging another file into the wrong folder as my phone buzzed nonstop.

Three unread messages from buyers, six from clients, an email from the inspector, and two voicemails from a seller who'd already called three times in the last hour. I noted upcoming appraisals on a yellow pad, pressing so hard the paper nearly tore. Deshaun's empty desk mocked me, a reminder that without him, I was my own assistant, scheduler, and analyst.

By Friday night, the candle on my bookshelf had tunneled into itself. Papers sprawled across my desk like a windstorm had passed. My phone vibrated again—another showing request. My stomach clenched with hunger. I thumbed through a delivery menu, debating pad thai or drive-thru fries, when a text banner slid across the top of my screen.

MALIK: Flying in soon. Miss those freckles.

ME: You saw them on FaceTime last night

MALIK: Doesn't count. I want the real deal.
Can I come thru?

Did I want to see him? Absolutely. Did I want him to know how badly? Not a chance.

My laptop looked like a crime scene—the city permit portal, comps, two spreadsheets fighting me on formulas, and a Zillow tab I swore I was only opening for five minutes. My stomach kept filing complaints I ignored. Hours ago, I'd texted Malik:

ME: Raisinets = respectable meals. Don't
judge me.

After hitting send, I buried my distracting phone under floor plans like evidence. I dove back into work, ignoring the hunger pangs, pausing only to hit the bathroom. On my way out, I decided to get more comfortable —trading my day clothes for cut-off sweat-pants and a cropped t-shirt.

I was halfway back to my office when a light knock sounded, then the doorbell. Not frantic—more like a polite tap that knew the hour was late. Two in the morning kind of late.

Every bone in my body told me not to open without checking

first. I padded to the entryway, my Hellcat's familiar weight in my hand.

"Who is it?" I called, sliding the chain across the door. "Delivery," a familiar baritone announced. "With a side of chocolate."

I peered through the peephole. The Tigers cap was low, concealing his eyes. But the asymmetrical dimples made his identity unmistakable. One hand held up a yellow Raisinets box, while the other balanced a paper takeout bag.

I cracked the door. "Malik, I didn't order anything."

"You kinda did." He lifted the box. "I'm not staying. I'm just gonna feed you."

He said it so simply that something loosened in my chest. "You have ten minutes," I warned.

"Twenty," he said, grin quick. "Non-negotiable." He stopped in my kitchen like he was on a field trip. "Plates are...where?"

"Upper right," I said, fighting a grin.

He set the bag down and started unpacking. "Pad thai, no peanuts, extra lime. Spring rolls. Mango sticky rice."

I squinted. "How would you know—"

"I cheated," he said, palms up, no swagger, no fronting. "Texted Cairo. Told her I didn't want to guess and show up wrong. If that's weird, I'll eat on the stoop, and you can say you never saw me."

My annoyance dissolved immediately. "It's not weird," I said.

"It's...considerate. Traitor," I added under my breath, referring to Cairo, though it softened me anyway.

He found a pan, added a splash of water, and warmed the noodles on the stove like someone who'd paid attention at least once in a kitchen. He rolled a lime under his palm, quartered it, and set the pieces by my plate. Then he tapped his phone; a faint chime sounded.

"What was that?"

"Twenty-minute timer," he said. "We eat, I'm gone."

"Bossy."

"Accurate." He slid the plate to me and passed a fork. "Drink?" He looked around; I pointed to the fridge. He reached in, grabbed a bottle of water, and set it by my elbow. "Begin."

The first bite hit like repentance and relief—sweet, salty, heat. I closed my eyes. When I opened them, he wasn't staring; he was watching to make sure I took a second bite.

"You haven't eaten since…?" he asked.

"Two-ish," I said. "Chips—"

"Twelve hours ago? Don't count." His gaze flicked to the sprawl in my living room. "This all today?"

"Permits. Appraiser with an attitude. A contractor who thinks 'tomorrow' is the norm." I took another bite. "I'm fine."

"You're a powerhouse," he stated—like a fact, not a line. "But even powerhouses refuel."

A laugh tripped out of me. "You practice speeches in the mirror?"

"Only when my barber's running late." He glanced at the stacks on my coffee table. I forgot I had papers there, too. "Mind if I…?" He mimed grouping things.

"Careful," I warned.

He made neat piles—City, Call, Paid, Asim—without peeking, just moving the water hazard out of the way of my laptop. Then he came back to the island and slid the Raisinets across the quartz like a trophy.

"Dessert if you finish." He paused. "Cairo also said you'll swear you don't want sticky rice and then eat half. I'm afraid of her, so."

I snorted. "As you should be."

We ate shoulder-to-shoulder without touching. He asked about my latest; I told him the permits and inspectors that Asim had warned about were becoming a problem. Transforming a whole block was challenging enough, but the red tape was a hassle I didn't need.

He didn't interrupt or fix; he listened with the experience of a person who led and still got blindsided. "At least you didn't have another mix-up like that sprinkler thing. It's like a perfect play blown by a loose screw in the rim. Not your fault. Don't let it make you play small."

My eyes shot to his face. "I don't play small. Ever."

"I know." The corner of his mouth tugged. "Watching you is kind of my new hobby."

Heat crawled up my throat; I pretended to care a lot about a spring roll. He nudged my water. "Drink."

"Bossy," I muttered, and drank. The timer ticked down on his screen; I could feel him monitoring them.

"I told Cairo I'd drop it and go. Plus, I gotta be at the gym early," he added, like he knew exactly where my brain would poke. "She said if I lingered, she'd FaceTime you and tell you to throw me out."

"That sounds right." I swallowed a sudden lump that wasn't food.

The idea that he'd done homework—quietly, through my people —pressed warm against a place I rarely let anyone touch.

He rinsed the knife he'd used, folded the paper bag and tucked it into the recycling, and wiped the counter left to right, like he had home training. Then he straightened, glanced at the phone. "Two minutes."

I set my fork down. "You really aren't staying?" He shook his head. "Respecting DC, not rejecting you." He came around the island slowly enough to let me stop him if I wanted more. Close enough to smell clean skin and citrus. He bent and pressed his mouth to my temple—warm, sure, gone too fast.

"I'll text when I leave practice tomorrow," he said. "You'll ignore me 'til you're starving and eventually remember I fed you. I'll pretend I'm not offended."

"You're very confident."

"I'm trying to be consistent." He pointed to the cap he left on a side table. "Collateral. I only get it back when you give yourself some downtime for one night."

"I have a terrible track record with downtime," I admitted, softer than I meant to.

"I noticed." He tipped his cap. "Thanks for letting me feed you."

"Thanks for asking Cairo," I said, meeting his eyes. "That part matters."

"I figured." He opened the door, looked back with that curve of a smile and those devilish dimples that made promises without saying a word. "Sleep, Bite-Size."

The door closed softly. I stood there breathing in lime and tamarind and something steadier. My kitchen felt warmer. My laptop still blinked like a needy child, but it was quieter in my head.

My phone buzzed.

MALIK: Drink water.

I laughed, finished the glass, and texted Cairo.

ME: You snitch.

CAIRO: A hungry snitch. Eat the rice.

I ate the rice. Then I set a real timer—twenty minutes to work, ten to stretch, eight to decide whether I'd let him earn his Tigers cap back. His cap-as-collateral stunt and the quiet way he looked after me were even better than the food.

When I finally hit the sack hours later, I kept replaying Malik's quiet kindness. I swore it was just dinner. My grin called bullshit.

After practice the next day, Malik sprawled on my turquoise sofa like he owned it, long legs stretched out. Martin reruns played, but his eyes stayed on me more than the screen. When Gina accidentally killed Mama's bird, I hopped up for more wine.

"You want a glass?"

"Nah, I'm good."

"Need anything else?"

"Nope. I'm full of that salmon, green beans, and cauliflower rice. That was good as hell. Just hurry up and bring your fine ass back."

I stepped over his legs with my bottle and glass, brushing his thigh on purpose. He didn't move—just smirked like he knew exactly what he was doing to me. "Let me ask you something. Which Martin character are you?"

He frowned. "No idea. Only thing I've got in common with him is being from Detroit."

"Aw, come on."

He tapped his chin, then grinned. "Got nothing. But I know who *you* are."

"Who?"

"Sheneneh Jenkins."

I almost choked. "Boy, what?! Ain't nothing about me close to her!"

"You're loud and sassy—you can't deny that."

"Pfft, well, no. But have you seen her outfits? I keep it classy."

"She's confident, got her own style—what's wrong with that?"

"That is not me."

He laughed. "Alright, Shortie, I'm kidding. You're Gina."

"Why?"

"Put-together but low-key chaotic. I can see you keeping me in check while enabling my nonsense."

"Mmm. If I'm Gina, you're Martin. But I don't know if you've got the comedic chops."

"You doubtin' me? I got jokes for days."

"I'll give you goofy. But Martin was extra—always starting something. That's you."

He grinned. "Exactly. So you admit I'm Martin, and you're my Gina."

I rolled my eyes. "Here you go. So... who's your Tommy and Cole?"

"Easy—Jackie's Tommy. Sharp dresser, mystery job." I laughed. "Seriously, what does your sister do for a living?"

"Nobody knows."

"Okay, so who's Cole?"

"Don't have one. Ain't nobody I roll with acting clueless 24/7."

"What about Jarvis Bentley?"

"Oh, facts. Doesn't matter how many NBA records JB breaks—Twinna runs his pockets and his schedule."

"No cap," I agreed.

"Thanks for indulging my silliness, Martin."

"Anytime," he said, his voice lower now, eyes dragging over me instead of the TV. "One of these days... you'll be my Gina for real."

The air tightened.

"So, are you saying what I think you're saying?"

"What do you think I'm saying?"

"That you're trying to make this more than hanging out."

"Maybe I'm saying I want to see more of you."

"See more of me how? Because if you recall, after my initial shock at your—" I gestured toward his lap, "—endowment, I was down for whatever. *You* took sex off the table. Not me."

He chuckled, low. "Yeah, I remember. But that's 'cause I told DC I'd keep things cool."

"And now?"

"Now, I might circle back... see if you're still talking all that noise."

"Please tell me you didn't go back to DC to ask if we could—"

"Nah, Shortie. It wasn't like that. I just let him know you and me...we've got a connection."

"That's what we're calling it? A connection?"

"A strong one. And it's worth seeing where it goes." His gaze lingered, pinning me until my pulse stuttered. I had to look away—because for the first time, I wasn't sure if I wanted to run from what he was offering—or straight into it.

Two days after Malik's visit, I still wasn't caught up on work. I skipped my yoga class on Saturday and played hooky from church on Sunday, which was sure to raise The Sisters' eyebrows. But I'd deal with that fallout later. All I wanted was to get back on track.

Early in the afternoon, I was sitting cross-legged on the floor in my living room, trying to refocus my mind by scrolling through real estate listings on my tablet. Instead, Malik's voice replayed in my head— steady, low, certain. "One of these days... you'll be my Gina for real." My heart thumped just remembering the weight in his eyes when he said it.

Suddenly, the front door clicked open. Cairo walked in, dropped her purse on the nearest chair, and kicked off her heels. She arched an eyebrow when she saw me on the floor, surrounded by property brochures and a half-finished glass of wine. I watched her eyeing the mess and braced myself for her trash talk.

"Damn, girl. This place looks like a paper mill exploded. You got a big sale coming up or what?"

I placed my tablet aside and sighed. "I do. But right now, I'm mostly just... distracted."

Cairo folded her arms. "Uh-huh. And by distracted, you mean Malik?"

I pressed my lips together. "So he told you?"

She shook her head and plopped down across from me. "Nope. Desmond might've hinted that Malik's been on pins and needles all weekend since he told you he wanted more."

Heat rose to my cheeks. Malik had been on my mind nonstop since then. His words weren't casual—they carried weight. And that rattled me. I'm used to being the one who sets the pace—and by pace, I mean hit it and quit it.

I leaned back against my sofa. "Yeah, he said it. And I...I didn't really give him a straight answer."

"Aren't you the one always preaching the benefits of good dick?"

"Yeah," I said, feeling defensive. "And?"

"Are you trying to tell me you didn't pick up on Malik's big dick energy?"

"Excuse you? Does Desmond know you're out here evaluating his friend's package?"

"Indy, shut up! And DC is not my man, remember? So, for now, he has no authority over my eyes."

"Anyway, CeeCee, where are you going with this?"

"I'm just trying to understand why you're playing so hard to get with Malik. The man is fine, sweet, paid out the ass—though I know that doesn't matter to you—and he's borderline obsessed with you. What's the worst that can happen—he bags you, then tricks you out with jewelry and purses?"

I pushed my lips toward my nose and considered my response. A lot could happen.

I could take him up on his offer, enjoy it until we'd both had our fill, and then move on. Or, I could give him something that would have his nose wide open, not wanting to move on at all.

Or worse—I could be the one who ended up sprung, head over heels, starving for his attention... only to watch him get tired of me.

But I didn't want to admit any of that, not even to my sister-friend.

Instead, I fiddled with a stray thread on my leggings, searching for an easier, safer explanation. "He's in the middle of the Playoffs, constantly in the spotlight... I'm already juggling my house flips and new clients. Jumping into something this public—" I exhaled slowly, "I don't want all of that to crash and burn."

"Look, I get it," CeeCee said softly. "The spotlight can be rough. But trust me, if Malik's serious, he'll work around your hustle. Have you told him why you're hesitating?"

Her question made me think about how I all but sidestepped his words, leaving him with a half-hearted, "I just need more time, okay?" The confusion on his face cut deep.

I rubbed my forehead. "No. I haven't explained in detail. How do I tell him I'm not just worried about the media—I'm worried about letting someone in? My real estate career is the one area I'm 100% sure about. Letting a superstar athlete into my personal life? That's a risk, one I don't know if I want to take."

Cairo nudged my arm. "And how did he react to what you did say?"

"He said he wanted to see more of me. But the way his smile faltered for a split second... yeah, he was hurt, even if he didn't say it outright."

"Girl, if you like him, you gotta meet him halfway. Keeping him guessing won't do either of you any good. Have the conversation. Tell him your fears. Lay it on the table."

I swallowed hard. "You're right. I just... I need to organize my thoughts first. There's so much to consider—groupies, the press, fans blowing up my mentions if they learn my name..."

Cairo smirked. "Don't forget the perks: courtside seats, VIP parties, those arms around you at night..."

I laughed despite myself. She knew how to push my buttons. And just like that, warmth spread through me at the thought of Malik's arms— steady, protective, impossible to ignore. Maybe it was time I stopped overthinking and trusted that he saw more in me than a fling.

"Alright, I'll talk to him. Soon. No more dodging." Cairo reached for my wine glass. "That's my girl. Now, can you share some of this vino? And maybe reconsider the mess around here before you invite Malik the Freak over?"

I rolled my eyes. "Whatever. Pass the wine—I've got a conversation to plan."

Chapter Fourteen

MALIK

People think the NBA is all talent and highlight reels. It's discipline. The league drills punctuality into you—be on time or pay for it. I don't do late. So sitting in an Ann Arbor bistro, checking my watch for the third time while Indira ran twenty minutes behind, had my jaw tight.

She'd picked a spot forty-five minutes from the city. Privacy. Fewer eyes. Fewer phones. I could work with that. Slade posted up out of the way because, as he told her, "Not during the Playoffs. Can't risk it." She hated the idea of security, but she let it ride.

The door opened and she came in fast—white leather dress with a clean plunge, rhinestoned fishnets catching the light, heels clicking like a metronome. The room shifted. I stood so quick I almost clipped my water glass.

"Indy," I said, pulling out her chair.

"Hey, Malik." A little breathless. "I'm so sorry I'm late. Client flaked, phone died, forgot my charger—"

"It's all good." And it was. Annoyance gone. I opened my arms. "May I?"

"You may," she laughed, stepping in. She smelled like honey-suckle on warm skin. Gone too fast.

"Have a seat," I said, trying not to stare like a rookie. She gave me a quick once-over. "You look good. You smell good. Dolce & Gabbana—The One?"

"You know it," I grinned. "Your hair's different."

"Air-dried. No heat today. Probably not what you're used to, right?"

"What's that supposed to mean?"

She lifted a shoulder. "You're around women with hair down their backs."

I huffed a laugh. "Did you just throw shade?"

"A little."

"For the record, I'm not that shallow." I reached, brushed the tapered side by her ear, let a coil slip between my fingers. "I've never seen a style on you I didn't like."

Her eyes softened. "Really?"

"Really."

The server came. She debated; I didn't. "Don't skimp," I told her when she couldn't choose.

"Latimer, I'm not wasting food."

"Who said anything about wasting? You order; I'll help." She got the salmon, broccolini, and truffled mash. I grabbed the lamb chops, extra garlic butter, and the bread I caught her eyeballing.

"If I eat too much, you're carrying me out," she warned. "Deal."

Plates landed, conversation loosened. She ate; I liked that about her.

No fake nibbling. When the server cleared, I leaned back.

"So does this place pass the test?"

"It does," she said. "And yes, I dragged you to the boondocks on purpose."

"That's why you haven't answered me?" I asked. "About making this more than... hanging out."

She tucked her hands under her thighs, glanced around the room, then back at me. "Kinda sorta."

"How so?"

"You want to define this. Make it… more formal."

"And what's wrong with that?"

"I like us low-key."

My chest pulled tight. "Nothing you'd change? It's perfect the way it is?"

A flush climbed her cheeks. "Not everything." She wet her lip, then blurted, "You haven't touched me since our first night."

I let out a low laugh. "You think I don't want to?" I leaned in, voice for her alone. "Indy, it's taking everything in me not to spread you out like a feast right now. But more than I want your body, I want to know you."

"You don't know me well enough?"

"To have sex? Sure. To handle the attention without us getting messy? I'm taking my time."

She sat with that. "So you're… pacing us."

"Yeah."

She exhaled. "What I'm worried about is the attention. When you say 'my girl,' you mean public. Photos. Blogs. People in my business. That's normal to you. It's not to me."

"White," I said.

She blinked. "What?"

"White. You like white. Cream. Ivory. You switch it up for special occasions." I cut my eyes at her. "My point? I pay attention. People pay attention to you, too. They're gonna look whether you're with me or not."

"I do care what people think," she shot back.

"I don't believe you," I said, and her eyes got wide. I held my hands up. "Hear me out. You're a head turner and you know it. You don't hide it. Those eyes. That mouth. The way you walk. You're a magnet. That's not on you—that's just true. And if I'm next to you, they'll look harder. But it doesn't have to run the show."

She stared, chin high. "Tell that to your ex at Della's party. Or to the women who act like I'm invisible while they shoot their shot in front of me. That's not ignorance—that's disrespect."

"Briana means nothing," I said, flat. "Fuck her."

She studied me, as if she were measuring whether I meant it. I did.

"Have I given you a reason to think I can't shut that down?" I asked. "That I won't keep my word?"

She hesitated. Something else lived behind her eyes. Then she looked away, traced the rim of her water. "It's not that. I just…" She shook her head. "Forget it."

"Say it."

"It's nothing," she said, but her voice said otherwise. Then: "I'm in."

"In how?"

"Boundaries," she said, finally meeting me. "For now: no photos, no tags, no sideline broadcasts. Private spaces. If one of us needs air, we take it. We build this quietly, and if it still feels right when the dust clears, we can stop hiding."

I nodded once. "Deal. I'll keep Slade close and invisible. I'll pick spots where we don't have to duck cameras. I'll make sure the people around me understand what 'off-limits' means."

She held my stare, testing for cracks. "And if they don't?"

"Then they're not around me."

The corner of her mouth lifted. "Okay, Martin."

I smirked. "Okay, Gina."

The check came. I didn't rush it. When we finally stood, I shrugged out of my jacket and settled it over her shoulders. Slade peeled from the wall like a shadow as we headed for the door.

Outside, the air had a bite. I walked her to her truck, opened the door, and waited while she slid in.

"Text me when you're home," I said.

"You'll ignore me till I'm starving and remember you fed me?" she teased.

"Nah," I said, grinning. "I'm trying to be consistent."

She rolled her eyes, but the smile sneaked out anyway. "Good night, Malik."

"Night, Indy."

She pulled away; Slade brought the truck around. I watched her taillights until they disappeared, then climbed in, thumbs hovering over my phone.

I didn't get everything I wanted. But I got what mattered— terms, not distance. A plan. And her "I'm in." I could work with that.

Chapter Fifteen

INDIRA

I cracked a little—not because of the meal, but because of the way he looked at me, like I was the most interesting thing in the room. And that scent—cedar and amber over warm skin, unmistakably him. Add the double dimple on the right and the single on the left—unfair, hypnotic—and suddenly I'm staring at his mouth. Clean-lined goatee, soft mouth. Pure trouble. Delicious trouble.

Which is exactly why I was supposed to remind him: I don't do ballers—the spotlight shifts, the gold-digger whispers start, and Tamara smells money.

I don't do relationships—because I learned early that somebody always leaves first.

Keep it casual—because I built my life so I'd never need anyone to take care of me again.

But tonight, I broke my own rule—the first one, the important one. Now it's only a matter of time before he proves me right. Relationships don't last—not really. It's a waiting game: who leaves first. Malik might think he's different, but when it gets rough, he'll do what everyone else did.

And there's this—I don't need a man. Consistent sex? Fine. Beyond that, I handle mine. Always have.

Since my first paycheck, the goal's been simple: make enough so no one ever has to carry me again—especially with Tamara circling whenever money is in the air. The Sisters did enough.

I put myself through college, built a career, and stacked my own money. That's who I am. That's what I trust.

I'd agreed, so I owed it an honest try. The way he listened—and those dimples—kept replaying until I was in Brush Park, facing the Gothic Victorian I'd seen listed two years ago. "Little Paris" then, mostly ghosts now. This one survived.

I dragged my eyes up the façade: a turret, a portico on carved columns, ironwork too delicate to have lasted this long. The place was meticulously restored—I knew that; it hit the market two years ago.

What I didn't know—what rooted me to the sidewalk—was who bought it:

Malik.

Not a glass box in Midtown. This. A survivor with history and bones. A house with weight.

Like dinner, the choice knocked me sideways. I'd filed him under flash and noise—ballers chasing what plays on camera and fades by Monday. This wasn't that. This was legacy, keeping something alive. Maybe—even—staying put.

And staying put isn't just an address; it's not running when things get messy. I speak that language, even when I pretend I don't.

That did something to me—something I didn't want to unpack.

Because Malik Latimer was supposed to be one thing—an NBA superstar, a man who lived for the cameras, for the next championship, for the next deal. But this house told a different story—one I wasn't sure I was ready to hear.

I exhaled, pushed past the hesitation, and stepped inside. The original banister, polished to a dark shine, led me up three flights—past the floors he rented out—toward the penthouse. Each step echoed off the high ceilings, my heartbeat settling a little more with every landing.

At the top landing, the penthouse's double doors—his—waited. I pressed the bell, rocking on my heels. A moment later, one swung open.

Malik leaned in the doorway, barefoot in gray sweats and a fitted black T-shirt, broad shoulders filling the frame. His eyes gave nothing away; the smirk said otherwise.

"Indy," he drawled, low and smooth. "Make it up those stairs okay?"

I rolled my eyes. "Barely. If I'd known it was leg day, I'd have stretched."

His chuckle was a warm rumble. "C'mon in."

I stepped in; the space stole my breath. Floor-to-ceiling glass ran the length of the room, Detroit spread out in lights. The skyline glowed against dusk. The living area felt expansive but warm— exposed brick, dark beams, a sunken charcoal sectional tying the old bones to the clean lines.

Tamara would see only dollar signs in this view, count the square footage, and plot how to work it. Me? I couldn't stop thinking about the choice behind it—the bones Malik decided to keep.

"This is... wow," I murmured, turning in a slow circle. "You live here?"

He shut the door and slipped his hands into his pockets. "Figured I'd invest in something worth keeping."

I glanced back at him, his eyes locked on mine, and it felt like he meant more than the house. Standing there, in his space, I felt something shift in me—something I wasn't sure I wanted.

I'd spent my whole life chasing stability, earning it, stacking it piece by piece. But this was something else entirely. Malik hadn't just bought a home; he'd restored one —a piece of the city's history, left behind but still standing, still worth saving.

Maybe that's why I felt off-balance. I've spent years swearing I don't need saving—no fixes, no rescue—but standing here made me wonder: did Malik see me the way he saw this place? Something with bones worth investing in, preserving, and keeping.

The thought rattled me.

I built my life on self-sufficiency—so I'd never need anyone, never hand someone the power to leave me stranded. And yet here I was, in a space Malik made, feeling something dangerously close to belonging. I looked at him again. Maybe this was a mistake. Or maybe it wasn't.

Standing in Malik's study, I traced the intricate woodwork of the fireplace mantel; the clean linen and polished oak scent wrapped around me. Lost in it, I didn't hear Malik until his voice cut through.

"You seem deep in thought."

I turned, offering a small smile. "Just admiring the work." He stepped closer, gaze steady. "It's more than that, isn't it?" I frowned. "What do you mean?"

"This place... changed how you see me."

I opened my mouth and closed it again.

He went on, softer. "You had me pegged as another athlete— fame over substance."

"I never said that."

"You didn't have to." He let the silence stretch. "But now the house doesn't fit the picture. Throws you."

I looked away, my fingers still resting on the mantel. "It's a lot."

"Let the old story go, Indy." Malik's voice softened. "I'm more than the box I'm in—and you know it."

I met his gaze. "It's not easy for me to... trust."

"I'm not asking for easy. Just a chance."

His words hung there, daring me to set down the fear I kept polished like armor. I didn't answer. He didn't move.

I turned back to the windows, but I felt him before I heard him. His warmth gathered close behind me, his breath a quiet thread. I swallowed, ignoring the goosebumps lifting along my arms.

"I wasn't expecting this," I said, keeping my voice steady.

"Expecting what?" he asked, lower now, closer. "This place. You. Any of it."

The air between us went dense, and then I felt it—his hand grazing my arm, fingertips barely there, enough to send a shiver down my spine. I should have stepped away, made space. I didn't.

His fingers slid down to my wrist, then back up—a lazy, deliberate line. Testing. Teasing. "You're tense," he murmured.

I let out a slow breath. "I'm not used to this."

"This?"

"You."

Silence stretched, not empty—charged, humming with what neither of us said. I tipped my head, my cheek almost grazing his chest. That scent —woodsy, warm, intoxicating—wrapped around me. My body leaned like it knew the way.

"Malik…" I started, the rest dissolving on my tongue. He didn't push. Didn't rush. But he didn't step back, either. And neither did I.

Malik's mouth met mine—slow, deliberate, like he had all the time in the world, and I finally believed I did, too. His hands—large, warm, sure —settled at my waist, flexing like he was mapping me. He let me set the pace. Somehow, that was the sexiest part.

I'm used to men chasing the moment—fast, careless, over just as quickly. Malik felt rooted. Present. That scared me, so I did what I do best: tested him.

My palms slid under his shirt, tracing hard planes. His breath hitched; he waited. I tipped my head, lips at his jaw. "You always this patient?"

A low chuckle vibrated against my skin. "Only when I know it's worth it."

I tugged his shirt over his head, taking in toffee skin and ink. He arched a brow. "You gonna keep looking, or do something about it?"

"Don't start something you can't finish, Latimer."

"Oh, Indy. I always finish."

His quiet certainty echoed inside me—like I wasn't just another conquest, but something he planned to keep seeing through.

Before I could give it more thought, he lifted me, hands firm at my thighs, pinning me lightly to the cool brick. The kiss went deeper, heat winding tight. Logic said stop. But the moment his lips trailed down my neck, slow and reverent, I let go.

"Indy," he murmured, thumb brushing my bottom lip. I could have pulled away, cracked a joke, dodged the real. Instead, I pressed into him. His restraint snapped.

The city view disappeared. There was only Malik—his weight, his warmth, his scent. I rolled my hips once; his curse rumbled against my skin.

Before I could do it again, he carried me to the bed. The mattress caught us; he covered me—solid, careful. One hand braced beside my head, the other skimming my thigh.

"You know how many times I've thought about this?" His voice was thick, unapologetic.

"Tell me."

"Nah." His smile ghosted my collarbone. "I'd rather show you." Our clothes found the floor. He paused, studying me like art. "How did I miss that belly ring?"

"Guess I forgot to share."

A fingertip traced my navel. "Any other surprises?"

"Lower-back tattoo. Did I mention that?"

He turned me, reading the script with a touch. "Resilient," he said softly. "That's me. Now, can we get to the good part?"

"You sassing me, Shortie?"

"Don't I always?"

He kissed down my spine, lips inching lower until his fingers hooked my panties and dragged them away. His palms gripped my hips, and then his mouth was on me—tongue and lips working with greedy precision.

A gasp broke from me, hips arching as he alternated flicks and circles, fingers sliding inside, curling just right. My back bowed, giving him full access. He didn't pause, didn't let me catch my breath, driving me higher until I was trembling and clenching around him.

"Mm, Malik, it's so good," I moaned.

"You like that, baby?"

"Yes."

"What else do you want?"

"Everything," I breathed.

"You gotta be specific." His mouth sealed over my clit again, suctioning while his fingers scissored deep.

"Yes, just like that—don't stop—"

"Give me one," he ordered, his pace quickening, "before we get to the good part."

I was gone in seconds, shattering around him, the orgasm ripping through me until I collapsed against the mattress.

When he kissed me again, it wasn't soft. It was deep. Consuming. A kiss that said I was his tonight.

"You ready for me?"

"I am."

The first thrust stole my breath—long, deep, stretching me open. Another, and another, filling me until I swore I felt him everywhere.

"You okay?" he rasped.

"I'm good. Please don't stop."

"Good," he said, spreading my legs wider and placing one on his shoulder. "I'm just getting started." Each stroke was slow, unrelenting, pulling me under until there was no going back.

Later, the city lights stretched beyond the glass. Malik's arm lay heavy over my waist, fingers idly tracing my hip. Neither of us spoke.

He pressed a kiss to my shoulder. "You okay?" I nodded because if I opened my mouth, I might say too much. He rolled onto his back, smirking. "Not much of a talker after."

"I talk."

"Mmm. Not yet, you don't."

"You always this smug?"

"Only when I'm right. That you wanted this as much as I did." I stretched, matching his smirk. "Maybe I need another round before I decide."

His laugh dropped low. "Careful what you ask for, Indy." The truth sat heavily in my chest. I wasn't just asking for another round. I was asking for more.

❦❦❦

Morning came pale and soft and smelling like him. The bed beside me was empty. I found him in the kitchen, fully dressed for the day, working a blender.

"You cook now?"

"Blending a smoothie isn't cooking, Indy."

The duffel by the door snagged my eye. "You're leaving."

"Practice."

It was already familiar—him moving on before I even had time to sort out what happened. His world didn't pause for mornings after. I forced a smirk. "So you're just gonna hit it and quit it?"

"First of all, you hit me."

"We both know that's not true."

He stepped in, fingers grazing my thigh. "Second—I never quit."

"And what is this, then?"

"You tell me."

His gaze was steady, unreadable. I broke it with a sip from his shaker. "This tastes like chalk."

"You're impossible."

"And yet, you like me anyway."

His smile softened. "Yeah. I do."

Before I could answer, he grabbed his bag. "I'll call you later." I nodded. Then he was gone.

I spent most of the afternoon convincing myself I wasn't waiting for Malik's call. That I didn't care. That I wasn't pacing my condo, half-starting paperwork, scrolling my phone without checking if he'd texted. Because I wasn't that girl.

Except—When his name lit up my screen at five o'clock, I damn near dropped my phone.

"Latimer," I said, masking the spike in my pulse. "Indy." His voice was a low chuckle, warm enough to curl through my stomach.

"You busy?"

"I might have plans."

"Oh yeah? Anything I should be worried about?"

"Maybe. A critically important date... with my couch." He laughed. "Well, damn. And here I was about to ask you to go shopping."

I blinked. "Shopping?"

"Yeah. Need a couple of things before we hit the road next week. Figured you could help."

"Help how? You can't pick your own sweatpants?"

"I could," he said, "but then I'd miss watching you judge everything I choose."

I hesitated, still curled in my couch cushions. Shopping wasn't a big deal... but it was still something.

"What time?"

"Seven."

"Seven," I agreed, ignoring the little flutter in my chest.

Chapter Sixteen

MALIK

I beat everybody to the gym and put myself on a circuit—corners, wings, top of the key. Ten at each spot, twenty up top, mixing in step-backs, pull-ups, and catch-and-shoots until I'd logged at least three hundred makes.

My teammates would say I was just grinding for the game, building muscle memory under my feet. Truth was, I was trying to outshoot my own thoughts, keep my mind from drifting back to last night and the way it felt to be inside Indira.

I was chasing down a rebound at the right wing when I finally spotted DC leaning against the wall near the baseline, rocking some drip from his new Valet line. He looked like he owned the place.

"What's a retired man doing at my practice?" I called out as I grabbed my water bottle.

"Retired, not dead," he shot back. "Besides, I'm here to watch you work and remind these young bucks how it's done. You know—community service."

I smirked, toweling off. "Community service, huh? Or you just needed an excuse to hang around the Pistons' facility?"

He shrugged. "Maybe. Or maybe I'm killing time before I see Cairo later."

I raised a brow. "Pillow-talking already?"

"Not like that," he said quickly, holding up his hands. "We haven't gone there. *Yet.* But we talk. A lot. And yeah, she's told me a little about you and Indira."

I narrowed my eyes. "Should I be worried?"

"Nah. Same deal with me and Cairo—it's not gossip. It's about knowing where I stand. I'm all in, even if she's not there yet. She's the one. Period."

I took a long drink of water, studying him. "Then you already know what I'm gonna say—don't half-step if you're serious. You start, you finish."

He grinned. "Look who's talking. You've got Indira in your life now. I can tell. Just... don't mess it up."

I tossed my towel at him. "Funny, I was about to tell you the same thing."

Somehow, I managed to lock in during practice, running plays and drilling like tomorrow's game was the only thing on my mind. But the second I slid into my ride, it was like she was still there—the ghost of her scent, the taste of her lips, the sound of her voice.

Indira.

The way she moaned my name like she was made for me. The way she let go last night, dropping that savage, guarded vibe and giving me every damn thing. And fuck, if that didn't make me want her even more.

She probably thinks she can tuck it away, pretend it was nothing but a slip—a lapse in control.

But she's wrong.

Because I meant what I said. I'm not interested in a one-night stand when it comes to her. She can tell herself it was just lust, but I know better. The way her body responded to me? The way she let me in? That wasn't just physical

That was trust.

And trust? That shit means everything.

Still, I have to be careful. Indira isn't like the others—she's got walls, and she's used to carrying it all alone. If I push too hard, she'll bolt. I have to show her—prove to her—that this isn't just about last night.

So yeah, maybe I've got something in mind. Something that'll make her see exactly where I stand.

And Desmond? He told me to be careful with her. Said if I came for her, I'd better mean it.

I do.

And since my word is bond, I'm gonna do this the right way. Not just take her—keep her.

She might not realize that last night sealed the deal for me, but she's about to find out—when I decide someone's mine, I make sure they know it.

❤️❤️❤️

I pulled up to the curb early; I couldn't help it. Sitting around waiting wasn't in me—not when I knew Indira was on the other end of the drive. She slid into the passenger seat, brows lifting.

"You're early."

"Traffic was light," I said, flashing her the grin I knew she pretended not to like. "You ready to shop?"

She shook her head, already plotting. "Almost. Can we make a quick stop first? There's a listing I want to peek at before the open house next week."

"Lead the way."

A few turns later, we pulled up in front of a worn-down bungalow. She was halfway up the walk before I even killed the engine, pointing things out like she already owned the place.

"The porch needs love, but the bones are good. Original windows like these? I'd refinish instead of replace. Floors too." Her voice picked up as she spoke, hands sketching the future like she could already see it. "Reminds me of another place I flipped—roof caved in, basement full of water—but I knew it had potential. This one does too."

I trailed a step behind, just watching. She lit up when she talked houses, brighter than I'd ever seen her in a room full of people. It wasn't about money or clout—it was vision. Her vision. And it pulled me in.

She caught me staring. "What?"

I shrugged, mouth tugging at the corner. "Just thinking about possibilities."

"Possibilities?"

"You'll see." I wasn't about to spell out the thoughts in my head —how I could already picture her taking on bigger projects, and me finding a way to put real backing behind her. That was for later. For now, I tipped my head toward the truck. "Come on—we've got a shopping date to get to."

The afternoon slid by in easy rhythm—warm light, glass store-fronts, her laughter bouncing off polished windows. I made a game of pulling clothes I swore would "change her life," just to see her roll her eyes. Truth? I liked the way she softened when she thought I wasn't looking, like my attention wasn't the nuisance she pretended it was.

We'd just stepped out of a shop when a sharp burst of white split the air. Camera flash.

I saw it before she did—the way her smile froze, how her body stiffened. Then another phone went up across the street, angling for a shot.

Her instinct was to bolt. I caught her hand before she could, steady grip, low voice. "Don't."

She didn't look at me, but her pulse was racing under my thumb. Out here, she wasn't in control—and that rattled her. She'd built her life on being untouchable, untied, answering to nobody. Now the world had a lens on her, and it scared her more than she'd admit.

I guided her toward the SUV, keeping it easy, casual. Opened the door for her like nothing had happened. But the way her shoulders stayed tight, eyes wary in the reflection of the glass—I clocked all of it.

And I hated that flash more than I let on. Not because of me—I was used to it. But because she wasn't. Because she deserved to choose what the world saw. And if they thought they could shake her, they'd have to go through me first.

Chapter Seventeen

INDIRA

Two days after Malik dropped a few racks shopping, we walked into Sonny's, the cozy diner he'd picked—low-key enough to avoid chaos, but visible enough people would notice.

My nerves buzzed from the moment we stepped inside. Malik, though? He looked at ease, like he belonged in any room.

"Relax," he murmured, brushing the small of my back as we moved toward a table by the window.

"That's easy for you to say," I muttered. "You do this all the time." He pulled out my chair before sitting across from me, unbothered as ever. "And now you do, too."

I shot him a look. "Don't push it, Latimer."

That grin. And those damn dimples. "Not pushing. Just letting you get used to it."

And—annoyingly—it worked.

A waitress came by, pad in hand, grinning like she'd been waiting for him. "Well, if it isn't Latimer," she said. "You slumming it with us today?"

Malik chuckled, easy as ever. "You know I can't stay away, Mavis. What's a man gotta do to get his usual?"

She rolled her eyes but was already scribbling. "Egg-white omelet, turkey sausage, black coffee. You're nothing if not predictable." Then her gaze flicked to me, curious but not unkind. "And for your friend?"

Before I could answer, Malik tipped his chin toward me. "She'll have the chai latte, soy milk, honey."

I blinked. "How do you—"

"You already know," he said, smirking. "I pay attention." Mavis arched a brow at me like she approved. "Good man. Anything else?"

"Maybe pancakes," I muttered, opening the menu for cover.

"Then bring the pancakes too," Malik said without missing a beat. Mavis chuckled on her way back to the counter, muttering, "Spoiled already."

I folded the menu shut. "You're impossible."

"And you're tense." He leaned back in his chair, completely unbothered by the couple at the next table whispering behind their menus. "You don't have to be."

"Says the man who's used to being stared at."

"Or," he countered easily, "says the man who stopped caring a long time ago."

I wanted to argue, but the calm in his voice made it hard. He wasn't brushing me off—he was modeling how to breathe through it, how to act like the world wasn't watching.

And after a while, I started to believe it—maybe this wasn't impossible. Maybe we could handle this. Together.

He didn't ask why my shoulders were stiff, didn't try to dig into what was rattling me. Instead, he treated it like background noise, like the whispers couldn't touch us. And somehow, that worked better than any reassurance he could've said out loud.

Still, I couldn't shake the truth: he made it look easy. But fame was never easy—it was brutal. And I wasn't sure I had the stomach for it.

Tamara would've thrived in this—eating up the attention, calculating the price tag on his smile. She'd see nothing but dollar signs. The thought twisted in my chest.

I wasn't her. I'd spent my whole life proving that.

The moment we stepped out of Sonny's, reality snapped back. Not flashing cameras this time, but phones—angled just so, thumbs pretending to scroll. A handful of strangers doing their best not to look obvious.

Malik didn't flinch. Slade hovered nearby. Malik's hand brushed my back again as he opened the car door, steady, like this was normal.

Like we weren't about to be dissected online.

By the time I got home, my phone was already buzzing.

@NBATea: Malik Latimer spotted with a new mystery woman...

@CourtSideChic: Okay, they look GOOD together. #Goals

@HatersGonnaHate: He's gonna drop 40 on the court and drop her in a month. Clock it.

@DetroitGossip: If she's just a fling, why does he look at her like that?

And then the DMs. Some nosy. Some supportive. Some cruel enough to make me want to delete the app.

I set my phone on *Do Not Disturb* and dropped it face down.

This was what I'd been afraid of.

And yet... I was still standing.

But standing wasn't the same as feeling steady. For every flicker of confidence I had sitting across from Malik, the noise in my phone threatened to drown it out.

The internet was a merciless beast. One moment, I was minding my business, helping Malik pick out some swag. The next moment, my phone buzzed nonstop, notifications lighting up the screen like a fireworks show I never signed up for.

Malik's hand on my hip, me not moving away—one snapshot turned me into a trending topic.

In hours, I'd become everything from a baddie to a clout chaser. Strangers dissected where I came from, how long I'd last, and whether I could handle the spotlight.

I wasn't sure I could.

And if the trolls weren't enough, then came the shadow of women from his past. Women like Briana.

Women like Briana knew how to smile for cameras, how to pose like they were untouchable. Me? I was just trying not to flinch. And what if that made me disposable?

So I did what I always do when the world presses too close: I retreated. Ignored Malik's texts. Declined his tickets. Let calls go to voicemail.

But Malik wasn't the type to let things slide.

When a knock came at my door—six a.m., no less—I knew who it was before I even checked. I froze, debating whether to play dead.

"Indy." His voice was calm, too calm. "I know you're in there." When I opened the door, he was standing there, tall and unbothered, holding a cup.

"Chai," he said. "Soy milk. Honey. Just how you like it." I blinked at him. "When did I ever—"

"You did." He pressed the cup into my hand, and damn it, it was perfect.

I let him in, bracing for an argument. Instead, he set a folder on my coffee table.

"What's this?" I asked, narrowing my eyes.

"Open it."

Inside: deeds. A whole block of houses I'd been talking about flipping, every title signed over. My name, on every page. My breath caught.

"Malik..."

He stepped closer, his voice steady. "This isn't a handout. It's an investment. In you. In us. I want you to know I'm serious, Indy. No headlines, no cameras—just me showing you where I stand."

The fight drained out of me, replaced by something terrifying and warm. He'd taken away my last excuse.

I swallowed hard. "I don't know what to say."

"Say yes."

"To what?"

He didn't hesitate. "To me. To this. To joining with me." His eyes held mine, unwavering. "Pack a bag. You're flying out with me this weekend."

I opened my mouth, ready to protest, but the words wouldn't come. He'd outmaneuvered me again—steady, patient, unshakable. And for the first time since that damn photo, I wasn't afraid.

We were stretched out on my couch, not long after he'd shown up, lounging like neither of us had work to do. My nerves hadn't fully settled, but there was something about Malik—steady, unshaken— that kept me from spiraling.

He'd already seen through my excuses, handed me chai exactly the way I liked it, and made it impossible to retreat back into silence. Now, with the cup empty on the table and his arm looped behind me, I tilted my head, studying him.

"Okay, break this down for me. Playoffs. I know they're important, but why does it feel like everybody's acting like the world's about to end?"

He chuckled, tugging me a little closer. "Because for some of us, it kinda is."

I raised a brow. "Dramatic much?"

"Nah. Think of it like this—regular season? That's the audition. You prove you belong, you fight for your spot. Playoffs?" He tapped my knee for emphasis. "That's opening night. Every possession matters. Lose four games, you're done. No do-overs. No second chances."

My lips parted slightly as I processed, and he softened his tone.

"Each round's a series. Best of seven. First to four wins moves on. Then you do it again until only two teams are left. Finals decide the champion. That's it. That's history."

I studied him, something flickering in my chest at the intensity in his voice. "And you've done this how many times?"

"Enough to know the pressure never changes." He held my gaze, steady and unflinching. "But this year? I want it more than ever." And the way he said it, I believed him.

Chapter Eighteen

MALIK

I should've been thinking about film breakdowns, defensive schemes, and how to lock down the next win. But the truth? I was thinking about her.

Indy.

Her sequined white tee. That bold lipstick. The way she'd sat courtside like she wasn't sure she belonged there—but still looked like she owned the whole damn arena.

I knew her hesitation hadn't disappeared. Not with the stares, the whispers, the cameras. Hell, not even with me right beside her. And if I left her to stew in it too long, she'd retreat. That was her pattern—step forward, then snatch it back.

That's why I gave her the block.

It wasn't a handout. It was a stake. A future. Proof that I wasn't chasing her for headlines or convenience—I was investing in her, in us.

And when I laid those deeds in her hands, she didn't curse me out or tell me I'd overstepped. She went silent. Speechless. That told me everything I needed to know. She felt it, too. She understood what it meant.

But gestures weren't enough. Not if she was still questioning whether she could handle the weight of my world. Now I needed this trip to prove something more. To show her that even with the eyes, the whispers, the flashing cameras, what we had could stand.

We hit a bump in the road, dropping Game 3 on Cleveland's home court. The locker room was heavy with frustration, but I wasn't pressed. We still held the advantage, and one more game here before heading back to Detroit was nothing to lose sleep over.

Besides, basketball wasn't the only thing on my mind. For the first time, I wasn't heading back to a hotel room alone—or with some random woman who saw me as a headline. Not one of the women sliding into my DMs promising a wild night, or the ones who thought a quick hookup and a selfie would buy them clout. That used to be my routine.

Not tonight. Tonight, I had Indira James by my side. Real, sharp-tongued, fine as hell—and completely uninterested in who I was on the court. She was the one woman who made me want to leave the game at the arena and focus on everything else I could have with her.

Back at the hotel, the game was already fading from my mind. All I saw was Indira, curled into the armchair by the window, shoes kicked off, her laugh soft as she teased me about my pre-game playlist.

I crossed the room, tugging her up with one hand. She landed against my chest, warm and familiar in a way that shouldn't have felt new —but it did. Her lips met mine, slow at first, then deeper, until I was tasting her smile.

I pressed her back against the wall, her fingers curling into my shirt like she didn't want to let go. My hands skimmed her waist, slid lower, memorizing the curve of her. She tilted her head, breath brushing my ear.

"You're supposed to be resting," she whispered. "I am," I murmured, kissing down the line of her neck. "You're the only thing I need."

Her laugh melted into a sigh as I lifted her, carrying her the few steps to the bed. We didn't rush. I'd had nights that blurred into mornings, names I barely remembered. But with Indira, every second carved itself into me. Just her. Always her.

When we finally came up for air, her hair was messy, her smile easy. We drifted to the couch with a bottle of wine for her and a bottle of water for me. My legs were sore, but I didn't care. I was still buzzing from Indy, the kind of high that didn't fade easy. She tucked her legs under herself, glass in hand, and her foot nudged my thigh like she was daring me to make her laugh again. But then her expression shifted, curiosity sharpening her features.

"Tell me what it was like being a twin, especially when you were younger?" Indira asked, her voice carrying that curious edge she got when she was interested in the answer.

I scratched at my chin, thinking. "You're wondering if we dressed alike. The answer? Yeah, but only briefly."

Her lips curled at the corner. "How brief?"

"Until we were four, maybe five. Marlene thought it was the cutest thing. We'd be matched from head to toe—same Jordans, same everything. And when we went to church? Fresh to death in our little suits and ties." I chuckled at the memory. "As soon as we were ready for school, my pops put an end to it. Said he wanted us to think and act independently. That was the end of our matchy-matchy phase."

Indira smirked, tucking her legs tighter.

"What about you?" I asked. "I know you were an only child. What was that like?"

I expected her to brush it off, but instead, she tilted her wine glass slightly, watching the deep red swirl before answering.

"Most people assume it was lonely. I mean, I didn't have cousins or anything, because even my mother was an only child." She paused, just for a beat, then exhaled. "But honestly? Granny was my world. She kept me company, distracted me from my mother's disappearances."

She swirled her wine again, eyes skimming the glass instead of me. "Granny made it easy to forget what was missing. She was the steady one. Without her..."

Her voice trailed, and she shook her head like she'd already said too much. Her tone was steady, but something in her eyes shifted—just a flicker, like a shadow passing through.

I leaned forward slightly. "Losing her must have hit you hard." She nodded, pressing her lips together for a second before saying, "It did. My mother was MIA as usual." Her voice was controlled, matter-of-fact, but I caught the way she gripped the stem of her glass a little tighter.

She let out a quiet sigh like she hadn't planned on saying that much."But Cairo's family took me in immediately. Later, when Cairo moved to Detroit, Ma'Dear swooped in and arranged for me to live with her and Aunt Millie, too. I was just glad to be back with Cairo and feel like I was part of a family again."

I studied her for a second. The way she framed it like it was all just a smooth transition—like she hadn't been grieving, like it wasn't a major adjustment. I knew better.

But I didn't push.

Instead, I twisted the cap back on my water, leaned into the couch, and let my eyes rest on her. "You know, the weather is finally starting to get warm."

Her gaze flicked to me, wary. "And?"

"That mean it's barbecue season. My family is known for having their summer get-togethers. Pops on the grill, Mama orchestrating everything, Malcolm talking too much—it's the whole crew." I let a smile tug at my mouth. "Next one we have I want you there."

Her brow rose. "Serious? You sure your mama's ready for me?" I didn't flinch. "She's gonna love you. And you'll see where I come from. What made me, you know... me."

She gave a little huff of a laugh, but I didn't miss the flicker in her eyes—the one that said she wasn't sure if *she* was ready for all that.

"Don't overthink it, Indy," I said, softer this time. "Just come eat. You'll like Mama's mac and cheese."

A smile tugged at her lips, small but real, before she shook her head at me like I was impossible.

Her smile lingered as she leaned back, wine glass balanced on her knee. "So, if I'd met you back then, would you have let me in? Or would I have had to prove myself?"

That got a real smile out of her. Small, but there. "Oh, you definitely would've had to prove yourself."

I chuckled. "Figures."

She lifted her glass in a mock toast. "I don't make it easy."

"Yeah," I murmured, my eyes lingering on her for a moment longer. "I'm starting to notice that."

I watched Indira create a tornado in her glass with her wine, her expression unreadable. "You ever wish you had a sibling?" I asked, curious. She didn't answer right away—just a tiny, almost imperceptible pause before she lifted the glass to her lips. "I guess. But I got used to doing my own thing."

It wasn't exactly an answer, and she knew I caught it. Most people would've said yes or no. Indira gave me just enough to keep me close, never more than she was ready to give.

"So you never wanted a built-in best friend?" I pressed, watching her reaction.

"I had one. Remember that Cairo and I have been besties since we both lived in Georgia. And I always had Granny." She took another sip, then shrugged like it was no big deal. "They were enough."

I rested my arm on the back of the couch, studying her. "I couldn't even imagine not having Malcolm around. We fought like hell, but we always had each other's backs. It was like having a shadow that talked too much."

That got a chuckle out of her. "A talking shadow sounds annoying as hell."

I grinned. "Oh, it was."

I told her about the time Malcolm and I switched places, thinking we were slick—until he bombed my math test and I got detention in his English class.

Indy's shoulders shook as she laughed. "And you just took the fall?"

"Hell no. I snitched immediately."

She cackled, her eyes shining, and something about it made me want to keep her laughing. Keep her talking.

I nudged her knee. "Hey, twin bond had limits. Especially when it came to strict-ass fathers."

She went quiet, just for a second, and it hit me—she'd never once mentioned her father. Every story was about someone else—her grandmother, Ma'Dear, The Sisters.

She stretched her legs out like she was shaking something off. "Honestly, I think being an only child made me adaptable. I learned how to handle things on my own and figure stuff out. So I never really felt like I was missing anything."

I didn't buy it. Not completely. But I let it slide. "Yeah. I could see that."

A beat of silence lingered between us—not uncomfortable, just... thick. Like there was something right there between us, but she wasn't ready to acknowledge it.

I tapped my fingers against my knee, then smirked at her. "But you know, if you ever needed a fake twin, I could step in."

She side-eyed me. "A fake twin?"

"Yeah. You got the height for it."

That earned me a playful swat on the arm. "Boy, shut up."

I chuckled, but I didn't miss the way her shoulders relaxed, the way she finally exhaled like she'd been holding something in.

Yeah. She had walls.

But I had time.

Chapter Nineteen

INDIRA

Back in Detroit, I finally caught Cairo on the phone. She'd been on the road all weekend with her team at a basketball tournament. I bet she'd been coaching hard and talking smack to every ref in sight.

"Look who finally decided to call me back," she said, her voice crackling through the speaker. "How's NBA Bae?"

I groaned, flopping onto the bed. "Don't start."

"Oh, I'm starting. You disappear for a whole weekend, and the next thing I know, social media's buzzing with blurry shots of you courtside in Cleveland, looking like a baddie—girl, you looked like money."

I rolled my eyes, even though I was smiling. "That's you, future-Mrs. Montague."

"Let's not get carried away. And you're just trying to deflect. So spill it. How was it?"

I hesitated, chewing the inside of my cheek. I could've brushed it off, played it cool—but Cairo would hear it in my voice anyway. "It was… different."

"Different good or different 'Lord, why did I do this'?"

"Different like..." I trailed off, then sighed. "He gave me a deed, Cee."

There was a beat of silence before she let out a sharp laugh. "A what?"

"A deed. Actually, multiple deeds. He bought the rest of the houses I've been eyeing on that block."

"Hold up. The man skipped roses, skipped jewelry, and went straight to real estate? Whew. That's some grown-man courting, Indy."

"I know," I said softly.

"And what did you do? Please tell me you didn't curse him out."

I smiled at the memory, the way I'd gone speechless. "For once, I didn't say much of anything."

Cairo went quiet, her teasing edge gone. "So how do you feel about it?"

I stared up at the ceiling, the weight of it pressing on me all over again. "Like it's too much. Like he's asking me to trust him in ways I'm not used to."

Cairo hummed. "Or maybe he sees something in you that you don't see in yourself yet. Don't let fear talk you out of something real."

I swallowed hard, blinking against the sudden sting in my eyes. Leave it to Cairo to slice right through my excuses.

"Anyway," she said, lightening her tone again, "you know I'll keep it real with you, Indy. Just...don't run. That's your move every time, isn't it? The second someone shows up for you, you pull back. You treat love like it's a trap when maybe this time, it's the key."

Her words hit harder than I wanted to admit. Running was easier. Until it wasn't.

"Yeah," I whispered. "I hear you."

Our conversation moved on, as we caught up on everything else in our world—Zahara, The Sisters, the usual. But when I hung up, the silence in my house felt heavier than usual. Cairo's voice still echoed in my ear— don't run from this one—but the truth was, standing still scared me just as much.

I set my phone down on the nightstand and curled deeper into the comforter, trying to block out the noise in my head. The Sisters would've called Malik's gesture a blessing. Cairo framed it like a challenge. And me? I couldn't decide if it was an invitation or a test.

Either way, the block was mine now. The deeds were mine. And so was the weight that came with it.

I closed my eyes, willing myself to believe what Cairo had said. That maybe he saw something in me I hadn't yet learned to see in myself.

By morning, I'd convinced myself I could hold onto that thought. That the world would let me hold onto him. I hoped I was right.

Two days after their Game 4 win, Malik asked me to have dinner with some of his teammates. I said yes before I could talk myself out of it. Now, riding shotgun in his car, I couldn't stop tugging at the hem of my shirt. Normally I'd be ready to turn up, to be the life of the party. But being out with Malik and his people felt like stepping closer to commitment, and it left me exposed—knocked clean off my square.

"You nervous?" he asked, side-eyeing me with that smirk that always made me feel seen and exposed all at once.

"No," I said too quickly. My voice sounded thin, too rehearsed.

He chuckled. "Nasir and Mirabel are cool. You'll like them."

"And the others?"

"They'll behave." His grin was easy, confident. Like I could borrow a little of it if I needed.

By the time we pulled up to a sprawling lakefront home in Northville, my chest was tight. The kind of house with more glass than walls and made the cars out front look like they belonged in a magazine spread. My throat went dry. This wasn't my world, not really. Not yet.

Inside, the room buzzed with guys talking over one another, plates clinking, bursts of laughter rising and breaking like waves.

Malik slipped into the chaos without a second thought, all wide shoulders and easy charm. His arm curved around my waist as he drew me forward.

"Y'all, this is my girl, Indira," he announced, voice steady, proud, like he was laying claim in front of the whole room. His dimples flashed as if it were the most natural thing in the world.

Relief washed through me. He hadn't forgotten me in all the noise— he'd planted me right at his side, made space for me where I wasn't sure I belonged. And then, just like that, the tide shifted.

His friends pulled at him—every laugh, every clap on the back, every head turning his way. He filled the space without even trying. Magnetic. Intimidating. A reminder of how far from my world this really was.

Before I could catch my breath, a voice boomed across the room.

"Damn, Latimer. You really got somebody putting up with you?"

Heads turned, including mine. And I had to tilt it way back to find the man who said it.

Nasir Walker. Seven feet of pure wrecking ball, smirking like he knew me already.

Beside him stood a woman whose curls framed a face so warm it disarmed me instantly.

"Don't listen to him," the woman said, nudging him. "He's just mad because I made him host instead of going to his usual wing spot."

That earned a ripple of laughter around the table, and I felt the corner of my mouth tug upward despite myself.

Malik gestured between us. "Indy, this is Nasir. And that's his girl, Mirabel."

Nasir's hand engulfed mine when I shook it. "Welcome to the circus."

"Appreciate it," I said, matching his grin.

Mirabel slid into the seat beside me, her eyes sparkling with curiosity. "So tell me—how's it feel dating Mr. MVP?"

I opened my mouth, not sure where to start, but Nasir cut in first.

"More importantly, how's it feel knowing you gotta behave now?" he teased, shooting Malik a look.

Malik rolled his eyes. "Y'all act like I was out here wildin'."

Nasir arched a brow. "Were you not?"

Mirabel leaned closer, stage-whispering to me, "He was."

I laughed, loud and real. Malik groaned, shaking his head, but I could see the faintest smile tugging at his mouth.

And just like that, the knot in my stomach loosened. The laughter was real, not polite. I didn't feel like such a stranger anymore.

I let myself breathe. Let myself imagine, just for a moment, what it would feel like to belong here—for real.

But deep down, I knew this was only one circle to win over. These people might accept me tonight, but the world outside this room was louder, sharper, and less forgiving.

And sooner or later, it would test me.

The test came quicker than I expected.

The next morning, sunlight cut through the blinds. I rolled over, groggy, and grabbed my phone. The screen lit up with a wall of notifications—missed calls, texts, tags. Honestly, I was hoping to see Malik's name. Instead, at the top was Cairo:

> CAIRO: Indy, don't let this get in your head.
> Call me when you wake up.

Malik was already gone, tied up with morning practice. I knew better than to expect him to be blowing up my phone—but a part of me still wanted his name at the top of that list.

Another message blinked in from an unknown number. Just a link.

I tapped it before I could stop myself.

The photos from Cleveland were bad enough. But the article didn't stop there. It had details—my business license, the houses I'd flipped, even the permits filed on the block Malik had just deeded to me.

My mind spun through the possibilities. Malik? No—he'd never. His brothers? Maybe, but what would they gain? Someone on his team? A manager? An agent? The more names I ticked off, the sicker I felt. Every circle around Malik was bleeding into mine, and any one of them could've been the crack that split me open. I was sure he wouldn't tell the, so how did anyone know what he did for me?

The headline blurred as I scrolled down, my pulse pounding in my ears. And then I saw it:

"According to sources close to Latimer's circle, Indira James has a history of chasing investments through her relationships."

Bile rose in my throat. *Sources close.*

I dropped the phone onto the bed like it burned. My chest ached, heat rushing under my skin.

I didn't even realize I was pacing until my sock caught the edge of the rug. I stopped, pressing both palms into my thighs, trying to catch my breath.

Something told me to check social media. See what else was being said. I searched for my name and thumbed through Instagram. And there it was—Briana's latest post.

"Some women confuse sitting courtside with being a cornerstone. Cute sequins don't make you wifey material."

Heat blazed up my neck. Sequins. She meant me.

The comments stacked up beneath her mirror selfie:

@CourtsideTea: *Another courtside chick, huh? She won't last.*

BrianaD: *Facts. The deed doesn't make the bond. Some people just want to play house.*

My breath hitched. The deed? How the hell would she know?

@PettyWithPurpose: *Not the property shade.* 😎 *You messy.*

BrianaD: *If the shoe fits...*

The ugly words glared back at me, my chest tightening like the walls were closing in. And damn it if I didn't hear Tamara in the back of my mind.

She would love this—being noticed, being gossiped about, even being dragged. Any attention was fuel for her. She'd smile for the cameras, twist the narrative, pocket whatever she could before the story moved on.

And I hated that a part of me understood that instinct. I'd spent my whole life swearing I wasn't her, that I'd never live on scraps of validation. But here I was, unraveling because strangers thought I was nothing more than sequins and a seat on the sideline.

Maybe that was the sickest part: Tamara had abandoned me, neglected me, broken every promise a mother should keep—yet she'd still left me with her sharp edges, her ability to survive a room that wanted to swallow her whole.

I despised her for it.

And I leaned on it anyway.

The screen blurred as another notification popped up—likes piling on Briana's post, laughing emojis multiplying in the comments. Humiliation pressed sharp against my ribs.

I thought about calling Malik, but what would be the point? He was at practice, locked in, unreachable. And even if he picked up, what could he say that would make this sting any less? Still, the ache of wanting his voice almost split me open.

When the phone buzzed again, Cairo's name lighting the screen, I didn't hesitate. This time I answered.

"Indy, I saw her post. She's not pulling that out of thin air. The deed? That's not random shade. Somebody handed her that information."

"Briana doesn't even know me," I whispered, though a part of me already knew better.

"Exactly. But guess who she follows?" Cairo's tone cooled. "Desmond's sister. And from there…"

The silence stretched between us until I forced the word out. "Twinna."

Cairo didn't confirm, didn't deny—just let out a long sigh. "I'm not saying it's definite. But it makes too much damn sense."

The name stuck in my chest like a stone. Twinna—Jarvis' wife, close enough to Malik's circle to hear the wrong thing at the wrong time. Maybe there'd been no malice in the telling. Pillow talk, casual slip. But Briana? She'd twisted it sharp, weaponized it, and aimed it straight at me.

The humiliation still burned, but beneath it something colder settled in my chest. Briana thought she'd scored a win. She had no idea what I was capable of when pushed.

I was still pacing when the sound of Malik's keycard hit the lock. My heart lurched into my throat. I didn't even think; I shoved the phone at him the second he stepped inside.

He took one look at the headline glowing across the screen, his jaw tightening. "Indy—"

"Don't 'Indy' me." My voice shook, sharp enough to sting my own ears. "Somebody in your circle talked. How else would Briana know about the deeds?"

His gaze flicked up, steady, but I could see the muscle working in his jaw. "You really think I'd let her get that close?"

I swallowed hard. "I think you've got people around you who don't know how to keep their mouths shut. And she's making me her target."

He dragged a hand down his face, muttering a curse under his breath. "Damn it."

I crossed my arms, hugging myself even as my words bit out. "Do you know how humiliating it is to wake up to strangers dissecting my business, calling me some clout-chasing groupie? "

His shoulders sagged, his hand twitching like he wanted to reach for me. I held up mine instead. "Don't. I don't need comfort right now. I need answers."

Silence stretched between us, thick with everything neither of us wanted to say.

Finally, he nodded once, the set of his mouth grim. "Alright. I'll find out where the leak came from. You've got my word."

That should've calmed me, but it didn't. Because this wasn't just about finding the leak—it was about trust. About whether I could survive in his world without being gutted by it.

I exhaled, slow and shaky. "You better. Because I'm not built to be anyone's punchline."

His eyes narrowed at that, something fierce flickering there. "And you're not. Not on my watch."

For the first time since I tapped that damn link, the bile in my throat eased. Just a little.

But the anger? The resolve? That stayed.

I thought of Tamara then, how she would've handled all this— smiling for the cameras, twisting the narrative to her advantage, pocketing whatever she could. She would've fed the fire.

But I wasn't her.

I couldn't be.

And if Malik was serious about me, then I had to find a way to survive this storm without turning into the woman I'd spent my whole life refusing to become.

Chapter Twenty

I couldn't sleep.

Indy was curled up next to me, her back to my chest, but my mind kept running laps like it was Game 7. The headline. The comments. The look on her face when she shoved that phone in my hands like it was a smoking gun.

I'd seen her fire before, but this was different. This was hurt.

And she was right. Somebody in my circle had been running their mouth. The deeds to the block—that wasn't public info. Too specific. Too sharp.

Jarvis was the only one I'd told. I hadn't planned to, but I'd needed his contact at the city to move the paperwork faster. It wasn't something I'd spread around, not even with my brothers.

So if Briana knew? That meant Twinna must've overheard something she shouldn't have.

My jaw tightened. Jarvis wouldn't have said a word—but his wife had a way of catching details and dropping them into conversation like they were harmless. Only this time, the fallout had landed square on Indy.

I glanced down at her. Even in sleep, her brow was furrowed, like she was still carrying it. My chest ached. She didn't deserve this weight—not from my world.

I reached out, brushing my thumb across her freckles, tracing them like a map only I was allowed to read. She stirred, lashes fluttering before she blinked up at me.

"Malik?" Her voice was soft, thick with sleep.

"Yeah, baby. I'm here."

She shifted slightly, about to roll over, but I caught her, easing her onto her back, my hand sliding across her waist. Her warmth seeped into me, untying the knot in my chest.

"I didn't mean to wake you," I murmured, kissing the corner of her mouth. "I just... needed to feel you."

Her lips curved into the faintest smile, sleep still clinging to her edges. "You're supposed to be resting," she whispered.

I shook my head, brushing my thumb over her bottom lip. "Not when all I can think about is you."

Her eyes softened, and I leaned down, kissing her slowly, like I was reminding myself she was real. Her hands brushed across my waves before looping around my neck, pulling me closer.

I kissed my way across her freckles, down her cheek, along her jaw, until she sighed beneath me. I wanted her to forget everything but this— forget Briana, forget the headlines, forget the weight pressing in from all sides.

Her legs tangled with mine, her body arching to meet me, and the sound that slipped from her throat nearly undid me. I fumbled for the drawer, tore open the foil, rolled the condom on, and then pressed inside her —slow at first, then deeper, until her gasp caught against my mouth.

"Malik," she breathed, nails catching on my back.

"Say it again." My thrusts found a rhythm, harder each time, chasing the sound of her voice.

"Malik..." The way she moaned my name had me gripping her

thighs, pushing them higher, opening her to me until she had no choice but to take all of me.

"You're mine, Indy," I growled, driving into her, rougher now, reclaiming every inch of her body. "Nobody gets to tell our story but us."

Her answer was the way she arched into me, the way her nails dragged down my shoulders, urging me on. Sweat slicked our skin, her breasts brushing my chest with every thrust. I bent, pulling a nipple into my mouth, circling my tongue until she shivered and gasped.

Her hips rolled up to meet me, matching my pace, the friction between us building sharp and fast. She clutched me tighter, biting down on my shoulder to muffle the cry tearing from her throat.

I didn't stop. I couldn't. I wanted her to feel it—how much I needed her, how badly I wanted to take back the power Briana had tried to steal.

Her body tightened around me, tremors rippling through her as she came, her voice breaking on my name. I drove into her through it, grinding deeper, until the heat coiled low in my gut. One last thrust, a groan torn from my chest, and I came hard, spilling into the condom as she clung to me like she'd never let go.

Release still pulsed through me, but I didn't pull away. I stayed buried in her, arms locked tight, holding her chest to chest while we gasped for air, as if letting go would undo the moment we'd just claimed.

For the first time since that headline, I felt steady. Anchored in her. Like nothing outside this room could touch us.

But when her breaths evened out and she drifted back to sleep, my eyes stayed open. Sleep wasn't touching me tonight. Not with the fire still burning in my gut.

Jarvis was solid. But the leak had come from somewhere close— and if it started with Twinna, I'd shut that down fast. Briana was out there running her mouth, loving every second of the spotlight, but giving her attention would only feed it.

Nah. Not yet.

First, I'd tighten the circle. Fix it before it broke any further. Because if Indy thought for one second I'd let her drown in this, she didn't know me at all.

I wasn't letting her go under. Not to gossip blogs. Not to leaks. Not to Briana. Not to anyone.

Chapter Twenty-One

Despite my name being dragged through headlines, the next morning, I realized how well I'd slept. I'd pushed back my first appointments and hadn't set an alarm, letting myself rest.

I had postponed site visits and showings to attend Malik's game in Cleveland, which made the next few days busier than usual—but worth it. Best of all, I was back in a familiar bed—Malik's, not a hotel mattress.

It was nearly 10 a.m. when I finally dragged myself from the sheets. On the nightstand sat a handwritten note.

You looked too damn good asleep—I almost missed practice. Almost.

Aww. That was cute.

I headed toward the kitchen when the doorbell rang. Too early for visitors, and honestly, who in the hell was Malik expecting anyway? Did he really let people show up at the Bat Cave unannounced?

I spun in his bedroom, searching for my robe, but settled on one of his t-shirts, which hung past my knees. I rushed to the door in my socks and nearly wiped out when my foot caught the base of the foyer table. Frazzled but upright, I opened it just after the second chime.

"Delivery," a man announced. His polo read Latimer Fine Dining.

No, he didn't.

"Good morning," the gentleman greeted me. "Indira, right?"

"This is so thoughtful. Thank you," I said, accepting a tray with a teapot and pastry box.

"Compliments from Mr. Latimer."

"Okay, let me find my wallet—"

"That won't be necessary. Bon appétit."

Grinning, I hauled the tray into the kitchen. Inside were pastries, egg bites, and cheeses. The ceramic pot steamed—chai, spicy and perfect. I poured a hefty cup and took a sip, warmth spreading through me.

My phone pinged with a text.

> MALIK: Bite-Size, I know you're busy. Don't
> forget to eat.

I smiled, reaching for my phone, but the screen lit with another name. My stomach tightened.

Tamara.

Mother's Day had already come and gone, and all I'd managed was a stiff text. Now she was calling like nothing had ever been broken between us, like we were just catching up after lost time instead of dragging chains of silence, guilt, and bad history.

I hesitated, then answered.

"Hey, baby girl."

My teeth clenched. Once, when I was little, I'd lived for hearing it. Now it felt like sugar-coated shrapnel.

Silence stretched until she sighed—dramatic, like I was the one who'd put her through something. "You still mad at me?"

Mad? I could've said so much, but I didn't waste my breath. "What do you want, Tamara?"

"Can't a mother check in on her daughter?"

I rolled my eyes. *A mother?* That was rich.

I waited. Tamara always showed her hand.

Right on cue, she said, "I was thinking... maybe we could have lunch. It's been too long, Indy. I miss you."

There it was.

I pinched the bridge of my nose. I couldn't do this. Not now. Between Malik, my career, and my fragile sense of privacy, I had no room for her.

"I'm busy," I said flatly.

She paused before sighing. Again. "Of course. You always are."

There it was again—that passive-aggressive dig, like I was the one who'd been absent.

"I gotta go," I said.

"Wait."

I froze.

"I know I wasn't... the mother you wanted me to be," she said, softer now. Calculated. "But I'm trying, Indy. I am. Can't you just meet me halfway?"

A flicker stirred—anger, guilt, exhaustion. For a second, I almost pictured it: her across from me, no lies, no drama. But the image collapsed under the weight of everything she'd already taken.

"I'll think about it," I said. A stall, not a promise.

I hung up before she could answer, dropping my phone onto the counter. My hand trembled even though my voice hadn't.

Tamara wanted back in my life. But I wasn't sure I could let her in. Not when I was still figuring out how to let Malik in, too.

One at a time.

And she wasn't first in line.

"The open house is Sunday. I need the house fully staged by Friday—cozy luxury: plush throws and layered texture. Kimura peonies in the entry —delicate but dramatic. Soft gold accents that catch light, no glitter. Table set casually, wine and charcuterie—not a wedding."

I paced my living room, phone to my ear, while Deshaun repeated the details back. This open house—always on calls, jumping at every ping— had me on edge. The glass of wine on my coffee table? Untouched, like a reward I hadn't earned.

Malik walked in from practice, sweatpants and a fitted tee, chest carved and tattooed arms distracting me enough to need that wine. He paused in the doorway, smirking.

I swiped the glass and kept talking. "And no fake fruit. Real lemons or limes. Organic if possible."

"Perfect. Send me pictures once it's in place. I'll walk through Friday evening." I hung up, exhaled, and turned to Malik, who was still smirking.

I dropped onto the couch with my wine. Malik sat beside me, stretching out his legs, nudging my knee.

"Kimura peonies, huh?"

"What about them?"

"Sounds expensive. Bougie ass."

"They are, and they're my favorite. But my sellers are motivated."

"And do you want to know what motivates me?" He plucked my glass and set it aside.

The air shifted. My chest tightened—not with stress this time, but with the weight of his gaze.

"No," I whispered. "Why don't you tell me?"

His lip dragged between his teeth. "I'll do you one better. I'll show you. Come here."

I crawled into his lap, straddling him. Control slipped the second my knees planted. He smacked my ass. "Good job, Bite-Size. I love it when you follow instructions."

"Gold star for me?"

"Absolutely. But first, sit on my face. I need dessert before dinner."

The air between us thickened, playful giving way to hunger. "You sure about that? Malcolm's teriyaki salmon is in there."

"Yeah, baby. I'm sure." His voice rumbled low against my skin.

Testing the game, I rolled my hips once, slow and deliberate. His breath hitched at the shift of my weight. In the same heartbeat, he flipped me, strength effortless; my back met the couch, his weight pressing me down.

"You trying to deny me?" His mouth grazed my throat.

I meant to answer; a moan came out instead when his teeth nipped and his tongue soothed the sting.

"You wear too many damn clothes," he muttered, bunching fabric.

"Then do something about it."

He did. One motion, shirt gone.

"Beautiful," he breathed, almost reverent.

I should've felt exposed. Instead, under his gaze, I felt wanted. Cherished.

His mouth moved lower, hot and insistent against me, tongue flicking until my back arched off the couch.

"Malik," I gasped, fingers fisting in his hair.

His grin curved against me. "MVP tongue, baby. Don't forget it."

I laughed—once. Then he made sure I couldn't.

Later, sprawled on the sectional with Malik's legs bracketing mine, his fingers toyed lazily in my curls. His warmth wrapped around me, cedar and amber in the air.

"Why do you wear white so often?" he asked suddenly.

I tilted my head up. "You noticed that?"

"Duh. Of course."

"You really want to know?" My stomach tightened. The answer wasn't simple.

"I'm just curious," he shrugged.

I gnawed my lip, stalling. "Yes. But first tell me why your family calls you MJ."

His grin spread. "When I was eight, I was convinced I was the next Michael Jackson. Had the whole 'Smooth Criminal' routine down—the lean, the glove, everything."

"Right. Because you couldn't be MJ without the famous glove."

"You know it. So one night, I snuck into my parents' room, grabbed my mom's church hat, and tried the spin-and-hat-toss. Except I launched it straight into the ceiling fan. The blades caught it, whipped it around, and smacked me dead in the forehead. Knocked me clean out. My mom found me on the floor, fan still spinning, her hat bow stuck in the blades like evidence of the crime."

I burst out laughing so hard I nearly spilled my wine. "Who gave you the hardest time? Malcolm?"

"Hell, no. My sister. All through middle school, they dared me to dance like MJ. Got old fast."

"That's cute. And now I definitely need to see that spin."

He winked. "I'll show you all the MJ moves you want. You already know I've got the hip thrust down."

Heat crept up my neck, and I swatted his chest.

"Whatever. My wearing white isn't nearly that funny. It started as rebellion."

"How so?"

"I was trying to be different. Or maybe invisible."

"Different from who?"

My throat went dry. This was the part I usually dodged—the part I kept buried. Malik had never pressed, never pointed out how little I talked about the woman who gave birth to me. And I'd been grateful for his silence.

"My mother. She and I were—are—complete opposites. She's

tall, model thin, and white is the last color she'd wear. She'd rather be caught dead than stepping out in something so plain." I paused.

But Malik pushed me forward. "So, what? She liked color?"

"I guess you could say that. The more color, the better. Bold, sexy, unapologetic. Before Megan Thee Stallion, there was my mother, Tamara Elle James, rocking curve-hugging silhouettes and statement prints."

"That's what's up," Malik nodded. "You got your hot girl confidence from your mama?"

I rolled my eyes. "I guess you could say that."

But he didn't know the difference. Megan had built an empire. My mother had burned every bridge she touched. Megan strutted with purpose. Tamara had run the streets chasing a pipe dream, literally. And me? I grew up learning that glitter faded and confidence cracked when you leaned too hard on it.

I expected him to joke. To brush past it like it was nothing. Instead, Malik tilted his head, gaze steady but soft.

"You don't have to spill it all tonight," he murmured. "But don't hold back thinking I can't handle it. I want every part of you, Indy— the good, the hard, the in-between."

That kind of reassurance felt like a vow, and it cracked something open in me. His patience wasn't distance—it was devotion.

I could have kept talking. Kept peeling back layers I wasn't sure I was ready to share. Or I could do something that felt infinitely easier.

So I kissed him.

Malik didn't hesitate—he never did. His lips claimed mine with the kind of confidence that made my stomach flip, his mouth coaxing me open, warm and sure. His hand slid up my back, fingers pressing into my spine, pulling me closer until there was no space left to hide.

The kiss deepened, slow and consuming, and I felt it everywhere — low in my belly, curling around my spine, setting fire to every nerve ending.

The water was warm, steam curling around us like a veil, wrapping us in heat and intimacy. My back rested against Malik's chest, his arms looped loosely around my waist as we stood under the spray.

Neither of us spoke. We didn't have to.

His fingers traced slow circles against my hip while water cascaded over us. My body still hummed from what we'd shared, but what lingered most was the way he held me—steady, grounding, like he'd done it a thousand times before and planned to do it a thousand more.

I tipped my head back against his shoulder. "Still think I wear too many clothes?" I murmured, voice rough with exhaustion and something softer.

His chuckle rumbled through me. "Definitely."

I smirked, letting my hands roam over slick skin, but instead of taking it further, he pressed a kiss to my temple and reached for the soap. He washed me slowly and methodically, his hands gliding in a way that felt like more than care.

It felt like devotion.

By the time we stepped out and dried off, my muscles had turned to liquid. Not just from the sex; from this—the way we could exist together, casual and close, like something I could sink into without losing myself.

I tugged one of his T-shirts over my head—because why bother with my own clothes when his smelled so damn good—and caught him watching me.

"What?" I asked.

He didn't answer right away. Instead, he reached for something on the nightstand—a small black box.

My stomach flipped.

He stepped closer, expression unreadable but warm, and flipped the lid.

Inside, nestled against velvet, was a layered gold chain. The shorter strand held a small Leo pendant; the longer, a slim engraved bar with an embedded diamond.

My throat tightened. "Malik…"

He shrugged. "Since you always wear white, I figured a little gold would set it off."

The words hit somewhere deep. This wasn't some flashy throwaway gift—he'd noticed. Really noticed.

My fingers brushed the bar. "Resilient," it read. My vision blurred before I blinked it away. "It's beautiful."

His lips quirked. "You gonna let me put it on you or what?"

I turned, tilting my head forward. His fingers grazed my skin as he clasped the chain, the intimacy settling over me like a second heartbeat.

When it was fastened, I touched it lightly, feeling the cool weight.

"Now you got a little something extra," he murmured near my ear. "A testimony to your strength."

My heart clenched. He'd remembered my tattoo.

I turned, not bothering to hide what I felt. "You're dangerous, Latimer," I whispered.

His grin was slow. "Yeah?"

I nodded. "Yeah."

And before he could say another word, I kissed him—the perfect response when a man sees you this clearly and chooses to honor you.

When we broke apart, I didn't say the thing sitting on my tongue.

But I felt it, deep and certain, settling into me like it had been there all along. I was already his.

Chapter Twenty-Two

MALIK

After everything Indy had given me, I wanted to give her something back—something lighter. A night where she could laugh with my crew, see where she fit in my world. Game night was supposed to be fun. We'd just breezed through the second round of Playoffs and were headed to the Eastern Conference Finals. That was worth celebrating—one night to relax before locking in again.

But with Twinna in the room? Nothing stayed simple. Honestly? After the way she'd been swapping secrets with Briana, I'd thought twice about inviting her.

Indy had found this game on Instagram, swearing it would be a good icebreaker. She'd been bouncing in her seat, hyped to host. I wanted her to see this—my people, my circle—and feel like she belonged in it.

Except the second she explained the rules, Twinna wrinkled her nose and asked, "A game? What are we, in high school?"

I felt Indy bristle beside me. I knew that look. She was ready. "Uppity Black girl, say what?" Indy shot back.

Laughter broke out around the room, but the air snapped tight. Twinna squared her shoulders. "You can't be talking to me."

"Oh, yes, Sweetie, I am," Indy fired, eyes cutting to Jarvis. "You might want to get your wife before I do."

Scattered "Daaamns" flew. Jarvis clenched his jaw, but said nothing.

I slipped a kiss to Indy's temple, hoping to pull some of the heat off her. "I got your refill, babe," I murmured, and took her glass to the kitchen.

By the time I came back, DC and Jarvus were arguing over teams. "Ladies against the gents," DC declared.

"Works for me," Jarvis said quickly, like agreeing would patch things over. But Twinna? Arms crossed, eyes rolling, full pout mode.

"You're still on that?" she snapped when Indy called her out.

Jarvis winced. I winced. Hell, everyone did. Indy set her glass down harder than she needed to.

"Look here, heifer. Why are you even here if you're just gonna kill the vibe? Drink yourself into oblivion and keep your comments to yourself."

That should've been the end of it, but Twinna pushed, voice rising. And for once, Jarvis didn't let it slide.

"That's enough!" he barked, giving her a look sharp enough to cut. "If you wanted to act like this, you should've stayed home."

The room went still. Twinna's eyes went wide. "Really, Jarvis? You're gonna take their side?"

He didn't even blink. "Yup."

She shot to her feet, wobbling. The espresso martinis had caught up to her. With a dramatic huff, she snatched her phone and stormed out.

Everybody laughed, but my gut stayed tight. Our crew used to be solid—no leaks, no problems. Lately, though? Twinna was proving that she was the weak link. She didn't just drink too much; she talked too much.

"Damn, I thought she'd never leave," CeeCee cracked, breaking the tension.

Indy high-fived her, smug and glowing, while Jarvis rubbed a hand over his face like he regretted breathing. I couldn't miss the way his shoulders sagged when Twinna's heels clicked down the hall.

That marriage was on thin ice. I knew it, and from the look on DC's face, so did he.

"Alright, listen up," I called, pulling the group back before the mood flatlined. "Rules are simple. Fill in the blank, thirty seconds, most accurate answers wins. Skip if you want, but you gotta circle back."

"Who wants to go first?"

"Ladies first, bruh," DC groaned.

CeeCee was already bouncing in her seat. "Let's go!"

Indy set the timer, grin wide. "Alright, first phrase: A hard head makes a soft—"

"Behind!"

"Yup! Next one—'Don't let your mouth write a check—'"

"That your ass can't cash!"

I laughed. "That one needs to be framed for Twinna."

The whole room cracked up, tension breaking. Even Jarvis wore a smile.

CeeCee shot me a glare. "Wait! Y'all can't talk during my time!"

Indy just reset, dimples flashing. "Next one: 'People in hell want—'"

"Ice water!"

And just like that, the game took off. CeeCee nailed half the board, missed only one question, and did a victory dance when Indy declared the ladies won the round.

I leaned back, soaking it in—Indy laughing with my friends, eyes sparkling, shoulders loose. After weeks of watching her hold herself tight, it was a damn good sight.

She leaned close, whispering, "This was a good idea."

I smirked. "Told you."

By the time the night wound down, the tension was gone. Even

Jarvis managed a real smile. When the last guest left, I pulled Indy aside, my hands brushing her waist.

"You had fun," I murmured.

She sighed against me. "Yeah, I did."

"See? My world isn't all bad."

Her smirk was pure Indy. "Let's not get ahead of ourselves, Latimer."

I kissed her temple, low so only she could hear. "Just say when, Shortie. I'm ready whenever you are."

And for the first time in a long time, I believed she might be ready too.

Chapter Twenty-Three

INDIRA

The days before Malik hit the road blurred together, and suddenly he was gone. Atlanta next—my old stomping grounds. The city where I went to Henderson College, where Cairo and I finally shook off some of our ghosts.

I wanted to be there. With him.

Instead, I was stuck in Detroit wrestling permits. Ace had tried, but nothing moved without me pushing it through. Until then, Atlanta would have to wait.

Malik and I squeezed in FaceTime calls and late-night texts. It wasn't the same—never enough—but it kept us tethered. Hopefully, I'd join him for Game 3.

Meanwhile, my project was bleeding me dry. The permit delays dragged on, and Ace's crew had already botched the flooring once, costing us time and budget. Electrical and plumbing issues had eaten through my contingency fund. Every call I made turned into excuses and red tape.

By the end of the week, I was pacing the kitchen, phone pressed to my ear, patience fraying. "Yes, I know permits can take time," I snapped, "but every day delayed is money lost. Can we expedite this?"

The answer was another wall of excuses. I disconnected the call and shoved my phone in my pocket before leaning against the counter. Seconds later I felt it vibrate against my thigh. I pulled it out and spotted my mother's name.

This was her second call within the same month, which was way too rare to be random.

"Tamara," I answered flatly.

"Baby girl, you sound tired. You working too hard?"

"What do you want?"

She sighed, all theatrics. "Can't a mother just check in?"

"You checking in or working an angle?"

Silence. Then she pivoted, voice softer. "Maybe it's time we see each other. Lunch or coffee. Five minutes, that's all."

"No." My voice was sharp. "You don't get to drop in and play mother when it suits you."

"You always were stubborn."

I let out a humorless laugh. "Wonder where I got that from?"

She didn't miss a beat. "Stubborn, but smart. I saw you've been stepping out with that baller boyfriend. My baby girl's finally living right."

The words hit like a warning, sugar-coated but sharp.

My stomach tightened. Compliments from Tamara were never free, and I wasn't about to let her sniff around Malik.

"Don't," I said quietly.

"Don't what? I'm just proud. You deserve someone who can take care of you."

"Tamara—" My voice cracked just enough to stop her. "This isn't about him. And it's not about you either. Respect that."

Her sigh dragged long, like smoke before a fire. "Alright, baby girl. If that's how you feel... we'll see."

The call ended, but the unease stayed. When the phone buzzed again, I snapped, "I'm not doing this with you!"

"Dang, did I do something?" Malik asked.

My chest loosened instantly. "Sorry. Wrong target."

"What's wrong?" he asked, concern threading through his deep voice.

"Permits," I deflected. "The whole project's a mess."

"Anything I can do?"

I wanted to say yes. To let him fix it. Instead, pride dug in. "I've got this."

"You don't always have to handle everything alone, Shortie."

His words sank deep, but I still shook my head. "This one's on me."

"Alright. But promise me you'll tell me if things change."

"I promise," I whispered, even though we both knew I probably wouldn't.

We caught up for a few minutes, sharing the highlights from each other's day. When we hung up, I stared at the phone, the ache of missing him mixing with the weight of everything I carried alone. Independence was a crown I wore heavily, even when help was just one call away.

Chapter Twenty-Four

MALIK

I dropped down onto Malcolm's plush leather sofa, tension easing a little as I sank back. My twin's spot was always the place where I needed to unload without judgment.

He poured himself a whiskey, the clink of ice sharp in the quiet. "You still on the wagon?"

I eyed the glass, temptation flickering. Relationship stress had me reconsidering my no-drinking-during-the-Playoffs rule. "I'm straight," I said finally, shaking my head.

"A'ight." He swirled his glass, studying me. "But something's chewing on you. Spit it out."

"It's Indy." The words came out heavier than I expected. "She hasn't been to any of the games in this series. At first, I told myself it was cool— she's grinding, got houses to flip, I respect that. But game two? Looking at the stands and not seeing her face? Man, it felt like I was running with one sneaker untied. Couldn't shake it. It's messing with my head."

Malcolm leaned forward, elbows on his knees, expression sharp. "So you think maybe you're in deeper than she is?"

I scrubbed a hand over my forehead. "Yeah. And that's crazy, right? First time I'm trying to settle down in years, and it feels like I'm putting everything on the line. What if I a m more invested than she is?"

Malcolm nodded slowly, sipping his drink. "You're worried about getting played again."

The words stung because they were true. "Yeah. Briana burned me once. I swore I'd never give anybody that much of me again. But here I am, back in it, hoping Indy's different."

He tapped the side of his glass, voice even. "Look, bruh, we come from a family that loves hard but keeps shit bottled up until it blows. Pops, Mama, even me. You? Same damn thing. But that's the cycle you gotta break. If you want Indy to know where you stand, you can't keep it locked in your head."

I let his words settle. He wasn't wrong. Communication had never been my strong suit, but silence wouldn't protect me either.

"You're right," I admitted, my voice low. "It's time I kept it a buck with her. It's scary as hell, but if I don't, she'll never know what she means to me."

Malcolm cracked a grin, leaning back in his chair. "That's what's up. And for the record—she's lucky to have you. Even though I'm still the better hooper."

I let out a brief laugh, feeling slightly relieved. "Man, whatever. Let's just hope Indy sees it that way, too."

I sat alone in the locker room, the noise of my teammates' celebration echoing faintly from down the hall. My head hung low, eyes locked on the tiled floor. We'd pulled out the win, but I couldn't shake the hollow pit in my gut. The way I played tonight—careless turnovers, shots I'd usually drain in my sleep—wasn't me.

And I knew why.

Indy wasn't there.

Every timeout, every trip to the line, my eyes went searching the stands, desperate for her face. Every empty seat I clocked chipped away at my focus until I barely recognized my own game.

I pushed up from the bench and moved to the mirror over the sink. The reflection staring back looked as drained as I felt—eyes clouded with disappointment. I knew better. Pressure was nothing new. Blocking out noise had been my specialty. But Indy? She was inside my head in a way no opponent had ever managed. Vulnerable wasn't a space I'd let myself live in for years. Not since Briana.

I splashed cold water over my face, gripping the sink until my knuckles whitened. I couldn't keep going like this—distracted, off my game, letting my team down. I cared about Indy more than I wanted to admit, but I owed it to my squad and myself to get this right.

Reaching for my phone, I scrolled until her name glowed on the screen. My thumb hovered, heart thudding like it was Game 7 already.

"Come on, Malik," I muttered under my breath. "Time to keep it real."

But doubt crept in, fast and sharp. What if she wasn't ready to hear it? What if I pushed too hard and lost her?

Still, one thing was clear: this couldn't go on. Indy needed to know exactly where I stood—no more guessing, no more silence.

When I got back to Detroit, I thought about hitting up Indy's spot, but ended up at the gym instead—focused on stepping up after messing up in that last game. Every rep burned out my frustration, but by the time I made it to my truck, I was wrecked.

I reached out to her twice. Both times, left on read. No congratulations on the win, no "good game." Nothing.

By the time I pulled into my driveway, it was almost one in the morning. I stripped down, dropped my bag by the closet, and collapsed into bed, still buzzing with restless energy. One more shot, I told myself. I had to hear her voice.

I scrolled to her number and pressed call. The tension in my chest climbed with every ring, and when she finally picked up, relief hit me— except something felt off immediately.

"Hey." Her voice was quiet. Distant.

"What's up, Bite-Size?" I tried to keep it light, hoping to tease her into softening, but the chill cut through the line.

"Nothing." Her response was short, clipped.

"You good?" I asked carefully, though I already knew the answer.

"I'm fine." No warmth, no playfulness. Just flat.

She was lying. We both knew it.

Before I could push, she cut me off. Said she needed her sleep and ended the call.

I stared at the screen, confusion twisting hard in my gut. Here I was, torn up because she skipped my game, and she's the one acting mad? The fuck?

I leaned back against the pillows, phone still in my hand, trying to piece it together. Indy never shied away from shutting me down when she disagreed—she usually came at me straight, no hesitation. But this? The distance in her voice, the way she kept something locked away... it hit different.

And for the first time all season, I felt more unsettled than any loss on the court.

Chapter Twenty-Five

Initially, the way Malik played had made me feel like shit. I had still been at one of my properties well after tip-off, but as soon as I got home, I tuned into the TV in search of game highlights.

During the commercial break, I sank into my plush sofa. I was finally relieved to be off my feet, which were throbbing from standing all day in back-to-back showings. I rolled my neck slowly, trying to release the tension that had settled deep into my muscles. With one hand cradling a glass of wine, I took a slow sip, savoring the momentary rest, while my other hand lazily scrolled through my phone.

The glow of the screen illuminated the dim room, bathing my fingertips in soft light. The first thing I did was check for tonight's box score, ready to analyze the game the way Malik taught me. The stats were brutally honest.

He'd had a bad shooting night, making less than thirty percent of his shots from the field, and his three-point percentage was just as bad. I could tell he allowed Atlanta's defense to pressure him, too, based on his turnovers for the night. His only redeeming accomplishment was the number of assists he managed.

Growing impatient with the TV commercials, I turned to the game highlights on my phone. Seeing his frustrated expression after a missed shot sent a sharp pang of guilt deep into my chest. I couldn't help but wonder if my failure to appear had been part of the reason he had looked so distracted.

It was possible, right? Or was I overestimating my influence on him? Malik had scored more than 20,000 points in his career. He'd played with the noise of just as many spectators firing sonic insults at him. Surely, my presence wouldn't have mattered much.

Just as I began to relax, my guilt subsiding, I searched for his post-game interview. Malik's face filled my screen, his familiar smile broad, although less confident than I was accustomed. Still, he looked effortlessly charming, displaying the charisma that drew people in so easily. The interview had already gone viral, and I ran to the comments section, eager to read his praises:

"MVP behavior."

"L'-Train is unstoppable!"

"This man is a walking highlight reel."

Given his less-than-stellar performance, I was surprised to find the comments so positive.

But then, my eyes snagged on a particular comment, sitting conspicuously at the top:

BrianaD: Some things never change. Proud of you, always. 

My stomach clenched tight. Heat flushed across my cheeks as my heart began beating a frantic rhythm. *Did Malik pin this heifer's post?*

I tapped Briana's profile before I could second-guess myself. Her latest story flashed onto the screen—a throwback photo of her sitting courtside, proudly wearing a vintage Malik Latimer jersey. The caption was simple but felt loaded with meaning:

"Once upon a time..."

A surge of irritation bubbled up inside me. What was she implying? Why did she feel the need to stake some kind of claim now?

I set my wine down harder than intended, the glass clinking loudly against the coffee table. My throat felt tight. Doubts crept in, whispering questions I wasn't ready to answer. Malik had always brushed Briana off whenever I'd asked, calling their history "old news." But if it was so old, why hadn't he shut this down?

I watched the interview again, knowing full well Briana wasn't part of it. Still, I searched his face for something I couldn't name—maybe proof that she no longer mattered. I hated feeling insecure and hated even more that Briana had triggered this uncertainty.

My thumb hovered over the keyboard, debating whether to text Malik. Should I confront him now or wait and see how he responds to this? Was confronting him the mature choice, or would I look paranoid and petty?

Frustration coiled tighter in my chest. My quiet evening had suddenly unraveled, replaced by anxiety and questions I wasn't sure I wanted answers to. The phone lit up with Malik's name, and for a split second, I thought about letting it ring. Instead, I picked up, offered clipped answers, then bailed before I could crack.

The sound of his voice had made the knot in my chest pull tighter. I dropped my phone on the nightstand like it burned. I wasn't certain if Malik had pinned Briana's post or if there was anything between them other than their past. But I couldn't explain my feelings, so I lied, said I was tired, and hung up.

Guilt pricked immediately. I wanted to call him back to smooth the sharp edge I'd left—but the words wouldn't come. How was I supposed to explain the fear that if I leaned in too far, I'd lose everything?

The silence stretched between us, heavy and unrelenting, even after I hung up. I curled into his t-shirt, burying myself in the scent of him, wishing it could quiet the noise in my head. Maybe tomorrow I'd find the words. Tonight, all I had was the ache of what I hadn't said.

By morning, the guilt from hanging up on Malik still clung to me like a second skin. I brewed my chai, scrolled my phone out of habit, and there it was—his name trending again. Normally, I'd brace myself for the usual highlight reels and fan chatter.

But this time it wasn't about the interview.

The comments hit different.

Because mixed in with the praise and photos was that bitch's name again.

Briana had dropped a heart emoji under a shot of Malik leaving the arena, casual as anything, like she still had a claim. And the replies? Full of speculation—old flames, unfinished business, the kind of noise that burrowed under your skin and refused to leave.

A few days went by without any communication between Malik and me—mostly because I couldn't bring myself to answer his calls. I was still salty about him pinning his ex-girlfriend's post. Maybe I was being childish —letting something so small get under my skin —but every time I thought about it doubt crept in.

I couldn't make the next game in Atlanta. After weeks of permit delays, I'd finally pushed through the red tape, and now the project needed my full attention before it unraveled again.

Truth? I didn't even know if the Pistons had won. I'd tuned out social media, TV, and radio on purpose. Because if I saw Malik smiling under the arena lights—or worse, laughing with Briana—I wasn't sure I could stomach it. After a few calls and texts, he gave up on reaching me, and my mind filled in the blanks with all the ways he could've spent those nights in my absence.

Maybe that was for the best. Malik had a career to chase, and I had mine. It wasn't like I could expect an NBA superstar to sidestep every panty-throwing, clout-chasing woman looking for her fifteen minutes. But me? I wasn't interested in sharing—his time, his focus, or his bed.

Malik wasn't the only one I'd been avoiding. Cairo couldn't wait to tell me that Ma'Dear and Aunt Millie had threatened to take a switch to me the next time they saw me if I didn't make an appearance.

The moment I pulled up to The Sisters' house, I felt it.

Something was off.

The air outside was too still. The usual warmth of home felt different. Even before I stepped onto the porch, my gut screamed.

Then I saw her—my mother.

Sitting right there beside Aunt Millie's blood-red caladiums. Georgia must've run out of people to annoy, because here she was— hours away from home.

Her endless legs were crossed—toned and deliberate—drawing attention just like she always did. One hand rested on her knee, the other flicking ash from a cigarette like she had all day to wait.

I froze.

She looked good. Too good.

Her silver-streaked hair was freshly styled into a wavy bob that brushed her shoulders. Casually chic, as always. When it came to color, Tamara never played it safe; bold and vibrant was her thing. The ruby-and-bubblegum-pink dress and designer heels might've looked good on her, but all I could see was the price tag. Money she didn't have. Priorities she'd never learn.

So yes, her exterior screamed confidence. But her eyes?

They gave her away.

A little too wide. A little too expectant. A little too desperate.

I swallowed, gripping my car keys tighter.

"You gonna just stand there, baby girl, or you gonna come say hey to your mama?"

Her voice was too casual, like she hadn't just shown up after ping-ponging in and out of my life for years.

I took a slow breath. "What are you doing here, Tamara?"

She sighed dramatically, flicking the cigarette to the ground and grinding it out with the toe of her shoe. "You act like I can't come see my own child."

The front door creaked open, and Aunt Millie stepped out, her expression tight. Guarded. Ma'Dear was on her heels in her wheelchair.

"I told her you weren't here," Aunt Millie informed me, eyes flicking between the two of us. "But she wouldn't leave. And she refused to come inside."

I exhaled slowly, glancing back at Tamara, whose lips curved into a smirk.

"What can I say? I'm persistent."

I didn't respond. Because I knew what this was. This wasn't about me. It never was.

She had waited for the right moment—waited until my name was in the media, waited until Malik and I were officially public, waited until she could make an entrance. And now? She wanted in.

I met her gaze head-on, my voice calm but firm. "You need to go."

She let out a soft, mocking laugh, shaking her head like I was a child throwing a tantrum. "Now, Indy, don't be like that. I just wanted to see you, baby. I miss you."

I clenched my jaw. "You *miss* me? Since when?"

Her smile faltered just slightly before she recovered. "Always."

A bitter laugh escaped me. "Right. That's why I only hear from you when it's convenient for you."

Her expression twitched, but she held steady. "Come on, Indy. Let's not do this out here on the porch. I'll go inside. We can sit down, talk like —"

"No."

Her lips parted, like she wasn't expecting me to be that blunt. But what did she think would happen?

That I'd welcome her with open arms?

That she could erase years of absence with a dramatic doorstep reunion?

She shook her head, her voice dropping lower. "Indy, baby, please. Just let me in."

The plea cracked open something small inside me, a whisper of vulnerability that I immediately silenced. It wasn't enough. It never was.

I heard the slightest waver in her voice. The tiniest crack.

But before I could process it, Aunt Millie stepped forward.

"She said 'no,' Tamara. You need to go."

My mother blinked, her expression shifting from pleading to cold. Her tongue clicked against the roof of her mouth, and she let out a sharp breath before pushing herself to her feet, smoothing her dress slowly, deliberately.

"Fine."

She didn't look at me or The Sisters. She just pivoted and walked off the porch, her heels clicking against the pavement as she disappeared down the street. I should have felt relieved. But all I felt was exhausted. Because I knew this wasn't over. Not by a long shot.

Chapter Twenty-Six

MALIK

I was determined to keep my focus and lead my team to a Game 4 win, even if I had to carry them on my back. Somehow, I managed to block Indira from my thoughts, even though she'd put me on ice days earlier. The silence between us still lingered, but I couldn't afford to let it affect my performance on the court—not tonight.

Earlier in the day, I'd confided in DC about not hearing from Indy, just like I'd opened up to Malcolm. But Desmond's feedback carried more weight because he'd walked in my shoes as an NBA player. He'd experienced firsthand how personal distractions could derail an entire season. Desmond listened patiently before offering me the kind of advice that only someone who'd been there could deliver.

"Malik," he'd said, gripping my shoulder firmly, his expression serious. "You can't control how Indira acts or what she's feeling right now. But you can control how you respond. Channel it. Use every ounce of that frustration, disappointment—whatever you're feeling —in your game. That's how you take your power back."

His words hit home. I knew he was right. Indy's distance had shaken me, but I couldn't let it break me—not with so much riding on tonight's outcome. Desmond's voice echoed in my mind as I stepped onto the court, determination fueling every step, every pass, every release. Each play felt personal, like I was proving something— not just to my team or the fans, but to myself.

By halftime, I felt locked in, laser-focused. The roar of the crowd, the rhythm of the game and the urgency of the moment, muted my concerns with Indira. I knew the silence would crash back once the adrenaline drained and the arena emptied. But for now, basketball was my sanctuary, and tonight, nothing else mattered.

Against my better judgment, I broke my rule. Normally, after a game I refused to look at social media, protecting myself from nasty trolls. But tonight, I couldn't help myself. Pathetic maybe, but I checked to see if Indy had even tapped a heart on my win post.

I didn't see any proof that she'd been on my page, but she'd been online, posting about real estate and commenting on other people's pictures. But not mine.

I missed talking to her, seeing her, being close enough to touch her. I debated whether to try reaching her and finally gave in. I opted to call instead of texting, and the call rang before going straight to voicemail. I tried again, but she still didn't pick up.

I hated this feeling, causing me to settle for a text message. "You avoiding me?" When a response didn't come, I broke.

I didn't chase women. I'd never had to. But this was Indira. And she was shutting me out.

As soon as the bus dropped us off in the player parking lot, desperation pushed me straight toward Indira's place. My heart hammered, anxiety twisting in my gut. The thought of losing her was eating me up.

I'd never felt this frantic, this out of control—not even on the court with seconds left on the clock. I couldn't shake the fear that I was already too late, that she might've decided we were done without even giving me a chance to fix whatever went wrong. I didn't care that it was almost three a.m.; I had to see her face-to-face and know exactly where we stood.

I pressed my forehead to the cool wood, counted to five, and knocked. I caught the footsteps, watched the peephole darken, and waited until the chain slid and the door cracked open.

Indy stood there in a short, spaghetti-strap nightgown, the thin fabric tracing curves I knew by heart. My thoughts scattered; blood rushed south, but I forced myself to refocus.

I reminded myself why I'd shown up here in the first place—I needed to know where we stood.

She looked surprised—but not shocked. Like she knew I'd come.

I pushed my way past her. "Alright, Indira. What the hell is going on?"

She followed on my heels as I took up residence in a kitchen chair, making myself comfortable. When she cocked her head and folded her arms, her breasts pressing together, the lace dipping low enough to test my control, I had to look away.

"What do you mean?" she demanded, leaning against the counter.

I snapped my attention back to her. "You know what the hell I mean. You barely talk to me; you ignore my calls—what did I do?"

Indira clenched her jaw defiantly, looking like she wasn't planning to have this conversation. I waited, gripping my patience.

"I ain't never known you to hold back, Indy. So, what is it?"

"You tell *me*, Latimer."

My eyebrows bunched. "You think I'd drag my ass over here at three in the morning if I knew what your problem was?!"

Her hand flew to her hip, and her voice rose. "Maybe ask your little friend on the 'Gram. Why is Briana acting like she still has a shot with you? And why the hell did you pin it?"

My expression tightened as I blew out a breath. "You're tripping over Briana Dillon? Indy, come on—"

"Don't 'Indy' me. She's out here acting like you two have unfinished business, and you're letting everybody think it's true!"

"You wanna know what *I* think looks unfinished? You not showing up. Game after game, Indy. I looked for you in the stands every damn time, and you're not there. Do you know what that does to me? I'm out there busting my ass, trying to keep my head straight, and all I can think about is how you don't bother to come!"

For a minute, I let the silence invade the room, filling in every cubic inch not occupied by me, her, or a stainless-steel appliance. The space shrank, suffocating me. I closed my eyes, wondering why it cut so deep that she hadn't been there, why I couldn't just brush it off. I second-guessed why I should even care this much about her being at my games.

I steeled myself before I spat something I couldn't take back or before sharing more than I really wanted to.

Finally, I glanced at Indy, who was staring at me like I was about to confess to first-degree murder—or some other crime that'd get me locked up. I scrubbed a hand over my head, then gripped the back of my neck.

I rose to my feet. "Indy, listen—I don't handle my social media. Never have. I don't check that shit in the postseason. Briana's comment was either an accident or someone on my team thought it was harmless."

Her eyes flashed. "I don't know, Malik." She looked away, voice tight. "It feels like you're making me look stupid out here—like I don't count."

"That's not true, Indy. You do count. You're the only one I'm trying to be with. But damn—" I shook my head. "Sometimes it feels like I don't count to you either. Not when you keep choosing everything else over being there."

She exhaled, shoulders sinking. "I just... don't know anymore."

Her words hit harder than I expected. After everything I'd shown her —every bit of my guard I'd let down—she still doubted me. It hurt more than I wanted to admit.

I stepped closer, my jaw tight. "Ain't nobody making you look stupid, Indira."

"So, I'm overreacting now?"

Silence stretched, between us, heavy and sharp, like one wrong word could cut us both open.

We were close now, breathing hard, eyes locked.

She looked like she wanted me to fix it, but I was angry too—not because of Briana, but because she didn't trust me.

"I don't know, Malik." She swallowed hard, and I could see her eyes filling with tears. "I honestly don't know anymore."

That hit like a gut punch.

I'd been trying to do right—committing, trusting, believing this time was different—and suddenly it felt one-sided. Maybe I'd been too caught up to see the cracks forming.

I stepped back, pulling in a deep breath, and ran a hand over my face. "You need time to figure it out? Fine. Take it."

I turned and walked out the door, slamming it behind me.

Chapter Twenty-Seven

He walked out the door, and my heart froze. I'd expected him to fight harder—to stay, to offer some explanation that made sense. But he didn't. What surprised me was the hurt in his eyes when I told him I didn't know if he'd disrespect me. And now, we were both hurting.

I replayed the conversation in my head on a loop, not sure where things went left. From the moment he walked out, a nagging voice whispered that I'd overreacted. But every time it rose, I shoved it down, replacing guilt with justification.

What proof did I really have that Malik wouldn't go behind my back —with Briana or someone else? His reputation said otherwise. Hell, was there a man alive who knew how to be faithful?

And even if he wasn't trying to rekindle things with his ex, I didn't believe this relationship would last. Maybe our argument just fast-forwarded the inevitable.

The only way to stop replaying his face at my door was to stay busy. So I filled my calendar with back-to-back showings until my feet ached.

One client in particular stood out—Luz Hanover.

Petite and stylish, she carried herself with a clipped New England polish that clung to every word. Even in Detroit, her Massachusetts accent bled through—vowels flat, r's swallowed. "Kyle's been doin' business here for years," she said as we toured a Victorian in Woodbridge, "but this is the first time we've really decided to settle."

I almost asked why now, what had finally tipped the scales. But the way she smoothed her coat and moved toward the staircase told me it wasn't a detail she planned to share. *Been around for years. Business in the area.* She hadn't offered more, and I didn't press, but something about the way she said it lingered in the back of my mind.

By the end of the tour, Luz was already mapping out where she'd hang her art—gesturing toward a sunlit parlor as if the decision were made. Client or not, I had a feeling she'd be easy to like.

Later, I swung by Cairo's place. She barely let me through the door before blurting, "So when are you gonna stop being stubborn and get my tickets?"

I dropped my bag on the counter. "Nice to see you too."

"I'm serious, Indy. Malik's on GSN every night, and you're over here acting like you don't miss him. Meanwhile, I'm ticketless. Don't make me beg."

"You're shameless."

"And you're distracted." She plopped onto the couch, eyeing me over the rim of her glass. "But anyway—I've got something bigger on my mind."

I narrowed my eyes. "Bigger than NBA tickets?" Her hesitation made me sit forward. "A prep school in Virginia reached out—one of those private, college-prep academies that's always ranked high. They've got a legendary basketball program. And they're recruiting Zahara."

I blinked. "Wait—*Zahara*? She hasn't even started at Farmington yet."

"I know," Cairo said, her mouth tight. "She's been counting down the days, talking about it nonstop. But this program wants her and Cheyenne. Full scholarships if they make the team. Exposure, training, facilities most schools can't touch. It's the kind of pipeline that sets kids up for college ball and beyond."

I let that sink in—Zahara, with her fire on the court and that sharp mouth off it, already catching the eye of recruiters. And Cheyenne right beside her.

"And what about her life here? The friends she's been waiting to start high school with?"

"That's what's messing me up," she admitted, rubbing her forehead.

"She's excited about Farmington. She finally feels like she belongs somewhere. Do I rip her out of that before it even starts—for a shot at... greatness? She's still just a kid, Indy. And Cheyenne too. They're best friends, not just prospects."

I nodded slowly, already hearing The Sisters' voices in my head.

"You know Ma'Dear won't go for it. Farmington was a big enough leap— private school, high tuition, all that. Not only is it out-of-state, but she's gonna see this prep school as taking Zahara even further away from her roots."

Cairo let out a dry laugh. "Don't I know it. I haven't even said a word yet, and I can already picture her face."

For a while, we just sat there, the weight of it hanging between us—the kind of decision that didn't have a clean answer.

When I drove home later, silence wrapped tight around me. I told myself to think about work—about Cairo, about listings, about anything else. But all I could see was Malik at my door, his eyes sharp with hurt.

And no matter how hard I tried, I couldn't shake him.

Chapter Twenty-Eight

MALIK

We'd just taken Game 1 of the Eastern Conference Finals, and the locker room was buzzing. Trainers handled post-game checkups, reporters stacked ten deep, and everybody was talking like we'd already taken the trophy.

I wasn't in the mood.

I slipped out after the interviews, towel slung over my shoulders, phone heavy in my hand. My body was still lit up from the game, but inside? Empty. The first person I wanted to share it with wasn't here —and hadn't been for a while.

"You bouncin' already?"

I turned and found Jarvis leaning against the wall, sweat still fresh on his face. He grinned, but there was no spark in it.

"Somebody's gotta keep y'all humble," I said. He chuckled, low.

"Truth is, I ain't feelin' it either." He scanned the hallway before dropping his voice. "I don't even wanna go home. Twinna's on some shit, bruh. Spending like crazy. Her friends been getting laced with everything from sunglasses to jewelry, and she's been footing bills like she got an unlimited card. She just bought one of them an extravagant gift I don't even wanna say out loud."

I stayed quiet, letting him keep going.

He exhaled hard. "And now—get this—she's suddenly besties with Briana. *Briana*! They've barely kept in touch all these years, and now they're posting selfies, going to lunch, laughing it up like old times. Don't make sense."

Briana's name stung, but I didn't flinch.

Jarvis rubbed a hand over his face. "Feels like she's doin' it on purpose. To get under my skin or... I don't know. To prove something. And I'm out here tryin' to lock in, and she's makin' me feel like a fool."

I leaned against the wall beside him, towel slipping around my neck. "You talk to her?"

"Tried. She brushed me off. Said I was overreacting." His laugh was bitter. "Like I'm imagining things."

I pressed my lips together, the words hitting harder than I wanted. Indira hadn't said those exact words, but the sting felt the same—being doubted, shut out, left standing on the outside of someone you love.

"Look," I said finally, "marriage ain't about playin' games. If something's off, you can't just swallow it. But if the trust's gone..." I trailed off, shaking my head.

Jarvis gave me a long look, like he knew I was talking about more than just him. Maybe I was.

When he left, silence pressed in around me. I leaned back against the wall, towel damp against my neck, and asked myself the one question I'd been dodging: *What was I getting out of this thing with Indy?*

Yeah, she was beautiful, sharp, had a fire that matched mine. But was that enough when every argument cut like glass? When she looked at me and saw the worst of my reputation instead of the man in front of her?

I wanted her—hell, I needed her—but wanting wasn't the same as trusting. And if we didn't figure out how to close that gap, how to stop making each other bleed, what were we really building?

I already knew what I needed. For her to believe me. To stop waiting on me to fail her and start seeing me as the man who'd never walk away.

I'd had my trust shattered once, years ago, and I'd carried the cracks ever since. I couldn't survive that kind of betrayal again—not from her.

I glanced down at my phone, thumb hovering over Indira's name. We'd won tonight, but none of it mattered without her in the stands. And no matter how hard I tried, I couldn't shake her.

Chapter Twenty-Nine

Since Malik walked out, I told myself I'd keep my distance. But damn, if that man wasn't constantly on my mind. Every night, the silence sat heavy on my chest, like an unanswered question. A week of no calls, no texts. Just absence.

So when Malcolm invited me to the soft launch of his new restaurant, Songbird, my gut twisted into knots. I knew Malik would be there, along with our usual crew—Cairo, Desmond, Jarvis, and Twinna. Avoiding him forever wasn't realistic. Maybe facing him would finally loosen the tightness lodged in my chest. Or maybe it would shatter me.

The moment I stepped inside, warmth wrapped around me. Songbird wasn't just a restaurant—it was Malcolm's love letter to Detroit. Big portraits of Aretha, Aaliyah, Stevie, and Eminem dominated the brick walls, like family watching over the space.

Instead of sleek, sterile lines, everything whispered comfort: wide leather armchairs, mismatched throw pillows, a bar trimmed in warm wood that glowed under soft light. It felt like stepping into somebody's kitchen and living room—only with a jazz trio in the corner and champagne flutes clinking across the room.

The place buzzed with life. Local notables brushed shoulders with a few of Malik's teammates, laughter and conversation weaving together like background music. Malcolm moved through it all with that effortless Latimer charm, pausing to shake hands and accept congratulations. For once, he was the star in the spotlight, and pride swelled in my chest seeing his dream come alive.

I caught sight of Cairo and Twinna tucked near a corner table, their laughter carrying above the hum, while Desmond held court by the stage, glass in hand. The sound made my stomach tighten.

Twinna's smile was wide, easy—like she hadn't been the one spilling tea to Briana. I reminded myself tonight wasn't the night for grudges. Still, my pulse jumped, the reminder of how quickly trust could turn into gossip scraping under my skin.

For a fleeting second, I thought maybe I could settle into the celebration—blend into the joy, let the night wash over me. But then my gaze drifted past them, and I froze. Malik stood at the bar, broad shoulders relaxed, smiling at something.

He was effortlessly handsome in that way that always knocked me off balance. The cozy glow of Songbird dimmed around him, and all I felt was the flutter in my chest and the ache of the distance between us.

His eyes flicked up, found mine across the room, and for the briefest second, he stilled. Then he looked away, leaving me rooted in place, heart pounding.

I lingered with Cairo and Twinna, laughing when they laughed, nodding when they nodded. But my ears caught none of it. Malik's presence pulled at me like a tide. Every cell in my body screamed to cross the room, but my pride ordered me to stay put.

Another ten minutes of pretending— another fake smile—and I couldn't take it anymore.

I wove through the crowd slowly, smiling, talking, though I hardly heard a word. My stomach knotted tighter with each step.

When I finally stood in front of him, silence pressed in, heavy and unyielding. He didn't speak, didn't even soften his expression. Just stared down at me, cool and unreadable, like I was a stranger.

"Congrats, Malik. You killed Game 1," I said, my voice steady even though my pulse betrayed me.

He hesitated, gaze guarded. "Thanks. Surprised you noticed." The words stung—not just because of the coolness in his tone, but because he was right.

"Just because we hit a bump in the road doesn't mean I don't care," I murmured, softer than I meant.

His jaw flexed, and for a moment he looked away, sipping his drink like it gave him more to say than I did. "Could've fooled me. You didn't give me a chance—you just assumed the worst."

Each word cut, because he wasn't wrong. "I was scared, Malik. Afraid of looking foolish. Afraid of losing you."

His eyes searched mine, but he didn't move closer. "Fear's one thing. Choosing not to believe me is another. After everything I've shown you, you still doubted me. That's the part that doesn't sit right."

Tears pressed against the back of my eyes, but I forced my chin up. "I wanna trust you," I whispered. "But it scares me."

He stayed still another beat, arms crossed like he was holding himself together. The noise of Songbird carried on around us— clinking glasses, bursts of laughter—while we stood locked in our own silent battle. Finally, he exhaled through his nose.

"Words are easy, Indy. Actions matter more."

My throat burned. "Then let me prove it." The words slipped out before I could lose my nerve.

The silence stretched, brittle as glass. I thought he might turn and walk away, leave me to drown in my own regret. But then, slowly, his arms fell to his sides. His fingers brushed mine—tentative, testing—like he wasn't ready to give me everything back, but maybe he hadn't given up either.

"I'll try," I whispered, nodding, the words fragile and fierce all at once.

Something in his eyes eased—cautious but still burning. "That's all I'm asking."

And just like that, the tightness in my chest loosened. For the first time in days, I felt like I could breathe again.

But even as I exhaled, I knew one touch wasn't enough to erase the distance between us. Still, it was a start.

Malik's mouth found mine the second the door clicked shut, and I let him—no hesitation, no second-guessing. Just heat, raw and relentless, spilling from every place we'd been holding back. His hands slid into my hair, down my spine, pulling me closer like he was trying to erase every mile, every silence, every bruise between us.

The kiss deepened—rough edges giving way to something softer. His breath mingled with mine, tasting of want and forgiveness, and the sound that escaped me wasn't anger anymore—it was relief. My fingers trembled as they fumbled for the hem of his shirt, desperate for skin, for proof that he was really here. That we hadn't broken beyond repair.

"I don't wanna fight anymore," I whispered against his lips, the confession catching between us.

"Then don't," he murmured, his voice low and rough, lifting me as though I weighed nothing. My legs wrapped around him instinctively, the motion familiar and new all at once. His body was solid and certain, but there was something different in the way he held me —like he wasn't just claiming, he was offering.

He laid me down with a care that contradicted the urgency between us, his fingers tracing my jaw before his mouth followed. Each kiss carried the echo of everything we'd said and everything we hadn't—anger cooling into apology, longing into promise.

Every touch blurred into something more than desire. It was a conversation without words, a slow unraveling of pride and pain. I clung to him, breathing him in, letting him remind me what it felt like to be chosen —not out of habit or heat, but out of hope.

When his forehead rested against mine, our breaths fell into rhythm. For the first time in days, the space between us disappeared, and the world went quiet.

Can I tell you how good makeup sex is? Reconciling with Malik worked wonders for my state of mind. I was wearing my mood like a brand-new purse I couldn't wait to show off. Nobody could tell me anything. I felt radiant—lighter, freer.

The next morning, sunlight slipped past the curtains, spilling across Malik's shoulders as he scrolled through his phone. His jaw flexed, the easy calm from last night vanishing.

"What's wrong?" I asked, propping up on one elbow.

He exhaled, tossing the phone onto the nightstand. "Jarvis. He's pissed. Said Twinna's out here dropping money on her friends like she's Oprah. Bought one of 'em a Cartier watch yesterday. And now she and Briana are posting like they've been best friends forever."

The name made my stomach pinch. Briana. Always hovering. "Since when are they even close?" I asked.

"Exactly," Malik muttered. "It's like Twinna's trying to stir up drama on purpose. Jarvis is tryna lock in for the Finals, but she's making it impossible. And Briana? She's the last person I need in our orbit right now."

The word *our* didn't slip past me.

I reached for his hand. "Then let Jarvis handle Twinna. You focus on what you can control."

His thumb brushed over mine absently, but his eyes stayed hard. "Yeah. Just saying—if Twinna drags Briana into our circle again, I'm not holding my tongue."

I squeezed his hand. "Fair. But we stay solid. That's what

matters." He gave a short nod—still tense—but the edge in his gaze softened

just a fraction.

I should have known that when Tamara James is your mama, a good mood is temporary. She wasn't done wreaking havoc, and she never accepted *no* for an answer.

Not when she wanted something.

Not when she thought she deserved something. And apparently, she'd decided she deserved a place in my life.

Whether she'd ever left or just circled the block all week, I'd felt her before I saw her.

On Sunday morning, I high-stepped into Shady Grove Church in the So Kates Malik gifted me. Even with him at my side, I felt ten feet tall from the vestibule, past the ushers, into the sanctuary.

I was barely settled in my pew before I spotted her. Fashionably late, unapologetic, she sauntered in, and my stomach dropped. Like always, she dressed for attention: a fitted floral dress that hugged her every line, stilettos too high for a Sunday morning, especially if you're already six feet tall, and a hat more declaration than shade. Heads turned as she moved down the aisle, her presence loud without a word.

My shoulders tightened on instinct. Malik, sitting beside me, must've noticed my shift in energy, his hand answering with the tightened grip on my thigh—a silent question, a steadying anchor. I exhaled, my jaw tightening as I whispered, "She's not supposed to be here."

Ma'Dear, positioned in her wheelchair at the end of the pew, and Aunt Millie, seated on the other side of me, had already noticed, too. When The Sisters disapproved, it meant all hell usually followed. I watched with apprehension as Ma'Dear's lips pressed together, her eyes narrowing just enough to send a silent warning across the sanctuary.

But Tamara?

She didn't care.

She slid into an empty pew near the front, crossed her legs, and settled as if she belonged, like she hadn't spent years avoiding the church house. Like she hadn't called church folks too judgmental, small-minded, and boring.

Pastor's voice blurred.

She didn't come for the service. She came for me. And worse? She came on a day when Malik was here. When Cairo, Zahara, and Desmond were present.

She wasn't just inserting herself into my life—she was inserting herself into my world. The life I built. The people I trust. The family that chose me when she didn't. I didn't know her next move. But I knew mine: I wasn't going to sit here and let her make it.

After service, we gathered in the bright, cozy annex. The walls had recently been painted mint green, and the odor of chemicals and pigments still hung in the air, mixing with the scent of freshly brewed coffee. The windows were open to let in the late spring air, barely masking the hodgepodge of scents.

Because it was Youth Sunday, the children's choir led the music. Most folks were bobbing their heads to the Christian rap, except for Ma'Dear and Aunt Millie, who preferred traditional gospel. As they sat together at the head of the table chatting, I imagined they were trading quiet gripes about the playlist.

My good mood returned after Pastor's sermon, which encouraged us to restore broken relationships and used the example of Jacob and Esau. The message loosened my frustration with Tamara's presence. So, despite my vow to foil her next move, I focused on enjoying the light fare the hospitality committee had provided and tried to soak up the love surrounding me.

Beside me, Cairo laughed at something Desmond whispered, her plate piled high with pastries. Zahara sat on my left, while Malik sat on the right, close enough for me to feel his warmth yet far enough to maintain a careful distance. I nursed a cup of tea, a far cry from my preferred chai, sipping slowly and savoring the atmosphere. For a minute, I let myself breathe.

Just as I started to relax, I felt a sudden shift. Heads turned toward the doorway, and my stomach plummeted. Heat crawled up my neck. When I was a child, and my mother swept into town, I'd be so ecstatic I'd practically leap for joy. Now, the only thing I wanted to leap on was *her*, and it wasn't joy driving me—it was fury.

My mother stood at the entrance, her vibrant dress and bold presence impossible to ignore. Her eyes zeroed in on me immediately, and my breath hitched. Conversations thinned, replaced by a tense silence.

"What do you want, Tamara?" I asked, my voice colder than I intended. "Because clearly, it ain't to hear the word." I know. It was judgy. But I never said I was a saint.

She smiled tightly, eyes flashing. "Indy, I'm your mother. Can't I just see how my baby's doing?"

"Your 'baby'?" My voice rose slightly, and I knew The Sisters now had eyes fastened on me. "Funny how I only become your baby when it suits you."

Malik leaned in closer, his subtle presence steadying me. He was still in the dark about my mother and me, but I felt his silent support.

"Indira, lower your voice," Tamara hissed, glancing around as if embarrassed.

"Oh, now you're worried about appearances?" I snapped, pushing to my feet. "You came here for an audience, so go ahead— say whatever it is you really came to say. But this? Trying to insert yourself now? Not happening."

"Indy," Cairo warned, knowing my fuse was as short as my height. Tamara straightened, defiance flashing in her eyes. "Careful, Indy. Don't forget where you came from."

"I haven't," I said, voice firm but quieter now. "That's why I know exactly where you belong—and it's nowhere near me."

We stared each other down, chests heaving, weighing the next words we'd throw. My comeback was on the tip of my tongue when Aunt Millie, all five feet of her, rose with force. "Tamara, you've said your piece. Now respect your daughter's wishes and leave."

"Y'all are so high and mighty!" Tamara spat. "You think you're too good to forgive. Maybe I have something important to discuss with *my* child."

"That might be the case," Aunt Millie conceded, "but this ain't the time nor place. You've caused enough trouble. Let Indira have her peace. She's a grown woman. If she wants to reach out to you, she knows how to find you."

I sank back into my chair, grateful once again for Aunt Millie's quiet strength that had always shielded me when I needed it most.

Malik hadn't said a word since Tamara left, but the quiet said enough. As we rode in the backseat of his SUV, I knew it wasn't about privacy—Slade had probably heard enough to write a tell-all if he wanted. Maybe Malik's silence was his way of protecting me. I glanced sideways at him, noting the tightness in his jaw and the crease between his brows. The gentle squeeze of his hand on mine was both comforting and grounding, but his eyes held questions he was too considerate to ask aloud.

I couldn't imagine what he was thinking.

He'd spent enough time around me and Cairo to know that my Detroit family was "normal." At least from the outside looking in. Our love and respect for each other were obvious in our interactions.

We celebrated one another. Showed up for one another. We were constant in each other's lives.

Malik knew that wasn't the case with my mother.

And he'd been patient with me, accepting my crazy schedule, my lack of trust, and my wavering commitment. I needed to fill in some of the blanks for him, at least.

"I guess I owe you an explanation, huh?" I whispered, glancing up at Malik, who watched me carefully. "You finally got to see my mother, a title she doesn't deserve. When I was little, she'd vanish for months, sometimes longer. When she'd show up again, she'd promise everything would be different. It never was."

Malik nodded, listening without judgment. "Sounds rough," he murmured, squeezing my fingers. "You don't have to tell me everything now."

"I want you to understand," I said softly, choosing my words carefully. "She's always been unpredictable, unreliable. I learned early not to expect much. I built walls, Malik, thick ones. And every time she shows up like this, those walls feel like they're crumbling."

He leaned in closer, his voice quiet yet firm. "You don't have to rebuild them alone this time. I'm here. I got you."

I leaned into him, cupping his face between my palms, and brushed a soft, lingering kiss against his lips. "And I got you."

Chapter Thirty

MALIK

When Indy started opening up about her childhood, I stayed quiet, giving her space to breathe. Still, I couldn't stop stealing glances—trying not to make it obvious how much it tore me up to see her hurting. Watching her with her mother told me everything I needed to know: their history was complicated, messy, raw.

My mind went to my own family—Pops, strict but steady. Mama, warm but firm. Jackie, who mothered us all. Malcolm, who never missed a chance to clown me for my Michael Jackson obsession. We weren't perfect, but we were solid. That foundation gave me something to stand on that Indy didn't have. Not until Detroit, not until now.

Damn. No wonder she builta fortress around her feelings. The fact that she'd let me inside at all felt bigger than any championship run. When she finally broke the silence and handed me pieces of her story, pride and tenderness hit me at once. She trusted me. That wasn't small.

So, when I told her I had her back, I meant it. Every damn word. And I'd prove it—not with promises, but with action.

I laced our fingers and studied my bite-size beauty. "I can make this shit with your mother go away you just say the word."

I felt her palm tense as she frowned. "Exactly what do you mean by go away?"

"I just want peace for you. If you don't want her to keep showing up, blowing up your spot, I can give her a big enough bag to keep her ass in ATL. I can loop Blaise. And he'll draft a mutual NDA—no-contact, teeth in every clause."

Indy studied me. "You would do that for me?" I looped my arm around her shoulder. "Hell, yeah. And I don't care how much it costs either. But I won't move without your consent. If you don't want a payout in it, we won't wire a cent. We'll just file and be done."

She chewed on my lip, considering my offer. I hoped she knew I meant ever word. This wasn't about managing her. It was about protecting her.

She exhaled. "If it comes to that, then do it. But I don't know when I can repay you."

"No need. Consider it done, Shortie."

I would do everything in my power to fill the void her mother left and to help heal her emotional scars. That's why, a couple of days later, I wanted her by my side at my parents' house.

Pops had the grill smoking before we even hit the driveway, and Mama's voice carried from the kitchen, fussing over the potato salad. My people didn't do anything halfway—especially family gatherings.

Good weather was all Mama needed to host a cookout and get Pops on the grill. And if my dad was known for anything, it was being a barbecue grill master. His sisters from Inkster drove in with slabs of ribs whenever he got the charcoal going. Malcolm handled the sides, with help from Jackie, while Mama orchestrated the whole affair, handing out orders now that she considered herself retired from cooking.

The crowd was thinner than usual, but my family was notoriously late. Slade pulled up to the curb in front of my parents' house. I spotted their Cadillac, Jackie's sedan, and a few of my aunties' cars. Classic R&B pumped from the DJ's speakers. Frankie Beverly's "Happy Feelings" floated through the air, setting the perfect vibe for a family cookout.

Before heading inside, I grabbed a box from the back seat. "Anybody home?" I called out, stepping into the front hall. Framed photos cluttered tables, keepsakes from years gone by. A jungle of plants filled every corner and my eyes instantly found the aloe vera Mama used for all our childhood scrapes.

I followed the smell of fruit and meat toward the kitchen, where my mother stood at the island, slicing cantaloupe.

She glanced up, immediately eyeing the box. "What you got there? I thought I told you just to bring yourself."

I leaned in, kissed her cheek, and pulled her into a hug. "Did I tell you you're the best mama in the world?"

"I better be since you only get one," she shot back, smiling, though her eyes stayed sharp. "You seem awfully chipper today."

"What's wrong with that? Can't a brother be happy?" "Yes, and you have plenty of reasons—my MVP!" She pinched my cheek.

"You seen Malcolm yet? I brought him some Macallan," I announced, pulling the bottle from the box. "I owe him after the damage I did at last year's cookout."

Mama swatted a dish towel, warning, "Just make sure you can drive home this time."

"I will, besides, Slade is here. Designated driver, right?"

"Where is he? He'd better come show me some love!"

"You know he'll come through, Mama. And he's not the only one I invited."

Her brows shot up. "Who else?"

"My girl, Indira. I can't wait for you to meet her." I started to walk away, but Mama called after me.

"Your girl? Is she the same one they keep talking about on @DetroitGossip?"

I almost tripped. "Mama, what you know about @DetroitGossip?"

She shrugged. "I read it…sometimes, you know. Just to keep up."

I laughed. "Does Pops know you're keeping up with that nonsense?"

"Pssh, and what's he gonna do about it?"

I shook my head, grinning, when my phone rang. My heartbeat raced at the caller ID.

"What up, Shortie?" I answered.

"I'm here. Should I come through the house or the yard?"

"Stay there. I'll come get you."

Excited to introduce her, I jogged to the front. My chest thumped faster with every step. When I opened her door and helped her out, her smile lit me up inside.

She wore a flowy white dress belted in gold at the waist, a sleeveless denim jacket, and yellow wedge sandals that gave her a boost. Knotless braids pulled back in a ponytail showed off her sun-kissed face, bronze and glowing.

"You ready, Bite-Size?" I asked, resting my hand at the small of her back. When I saw her chewing her lip, I said, "They don't bite."

"Are you sure?" she asked under her breath, eyeing the house.

"I'm sure."

"Okay, then." Indira flashed a beautiful smile. "I'm ready. Bring it on."

I felt my chest squeeze. My girl was confident, outgoing, and enjoyed turning up. I inhaled and hoped my family would appreciate her company as much as I did. I slid my free hand into hers and led her toward the backyard, catching spicy, smoky scents of grilled meat along the way.

The first thing I spotted was Pops at the barbecue pit, holding court while schooling Malcolm on how to grill the perfect slab of meat. I chuckled, considering my brother was a master chef who could cook anything. I took my time walking over, matching Indy's shorter stride in her wedges.

"What up, fam?" I called as Pops closed the lid on the grill.

His face lit up. "Hey now, Son. Good to see you." He pulled me into a bear hug—same move whether I'd seen him yesterday or two weeks ago. Then he turned to Indy. "And who do we have here? Is this the girl you've been crushing on?"

We all broke into laughter, Indy included, before Malcolm jumped in to clown him. "Crushing on, Pops? You're dating yourself."

"Whatever," Pops shot back. "That's what we called it when I was chasing your mama." He extended his hand toward Indy. "Young lady, I'm Joe. Or Papa Joe to these knuckleheads." He jerked his thumb at Malcolm, making the point stick.

"Dad, this is my lady, Indira."

"Pleased to meet you, Mr. Latimer. You can call me Indy."

"And you can call me Papa Joe, like I said."

She flashed a grin. "Okay then. I stand corrected." She gave Malcolm a wave. "Good to see you again."

She kept it light, and that was fine by me. Indy was mine, and everybody here needed to know it. Before I could say more, a familiar voice cut through the music. "Unc! You finally showed up."

I turned to see Jaeden Bentley making his way over, football in hand, grinning easy. The kid had stretched out since the last time I saw him— broad shoulders, lean muscle, confidence dripping off him. Farmington Country Day's golden boy, fresh off a 14–0 season and headed to college on a full ride. Jarvis was amped, proud his kid had carved out his own lane.

And me? I was stoked too.. Jaeden wasn't just my godson—I'd embraced him like he was my own.

"Look at you," I called out, shaking my head. "You trying to make me feel old?"

He laughed, spinning the ball between his hands. "Nah, Uncle L. Just trying to keep you on your toes."

"Boy, please. You think you can get a pass past me?" I dropped into a mock defensive stance, spreading my arms.

Indy chuckled under her breath, but Jaeden was locked in, cocky grin plastered on his face. "Bet I can."

"Go ahead then."

The ball zipped past, fast and clean, but my reflexes were sharp. I snatched it out of the air, tucked it under my arm, and grinned. "That all you got? You must've left your arm back at Farmington."

Jaeden lunged, laughing as he tried to grab it back, but I held it high overhead. "C'mon now, you gotta want it more than that! Think college corners are just gonna let you slide by?"

We tussled light, both of us cracking up, until I finally shoved the ball back into his chest. "Alright, alright. You get to keep your scholarship. For now."

"Unc, you're crazy," he said, shaking his head with a grin.

I clapped him on the shoulder. "I'm proud of you, man. You've got a good head on your shoulders. Keep it there, and the sky's yours."

"Yes, sir." His voice had that steady weight that reminded me he was more man than boy now.

When he jogged off to find his brothers, I felt Indy's eyes on me. Her smile was soft, dimples showing, as she teased, "So that's the side of you the cameras never get to see, huh?"

I shrugged, trying to play it off, though my chest warmed under her

gaze. "What can I say? That's my godson. Gotta keep him honest."

"Honest?" she repeated, eyes glimmering. "Looked to me like you were teaching him how to cheat."

I laughed, sliding an arm around her waist. "Nah. Just showing him the rules come harder when you're playing against me."

She leaned into me, still smiling, but I caught the flicker in her eyes—like she'd just seen me in a different light. Not as Malik the MVP, not even as her man. But as something more.

"Come on. Let's go meet Mama." I tugged her along by the hand

and crossed the yard. We climbed the deck stairs and entered the house through the sliding door off the kitchen.

My queen was still in the wide grin split her face. "Mama, look who made it. This is Indira."

A wide grin split her face as she wiped her hands on a towel. "Well, Indira, I have been looking forward to this day."

Indy's eyes darted over to me, and she appeared nervous, similar to when she first met my friends. Mama reached for her and smothered her in a hug, causing Indy to squeal in surprise. "You must be special if Malik brought you home to meet us. Welcome," she added before setting Indira free.

"Thank you, Mrs. Latimer," Indy giggled. I didn't realize Malik had told everyone about me."

"He's been pretty tight-lipped, but Malcolm spilled the beans. You're just as beautiful as he said."

"Oh, that's sweet." She smiled before turning back to Mama. "I've heard a lot about you. It's great to finally meet you in person."

"Same here. Now, Honey, don't be shy up in here. Fix yourself a plate. There's plenty of food."

"Ma'am, I'm not shy when it comes to food."

I nodded my head. "Trust me, she's telling the truth. The girl can eat."

"Hmph. It sure don't look like it. You must have one of those high metabolisms I wasn't blessed with."

"Something like that," Indy smiled proudly.

"Oh, and Malik, I meant to ask you what else was in the box. Tell me it's not all liquor. "

"Not at all," I added, handing her the box of chocolate pecan pies from Sonny's. After setting them on the island, Mama pulled at the baker's twine. When she flipped back the lid, her look of satisfaction made my day. "Boy, you sure do spoil me."

"I try to, Mama. That's why I'm your favorite."

"Hush, chile. I don't have favorites. I'll tell you who my favorite is. Whichever one of y'all brings me some grandbabies."

Aww, shit. "Grandbabies?" My eyes widened, and I quickly raised my hands defensively. "Mama, slow your roll. Can a brother get married first?"

We laughed in unison before I announced. "On that note, I'm going to see if I can find Jackie. Indy, you coming?"

She glanced around the kitchen as if making up her mind. "I think I'm going to stay in here and help your mom. Is that okay?"

"Sure, I'll be back to check on you." I liked the idea of her feeling comfortable with my mother. As far as I was concerned, Indira was endgame, so the sooner she got to know everyone, the better.

I made my way back outside, where the scent of barbecue had my stomach growling. Malcolm was on the grill, which was a surprise because my father rarely relinquished the rights. I scanned the yard and found my old man struggling to assemble the volleyball net. He looked up, noticing my approach. "Son, you're just in time. Your sister usually helps me with this."

"Where is Jackie anyway? I thought I saw her car," I asked while reaching for the aluminum poles lying on the ground.

"She was here, but that new rascal of hers swung by and ran her to the store. I've got a mind to make him put it together when he gets here."

"What you got against this guy, Pops?"

"Shoot, nothing specific. I guess he treats her good enough."

I chuckled. "Mama always said you never thought anyone was ever good enough for your baby girl, not even James."

Joseph pounded a stake in the ground and then stepped back to survey his work. Satisfied, he shielded the sun with his hands and glanced over at me. "I suppose that's true, but I'm wrong sometimes, like with James. He was a damn good husband and father to Jamal and Jarrell. He was just gone too soon."

"Yeah, I miss James, too." I grew silent for a minute and then added, "My first beef with the new guy is I haven't met him."

"Malik, you've been busy trying to get your team to the championship." He nodded his approval while pounding the final stake.

"You're almost there. I know I already told you, but I'm proud of you."

"Thanks, Pops."

"Now I know the other reason you've been busy. That young lady got your nose wide open."

I sucked my teeth. "You make it sound like I'm sprung or something."

"Son, that ain't necessarily a bad thing. Hell, I'm so glad all of the headlines stopped talking about you being surrounded by skeezers."

I threw my head back and laughed. "Skeezers, Dad? I ain't heard that word in a minute."

"Good. Let's keep it that way. You told me Indira is a good woman. She's not a gold-digger, right?"

I chuckled. *This guy.* "No, Pops. She's got a career and she's very ambitious. And she's pretty independent. She likes having her own money."

"That's good to hear. After you meet a woman like her, you won't settle for second-rate."

"I know. Now let's get this net up. I plan on whooping Malcolm in a match."

"Good luck with that, Son. You may have more luck with the ladies than your brother, but when was the last time you beat him at anything?"

"Fine pops, you don't have to rub it in." I may have been fighting for an NBA championship, but family had a way of humbling you. And Pops was right. Malcolm beat me at any sport we played. Every time.

Chapter Thirty-One

It wasn't until my stomach started growling that I realized how long I'd been chopping it up with Mama Latimer.

I stepped onto the deck to check out what I was sure would be a huge spread of food. The Latimers' backyard stretched wide, emerald grass and neatly trimmed hedges lining the fence. The late spring air carried the scent of grilled meat and the faint perfume of fresh blooms arranged around the patio. In the background, laughter mixed with the melody of a 90s R&B playlist floating from the speakers.

I hit the patio, and a dozen eyes hit back. Malik had sworn it would be casual—Sunday chill—but his family had multiplied while I was parking.

Before I could blink, she beelined toward me—tall, impossible to miss, lemon-yellow sundress, curls springing, a smirk that promised trouble.

"You must be Indira," she said, barely waiting for my nod before pressing a glass of deep red into my hand. "Here. You're gonna need this."

I huffed a laugh, thrown but amused. "Uh... thank you?" I glanced at Malik as he closed the distance.

"Jackie," he said, shaking his head, fondness leaking through. "Let's not scare her off."

Jackie flicked him away. "What? I'm welcoming her properly." She turned back to me, eyes twinkling. "I'm Malik's favorite sister."

I took a cautious sip while she watched me, taking my measure —not unkind, more like checking if I could hold my own.

"You're my only sister," Malik said, deadpan.

"And yet, still the favorite." Jackie winked at me before looping an arm through mine.

"Have you met my aunties yet?"

"Nope," I answered.

"Well, let's get you introduced before they start making bets on how long you'll last."

I almost choked on my wine, coughing slightly. "Wait—did you say bets?"

Jackie just grinned. "You'll be fine. If you're already drinking, you're halfway there."

I felt a flutter of nerves mixed with amusement. Jackie's confidence was contagious, but I couldn't shake the feeling of stepping into a test I wasn't fully prepared for. Sure enough, a half-circle of aunties was waiting, names flying at me faster than I could catch them. I smiled, nodded, and hoped I'd remember at least two.

Malik caught my eye, giving me a look that was both apologetic and encouraging. He followed us toward the rest of the family, and I couldn't help the small smile tugging at my lips.

After the barbecue wrapped up, Malik and I headed back to his place. Even though I'd enjoyed the day, I was drained—emotionally more than physically. Sitting on Malik's plush sofa, nestled comfortably against him, I quietly listened as he recounted funny stories about his family, laughter still lingering in his voice.

The warmth and connection I'd felt in Malik's backyard suddenly made me realize all I'd missed growing up. An ache settled deep in my chest, reminding me of everything Tamara couldn't or wouldn't give me.

"You good, Indy?" Malik asked softly, pulling me from my thoughts.

I hesitated for a second, unsure how much I wanted to share. But Malik had earned it—he'd earned my honesty. "Today was beautiful," I finally whispered, looking up at him. "Your family, the way you all just...belong together. I loved it. But seeing it up close made me realize how much I missed."

His brow furrowed gently, his voice cautious but tender. "You mean because of Tamara?"

I nodded slowly, feeling my throat tighten. "I was about nine or ten when Tamara promised to take me to a family reunion up in Atlanta. It felt like more than just a trip, like maybe she was finally ready to be the mom I needed. I picked out my clothes weeks ahead and told Cairo and my friends I was finally gonna see the big city, leave the country behind, and have a real adventure.

"When the day came, I woke up early, ready to go. But Tamara..." I paused, shaking my head. "Tamara never showed. No call, no explanation, nothing."

Malik squeezed my hand gently, urging me to continue without pushing.

"I sat at that window all day, waiting. Granny tried to get me to play outside with Cairo, but I refused. Finally, Ma'Dear came and got me. She took me for ice cream, trying her best to ease the pain. But even then, I knew—I knew Tamara wasn't coming back anytime soon."

Malik's expression softened further, his voice quiet yet strong. "You deserved better than that."

"Maybe," I admitted quietly. "But Granny, and then later The

Sisters, taught me more than just surviving disappointment. They gave me love, stability—everything Tamara couldn't. Without them, I don't know who I'd be today."

Malik wrapped his arm around me, pulling me closer. I relaxed into him, letting myself accept the comfort and security I'd long craved.

"I don't have to tell you how resilient you are, Indy," he murmured against my braids. "But you don't have to carry it alone anymore."

I looked up at him, seeing sincerity in his eyes and feeling warmth flood my chest. I wanted to believe him, desperately wanting to trust that he'd be here.

"I'm starting to realize that," I whispered, resting my head on his shoulder again, breathing in the comfort and safety he provided.

And once again, I noticed that trusting felt less scary than the thought of losing this warmth.

Maybe Jackie was right—if I'd made it through the day without running, I was already halfway there.

Chapter Thirty-Two

MALIK

I needed a vacation. Bad. Don't get me wrong—I wasn't complaining. But it had been a long, grueling season, and right now, all I could think about was finally getting some real downtime. I could see the light at the end of the tunnel, and I was confident it would end with a dub. Then I'd take that well-deserved break, savoring every fleeting second before the grind started all over again.

During the offseason, the guys and I unwind—Mykonos, Venice, Ibiza. Sometimes Paris for Fashion Week or just the sights. We're blessed to hit places most folks see only in their dreams.

What people don't see is how short the break is when you go deep in the playoffs. Those five months shrink to three, and even then, it isn't all sun. It's individual work, mini-camps, Summer League in July, sponsor days. If you're lucky, you're repping your country at the Olympics or the FIBA World Cup. The offseason is precious. Most days it feels like a race against the clock to enjoy.

I was stretched out on the bed, scrolling through my phone, checking out potential vacation spots, when Indy walked in. She was rocking a cropped top and tiny shorts that hugged her curves, making her ass look like a peach ready to be plucked. Suddenly, planning a vacation didn't feel so urgent.

"What you doing?" she asked playfully, climbing onto the bed and snuggling close. Fresh out of the shower, she smelled floral and tempting.

"I know what I'd rather be doing," I said, sliding an arm around her waist. "But since you asked, I was thinking about vacation spots —and I want you there with me."

Her smile softened, intrigued. "And where exactly do you have in mind?"

"I'm thinking Santorini or St. Lucia. Somewhere we can recharge."Indy's eyes flicked toward the screen. "You really planning all that already?"

"I gotta have something to look forward to. Offseason's a blink. Three months if we're lucky. The grind never really stops." I paused, flipping past another overpriced resort. "Truth is, I don't even know if I'll enjoy any of it if I don't win this thing. It's not just about the ring anymore. It's about finishing what I started—for my squad, for me... and you."

She reached over, her hand warm on my forearm. "You already won, Malik. Maybe not the trophy—yet. But the way you've shown up? That means something."

Her words hit me different—not like a fan hyping me, but like someone who really saw me.

I kissed her temple, holding that moment close. "Then be there when I finish it. I want you in the stands when I take it all home."

She looked up at me, steady, thoughtful. "I know. I'm working out my schedule."

And the way she said it? It sounded a whole lot like yes.

We breezed through the Eastern Conference Finals, sweeping Atlanta on our home court. Just like that, eight days after the cookout, we were headed to a shot at the crown.

The night before I had to fly West, I moved around my bedroom, tossing clothes and sneakers into an open suitcase. My mind was racing, but not just with basketball. What kept circling back was Indy—the way her eyes had softened when she'd opened up to me after the barbecue, the mix of strength and fragility I'd seen in her.

I looked up when she slipped quietly into the room, a soft smile tugging at her lips. She perched on the edge of the bed, watching me pack.

"You sure you've got enough in there?" she teased. I chuckled. "Probably enough for three trips." But my smile dimmed as I caught the faraway look in her eyes. Something was bothering her—I could tell. "Talk to me, Bite-Size. What's on your mind?"

Indy's gaze dropped to her hands. "It's silly, really, but...part of me worries when you leave." She shook her head lightly. "It's not you. It's just..."

Her voice trailed off, but I knew. My chest tightened. "Because people have always left you," I finished for her.

Her eyes lifted to mine, vulnerable and raw. She nodded. I set the clothes aside and sat beside her, threading my fingers through hers. "I'll be back, Indy. I don't disappear on the people I love."

The word slipped out before I could catch it. My chest tightened, but I didn't take it back. Couldn't.

Her eyes widened just a fraction, the kind of blink you'd miss if you weren't looking right at her. She didn't call me on it, didn't flinch or pull away. She just let it hang there between us, heavier than air, heavier than I'd meant, but true all the same.

She smiled faintly, equal parts hope and doubt. "That's good to know."

I pulled her against me, holding her tight, wishing I could bottle this moment for her. "You could come with me. The Finals are a big deal. I'd love to have you there."

She hesitated, chewing on her bottom lip. "I want to, Malik. I really do. But work... and honestly, I think I still need a little time. I don't want to show up for you halfway. When I'm there, I want to be all in."

I nodded, respecting it even though it stung. "I get it, Indy. And when you're ready, I'll be waiting."

She nestled her head on my shoulder, and I wrapped my arms around her. Indira had carved out space in me that I didn't want to close off —not now, not ever.

Leaving her the next morning wasn't easy. She stood in the doorway wrapped in my hoodie, waving as I tossed my bag into the trunk. I promised I'd call every night. Promised I'd come back better than ever. Promised things I didn't even know how to say yet.

By the time I checked into the team hotel out West, with basketball's biggest stage looming, all I could think about was getting back to her. The L-word I let slip kept echoing in my head, the one I hadn't planned on saying out loud yet.

And maybe, once the dust settled, I'd find the right way—and the right moment—to make sure she knew I meant it.

Chapter
Thirty-Three

INDIRA

Malik texted me when he touched down in Vegas, the home of the league's newest expansion team and his Finals opponent. Knowing he landed safely should have made me feel better. But instead, I felt worse. I hated not being there. That's why I jumped at Cairo's invitation to meet at our favorite café. I needed to talk, and she was my person.

The scent of roasted coffee beans and cinnamon wrapped around me as I stepped into Books, Beans, and Berries. I slid into a booth by the window and placed my order. It was five o'clock somewhere, so I considered a glass of wine, but I settled on an iced chai latte. I swirled it around nervously before sipping through the straw, already rehearsing what I wanted to say.

I spotted Cairo approaching. Tall and striking as always, her stride confident, she wore red and black gear in tribute to Zahara's basketball team, which she coached. The Farmington Fire logo appeared boldly on her hoodie. I smiled, genuinely happy to see my sister-friend. It had been weeks since we'd had more than a rushed FaceTime call—her travel schedule was no joke.

She flopped into the seat across from me, and I took in the puffiness beneath her eyes and the tension in her shoulders. "You look tired, CeeCee," I said, not bothering to sugarcoat it. "Y'all running games or marathons?"

She laughed and tugged her hoodie back. "Girl, I don't know what time zone I'm in anymore. We've been everywhere—Chicago, Louisville, Orlando. I miss my mattress."

"I understand," I murmured. "And I miss you. I barely saw you at church, and then, poof—you were gone again."

Cairo met my eyes and smiled. "I missed you, too. But enough about my road dog life. Spill the tea. What's going on in the land of real estate and baller drama?"

I rolled my eyes, though I knew the smile tugging at my lips betrayed me. "Real estate's busy. I'm still tracking to hit my sales goal. The block on Fielding is coming along. And there's no drama. Not really."

She raised an eyebrow. "So... Malik's name doesn't ring a bell?" I hesitated, lifting my cup to my lips. "Things are good... I guess."

"Mmhmm." She leaned in with a knowing grin. "You're feeling him."

I smirked, looking away. "Maybe. He's been... sweet. Steady. Checks in even when he's traveling." I paused, narrowing my eyes. "And I know you're feeling D.C., too."

"Maybe," Cairo said, dragging out the word. "We're trying to figure things out." She shrugged. "Sounds like you are, too."

I leaned back and glanced out the window. "It's just... I don't know what this is yet. I like him. But naming it makes it real. And once it's real..."

"You risk losing it," Cairo finished softly.

We sat in that truth for a moment, letting it settle. And I couldn't help thinking of Tamara—how she never showed up, how I'd spent too many nights waiting on a love that never came. Some ghosts were hard to shake.

"Speaking of risking things," I said slowly, forcing the thought away, "Game 1 is tomorrow."

Cairo lifted her brow. "And you're thinking about going?"

"I don't know." I picked at the corner of my napkin. "Showing up feels... big. Public. You know how much I hate the reaction. But not going feels petty."

"You want to go?"

I met her eyes. "Yeah. I do. But I don't want to look thirsty." Cairo burst out laughing. "Girl, you're not thirsty. You're interested.

That man is crazy about you, and everybody sees it—even the damn camera crew that caught y'all shopping at the mall."

I laughed despite myself, heat rising to my cheeks. "I just don't want to get caught slipping."

She reached across the table and gave my hand a gentle squeeze. "Then go. Not for what people might say. Not even for him. Go because you want to see him play. You deserve joy, too, Indy."

I nodded, quiet for a beat. Then, a smile curled across my lips. "Alright then. I guess I've got some tickets to claim." I glanced down at my watch.

Cairo grinned. "Now that's the Indy I know. Just make sure you get two, because I'm going!"

When we stepped off the jet, the desert heat wrapped around us. Not the sticky, unbearable kind—this was dry, heavy, the kind that licked at your skin and smothered like a weighted blanket. I was eager to reach the air-conditioned refuge waiting beyond the tarmac, but even more eager to see Malik.

It was my first time flying private, and judging by Cairo's wide grin, hers too. We'd been up since four a.m. for a six o'clock departure, but exhaustion didn't matter. The adrenaline of being here carried us.

"We 'bout to turn up in this desert!" Cairo hollered, already halfway down the stairs. She didn't wait for me or Desmond, bouncing toward the runway like she owned it.

I lingered, juggling my bags. Of course, I'd overpacked—one suitcase for clothes, another for shoes, plus my Neverfull and oversized Telfar stuffed to the brim. Ridiculous, I know. But saying yes to this trip at the last minute had me packing like I had to prepare for every possibility. Too many outfits, too many "just-in-case" items. Truth was, it wasn't about luggage—it was about nerves.

Finally, when I stepped onto the tarmac, there he was. Malik looked like a GQ cover—khaki cargo shorts, a yellow graphic tee, black leather slides. His sunglasses were pushed low on his nose, revealing that familiar gleam in his eyes as he leaned against a sleek, black SUV.

"Well, look who actually got on the plane," he teased. I rolled my eyes, though my smirk gave me away. "You're lucky I like warm weather."

He pushed off the truck, closing the space between us. His arms slid around me in a warm hug. He smelled like citrus and musk, clean and magnetic, a scent I'd missed more than I wanted to admit.

Instinct took over. I tilted my head, lifted onto my toes, and let his lips meet mine. It wasn't a show, not some public claim for cameras—it was just us, the kind of kiss you give someone you've missed. Like I belonged here.

For once, I didn't think about what the blogs might say or whether Briana was lurking somewhere in the shadows. I didn't even think about the word Malik had let slip before he left. I just let myself want him.

Cairo's wolf whistle broke the moment, followed by a sharp catcall. "That's what I'm talking about!" she shouted.

I laughed against Malik's shoulder, heat rushing to my cheeks. "Let's get out of here," he murmured, low enough for only me to hear, his palm firm at the small of my back as he steered me toward the SUV.

Technically, Malik was required to stay at the team hotel. It was part of the organization's Finals protocol—curfews, check-ins, team meetings, the whole thing.

But he wasn't the only one who found a workaround. Somehow, DC and Cairo managed to snag a suite at The Venetian too, just a few doors down from ours.

Our suite came with a wraparound balcony overlooking the Vegas fountains—prime view, one of those rare angles where you could see both the Bellagio show and the Strip stretching out in glittering lines.

I couldn't wait to watch the fountains burst against the neon skyline later that night. For now, though, this space felt like ours.

The second we stepped inside, I let out a low whistle. "Not bad, Latimer."

He smirked, tossing his bag onto the couch. "Figured you deserved the full experience."

I arched a brow. "And what experience is that?" He stepped closer, slow and deliberate, his fingers brushing my wrist before linking with mine. "One where you actually relax," he murmured.

I exhaled, smiling despite myself. "I plan to."

"Good. I need to nap before I get to the arena. I booked a spa appointment for you, but feel free to cancel if you'd rather do something else."

I stared at him like he'd lost his mind. "Oh, I'm already there." Then, with a wicked grin, I shoved him playfully. He stumbled back, laughing as he dropped onto the couch.

"Perfect," I teased, heat sparking low in my belly. Maybe it was the desert air, maybe it was the way he'd been looking at me since I stepped off that plane—but I wasn't waiting.

Sliding to my knees between his legs, I tugged at his shorts, dragging them down in one smooth motion. His breath caught, rough and unguarded, just before I took him into my mouth.

Chapter Thirty-Four

MALIK

Jarvis elbowed me in the ribs, and it hurt like hell. "What the fuck, JB?" I snapped, rubbing my side.

"I've been trying to get your attention. You over there acting like you can't hear me."

"Whateva," I muttered. Truth was, it wasn't that I couldn't hear him. My earbuds were in, but no music was playing—just static, white noise to drown out everything else. I'd been meditating, resting my eyes, trying to block it all out.

We were flying home from Vegas after losing Game 2. When we boarded, a few of my starters had their heads down, even some reserves looked gutted. But not me. The Rattlers were a tough squad —they'd earned their win. We'd stolen one on opening night; I knew it wouldn't be easy to repeat.

I wasn't here to sulk. I was here to soak it in, because deep down I knew... this might be the last time. Hell, maybe one of the last times I stepped on the hardwood period.

That thought had crept in that morning. Realistically, my clock was winding down. I could chase twenty years like some of the greats—but for what? Another line in the record books? Another bill my body has to pay?

And honestly?

I don't have the usual reasons to hang it up. No wife asking me to be home. No kids I'm missing. Nothing pulling me harder than the game itself.

But lately, time with Indy had me questioning all of it. She made me wonder if—maybe—I'd been missing more than I realized.

I popped out an earbud and turned to Jarvis. "Let me ask you something. We haven't talked about it in a while."

"Shoot," JB said, giving me his full attention.

"You ever think about how much longer you got?"

He raised an eyebrow. "Damn. One loss got you thinking about hanging it up? You've been playing like you'll never slow down."

I huffed a laugh. "Never planned to. But my body's speaking a new language—and my knees? They don't lie."

Jarvis nodded. "Father Time's undefeated." He leaned back. "Real question is: what's next for you?"

I stared at the ceiling, stretching my legs out. "That's what I'm trying to figure out. Basketball's been everything. So... what the hell comes after everything?"

Jarvis turned to face me. "You've got options, Malik. Broadcasting. Coaching. Business. You got the charisma for TV, too."

I snorted. "TV, huh? You know they approached me and Malc about a reality series. I didn't pay it any mind."

Jarvis laughed. "Man, that would be ratings gold. But real talk—you gotta find something that feeds you the way the game does. Otherwise, the void will eat at you."

I nodded slowly. "And the void... you think we ever really fill it?" Jarvis rubbed his jaw, thoughtful. "Not completely. But you can reshape it. The game's one chapter. A great one—not the whole book. Sometimes you gotta add more chapters. New characters. Different stakes."

I sat with it.

New characters.

Different stakes.

"Yeah—I get you."

Jarvis grinned and clapped me on the shoulder. "You want a surefire way to stay busy?"

I raised an eyebrow. "What's that?"

He chuckled. "Have some babies. They'll wear your ass out—in a good way."

I barked a laugh, Indy's face flashing, but the thought lingered longer than expected.

"I appreciate you, JB. For real. Time to figure out what my next chapter looks like."

Jarvis nodded, going serious. "Just know whatever you choose—you're built for it. And you've got people in your corner—starting right here."

New characters. Different stakes. I knew who I wanted on the page.

Chapter Thirty-Five

I breezed through my post-game routine—and the interview. The minute I sat down, I decided to keep it short. No point wasting words with my mind already somewhere else—on Indy, and on the clock running down on the night we had left. Practice in the morning. Flight to Vegas for Game 5. Every minute counted.

On the ride over, Slade said they were pushing the "girlfriend" tag on TV. I didn't need the clips; I saw it in the way she breathed when I walked in—like I turned the noise off.

Didn't take long for me to get spoiled by her. Indy waiting in the tunnel had become routine—something I craved. Hers was the first face I wanted after the buzzer, the one that pulled me out of game mode and back into life. Lately, she'd been there—with Slade lurking close enough to play watchdog.

I expected tonight to be no different. My Shortie in that black catsuit with silver pinstripes, leather jacket slipping off her shoulders.

During shootaround, I'd already clocked her drip—the new diamond tennis bracelet, the rhinestone Louboutins that made her look two inches taller. I'd stolen a kiss before the anthem, and the crowd reaction told me everybody saw it. Didn't bother me. Let 'em talk.

All I could think about was peeling her out of that outfit the second the game ended.

Jarvis and I were the last ones in the locker room. "What's taking you so long, JB?"

"Shit, I ain't moving no slower than you. Thought you'd be the one rushing."

"Oh, I am. No cap."

He smirked, shaking his head. "Yeah, well, Twinna been blowing up my phone—nagging me like she don't know where the fuck I'm at."

"She's just trying to make sure you get home and handle business. She didn't make it to the game, right?"

"She wasn't supposed to, but she pulled a last minute pop-up. Gotta keep an eye on me."

I chuckled, swinging my backpack over my shoulder. "Don't T know by now you ain't going nowhere?"

He muttered, "I don't know about that. If she keeps stressing me, she gon' fuck around and find out."

"Whatever, JB. Let's get up outta here."

We pushed through the doors together—me buzzing to see Indy, JB bracing for his wife. Twinna rushed Jarvis the second she spotted him, arms hooked tight around his neck. I cut past them, eyes scanning for my girl.

And then I saw her.

Not Indy.

Briana.

Poised. Confident. Standing in the tunnel like she had the right. Like she hadn't torched my life years ago. For a second, I blamed fatigue. But nah—she was real. And walking straight toward me.

"Malik." Her voice had too much history.

My stomach dropped. "Briana."

She tilted her head, smiling like we were cool. "It's been a long time."

"Not long enough."

"Come on, now." She laughed softly. "Is that any way to greet an old friend?"

I folded my arms. "What do you want?"

Her eyes flickered, then steadied. "Damn, straight to business? Can't I just say hello?"

"You never just do anything. So let's hear it."

She sighed like I was the unreasonable one. "Alright, fine. I'm back in Detroit handling some family stuff and…I wanted to see you. Catch up."

Bullshit.

Briana was calculating. Always had a motive.

"There's nothing to catch up on."

Her smile thinned. "So that's how it is?"

"That's exactly how it is."

She shifted, tone softening. "Look, Malik, I know things ended badly. But I don't want there to be bad blood between us."

I barked out a laugh. "Bad blood? That's what you call what you did to me?"

Her expression pinched—like she hadn't expected me to put it that plain. "I didn't come here to fight."

"Then why are you here?"

She hesitated. And that's when I knew—she wanted something. Before she could answer, a voice behind me cut in. "What's going on?"

My chest tightened. I didn't even have to turn. Indy.

I faced her anyway, caught the way her eyes flicked between me and Briana. Her expression was unreadable.

And just like that, the night blew up.

When we got home, Indy fucked me like she had something to prove. And I let her. She wanted to control the tempo, test me, show me she could go head-to-head.

We barely made it inside before she dropped her purse on the hardwood. Lipsticks and whatever else rolled across the floor, but she didn't even glance down. Heels off, five feet of woman standing there with the swagger of a giant.

I leaned back, arms crossed, watching her peel out of the catsuit like it was a damn competition. Slow, deliberate. Nipples poking through her bra, curves spilling against brown skin. Every inch of her made my dick harder.

By the time she shoved the fabric past her thighs, I was ready to take her against the glass, make her scream loud enough for the city to hear. But she beat me to it.

"Strip." Her voice was sharp, commanding.

I kicked my sweats and boxers off in one move, my dick springing up, heavy and eager. She smirked, eyes dragging over me like she was judging form.

"Where do you want me to fuck you?"

"Anywhere you want, Boss," I shot back, dick throbbing. She didn't hesitate. "On the sectional. I'm riding you."

I grinned. She'd never perfected that move, but her fire alone had me ready. "Say less."

I laced my fingers through hers, led her over, and dropped onto the cushions. "But first? Sit on my face."

Her mouth curved. "That works."

I yanked her higher, buried my tongue in her, worked her until she was grinding down, shaking, soaking my mouth like she was trying to drown me. I didn't stop until her thighs trembled, and her moans cracked.

When she finally slid lower, she grabbed my shoulders, eyes locked on mine like she wasn't backing down. She guided me inside —tight, wet, perfect.

And then she rode me like she had money on it. I gripped her hips, helped her bounce, met her stroke for stroke.

Every smack of her ass against me lit the room with heat. She was putting in work, trying to make me forget Briana ever existed.

But my ex-girlfriend couldn't be further from my mind. Because I was knee-deep in Indy, giving her every inch, every thrust, every reason to accept our fate.

By the time she came apart around me, nails digging into my chest, I learned something—Indy didn't just fuck for pleasure. She fucked for bragging rights.

And I loved every damn second of it.

Chapter Thirty-Six

I wasn't fooling anyone. Definitely not Malik. We left the arena like everything was cool, and I acted like Briana's showing up didn't faze me.

At his penthouse, I doubled down. I was determined to prove I didn't care.

That's why I jumped his bones the second the door shut. Call it petty, call it overkill—I called it erasing any trace of Briana from his brain.

I almost convinced myself. After a shower and one of his T-shirts, I was in the kitchen pouring wine when Malik finally called me out.

"You don't believe me."

My hand stilled midair. "What?"

His jaw flexed. "You don't believe me. About Briana." I set the glass down. "I didn't say that."

"You didn't have to."

I licked a drop of wine from my lip, stalling. "It's not... Look, I'm learning to trust you, Malik. I am. But when women like her keep coming back—" I hesitated. "There must be a reason."

His face hardened. "I'm not giving her any reasons. I can't

explain why she's here, but I need you to believe me when I say she doesn't matter." His voice dropped, firm, certain. "You're the only woman I want."

His phone buzzed. He turned the screen so I could read.

SLADE: Incident filed. She came in on Twinna's family-lounge escort. Briana's banned. If she tries again, it's trespass.

"Blaise sent the no-contact letter this morning," Malik said, steady."They pulled her access. Door's shut." He locked the screen and set the phone beside my glass.

Briana was handled. The only door still cracked was the one with my mother behind it. Heat rose in my throat. I wanted to believe him. But believing meant risking everything.

"You sure about that?" I asked.

He pushed off the counter, closing the space between us, tilting my chin so I had to look at him.

"I don't entertain ghosts, Indy. My past doesn't control me. And I'll be damned if I let yours control you."

I blinked. "What's that supposed to mean?"

"It means," he said, steady as ever, "I know you're scared. But I'm not leaving. I need you to trust that what we have is different."

His words landed dead center. He wasn't just asking me to believe him about Briana. He was asking me to believe in us. That's where I stumbled. Because I still didn't know how.

For a while, neither of us spoke. The air between us softened— still heavy, but less sharp. He reached for his glass, took a slow sip, eyes on the counter instead of me. I thought maybe that was the end of it, that we'd said enough for one night.

But when the quiet stretched too long, he pressed again. "Why is it so hard for you to believe me?"

I stared at him, only one answer surfacing. "Give me one reason I should."

His eyes didn't flinch. "Tell me why you shouldn't."

"That, I can answer. Number one? We both know your nick-names—Malik the Freak, L-Train. I don't want to know how you earned those—"

"Indy—"

I held up a hand. "Let me finish. Number two: you have a playboy reputation."

"That's the same as your number one."

"Maybe. Maybe not." I shrugged. "It's hard to believe you'd turn women away."

His eyes went wide. "Indira, if you only knew…"

"Knew what?"

"I can't tell you how many women I turn away. Not just face-to-face—DMs, texts, all of it. I ghost them. I'm not interested in anyone but you."

I shook my head. "I don't understand how you can just change overnight."

"I didn't change. I chose. For years, I kept it casual because that's all I trusted myself with. But there was a time I was a one-woman man. Perfect boyfriend, even."

"That's what Jackie told me," I admitted.

"Psssh. My sister thinks she knows, but she doesn't know the whole story."

"You want to tell me?"

He exhaled. "You already know it was Briana. I was devoted to her.

Never messed around. I loved her. But in the end… she crushed me. And I've been ruined ever since."

The words were heavy, dragging me toward his past. "It must've been bad," I whispered.

"Bad doesn't even cover it." His voice cracked, the weight of it spilling into the room. For the first time, I saw Malik not as the Freak, not as the MVP, but as a man who'd been broken before me.

"Can I ask what happened?" My voice came out smaller than I meant, like I wasn't sure I wanted the answer.

He dragged a hand down his jaw, eyes narrowing like he was rolling the film in his head. "We'd been together since my sophomore year. Student-athletes—practice, classes, locked in. She came to church with me and ate Sunday dinner with my family. By senior year, we were prom royalty and homecoming royalty. People thought we were #relationshipgoals." He sounded bitter, not proud.

"We promised to stick it out through college. But near the end of my freshman year, I got hurt. Bad. I spiraled—bitter, angry. Took it out on her until she finally left."

My chest pulled tight.

"I rehabbed, came crawling back around Christmas. We reconciled. A few months later, she told me she was pregnant."

My breath caught. "Wait—you had a child?"

His gaze flickered. "That's what I thought. On draft night, she was right there beside me. Belly showing. My family knew. Cameras caught it. Highest high of my life—top-five draft pick and about to be a father."

I pictured it—Malik glowing, carrying a future he didn't know would collapse. "Where is he now?"

His jaw flexed. His voice dropped. "He wasn't mine." Air left my lungs.

"She delivered on media day," he said, quieter. "Should've been a good omen, right? New life. Fresh start. But by the first regular-season game, we knew something was off. The baby had sickle cell—the kind that only happens when a kid gets an abnormal gene from both parents." He met my eyes. "Briana carried the trait. I didn't."

I swallowed. "Did she know?"

"Honestly? I don't think so. She'd been with another dude around the holidays, right before we got back together. When we reconciled, things were still shaky. But by the time she realized she was pregnant, we were stable." His voice caught.

My throat ached.

"The worst part?" He gave a humorless laugh. "She named the baby after me. First and middle."

My hand pressed to my chest. "That's... a lot."

"Yeah. And when the truth came out, I still had to pay to get my name off—lawyers, filings, whatever it took to amend the birth certificate. It wasn't about the money. It was about not letting a lie follow that kid—or me."

"Yeah. So, while everybody else celebrated my rookie season, I was in court rescinding paternity. Took damn near a year. I couldn't lock in on the game the way I wanted until it was done."

Silence stretched. The betrayal, the spectacle, the grief—it explained so much about his walls.

"When it was finally over, I came back for my second season like a man possessed. Made it my mission to crush every rookie stat from the year before. On the court, I was locked in.

"Off the court?" He shook his head. "That's when Malik the Freak was born. Headlines. Rumors. And I didn't care.

"If a woman came my way, I had her. Didn't matter her race, didn't matter the place—club, elevator, locker room. It was about control. Proving nobody could play me again."

He looked at me then, eyes sharp and wet, daring me to flinch. "Yeah, I earned that nickname. But here's the part nobody gets—I never stopped chasing what I lost: loyalty. A one-woman life. I didn't believe it existed anymore."

A lump formed in my throat.

Then his voice dropped, rough but steady. "Until you."

The words cut straight through me.

I wanted to believe him. God, I did. But believing meant risking everything. "You sure about that?" I whispered.

"Damn right I am. I love you, Indy. I don't want anybody else. I don't need anybody else. That's the only truth that matters."

My heart lurched. His words filled me, but fear still clung like a shadow. I opened my mouth, searching for something—anything— that wouldn't make me sound scared or small. The truth sat on the edge of my tongue, heavy, unsaid.

"But what?" he cut in, voice low, rough. "You can keep doubting me, but you haven't even said it back."

I stalled. "Said what?"

"You know damn well what." His jaw clenched. "You haven't told me you love me. Not once."

The floor tilted. He was right. I hadn't.

And now, with the man bearing his deepest scars to me, I had nowhere left to hide.

I had no words. No quick comeback, no teasing deflect. Nothing to throw between us.

He sat there—shoulders tense, jaw locked—like he was bracing for impact. Like maybe he regretted telling me. Like maybe he thought I'd see him differently now.

All I saw was a man who had carried this hurt too long. I moved before I could second-guess it, closing the space between us. At first, he didn't react—eyes on the floor, fingers pressing into his palms like he could squeeze the pain away.

So, I did what I always wished someone had done for me when I was breaking. I took his hand, threading my fingers through his.

His eyes snapped to mine, startled. He didn't pull away. I squeezed. "I'm sorry, Malik," I said softly.

His throat worked, but he stayed quiet.

I shifted closer, brushed my other hand along his jaw, my thumb easing the tension there. "I don't just mean about her." My voice dropped. "I mean all of it. What it did to you."

His breath hitched.

I knew then—no one had ever told him that. No one had cared what that betrayal did to him as a man, not just as an athlete.

For a long beat, he didn't move. Then he exhaled and rested his forehead against mine, his grip tightening like I was something steady. Something real.

"I didn't think it still got to me like this," he murmured. "Because you never let yourself deal with it," I said, stroking over his knuckles.

"That whole relationship, that whole situation—" his voice went lower—"it's the reason I stopped trusting people."

He pulled back just enough to meet my eyes, his fingers brushing my wrist, searching. "But with you?" His voice steadied. "I don't doubt you, Indy."

The words sank so deep I almost couldn't breathe. He wasn't just saying he wanted me. He was saying he trusted me.

There it was—the thing I hadn't said back. The thing lodged like a stone in my throat every time he opened himself up.

"Good," I managed.

Then I kissed him. Slow. Soft. His mouth moved against mine like he had nowhere else to be, his arms wrapping around me, holding me like I was the safest place he'd ever been.

Maybe I was. Maybe he was mine, too.

Relief eased through me. His story made sense now. No wonder he'd gone wild. Betrayal like that could break anyone. Maybe we weren't so different—he got burned in love; I learned too young that trust is just an opening for heartbreak.

Still, I couldn't let him off easy.

"You know... I think you still have some freakish tendencies." His head snapped up. "Like what?"

I smirked. "We did have sex in a car. That sounds like something 'Malik the Freak' would do."

He gave me a look. "True. But I haven't touched another woman since I met you. And I plan to keep it that way."

I arched a brow. "We'll see," I murmured, fighting a smile. "You've got a long way to go, L-Train."

Being back in the arena, sitting courtside, felt surreal. Thousands of fans screaming, cameras flashing, the whole production—it should've drowned out everything else. But Malik's words from last night still rang louder in my head.

You haven't told me you love me. Not once.

It was ridiculous how those words clung to me harder than the jersey I was wearing. I'd apologized for what he'd endured, hoping it was enough, hoping he'd feel what I couldn't say. But sitting here, surrounded by noise and spectacle, I couldn't stop wondering if my silence spoke louder than anything I'd managed to say.

Malik had made sure I was set up with everything—private access, perfect seats, and just enough space so I wouldn't feel completely suffocated by attention. But people still noticed. The cameras still lingered on me. The influencers still mentioned my name.

And when Malik hit a deep three-pointer and immediately glanced in my direction, the arena went crazy. My chest swelled, the doubt curling tighter inside me. He was out there telling the whole world what he wanted. Meanwhile, I was still keeping the most important words locked behind my teeth.

By the end of the first quarter, I was able to get into the game without worrying about being under a microscope. Honestly, the competition had been so intense that it was impossible not to. Things got heated between Nasir and Vegas' center, and they both received double techs. And Malik was in his bag, playing with a no-fear mentality.

Cairo and DC were having a great time, too, arguing over the fairness of play calls. When Cairo cursed out a referee for continuously assessing penalties against Detroit, I just knew we were going to get tossed out on our asses. But that was the beauty of being so close to the court—talking trash and watching the trash talk.

The second quarter was more of the same, and I was practically biting my nails when the game went into the half with the score still tied. DC predicted that the Detroit-Vegas match would go down to the wire. I was still learning about this game, but I knew enough to know that Malik preferred to wrap this up in five or six games at most. Our Santorini vacation was waiting.

After the game, we decided to hit the strip with Malik, DC, and their security in tow. Jarvis, Twinna, Nasir, and Mirabel joined us, along with a few other players and their dates. The guys hung back with Diesel, DC's bodyguard, to smoke a stogie, while Slade accompanied us into the club. We were ushered to a VIP section, the kind of treatment a girl could get used to.

Mirabel and Cairo hopped into the tall barstools at a high-top table while I struggled, even in my spiky Daffodiles, to reach mine. Cairo couldn't resist a crack about my size, but she realized quickly that the longer she delayed, the longer it took to place our drink orders.

"You need a hand?" she teased.

I leaned toward her, yelling over Kendrick Lamar blasting through the speakers. "You always got jokes, Cee."

As I wrestled with the stool, Malik sauntered over, grinning like he had the punchline ready. "Need me to ask security to bring you a booster seat, Bite-Size?"

Laughter rippled around the group. I narrowed my eyes, pretending to be annoyed, but his words from last night echoed too loudly in my head. *You haven't told me you love me. Not once.*

I pasted on a smile anyway. "Keep talking, Latimer. Slade won't be enough security for you."

DC chuckled, shaking his head. "Better watch out, Malik. You know, they say dynamite comes in small packages."

Cairo's laugh was clipped, sharp. Her eyes flicked to DC and back again, and I knew she was in a mood. "Oh, hush," she muttered.

I guessed they must've argued on the way, but I'd be damned if I was going to let it ruin my good time. "I think we should order some food."

"I'm not hungry," Cairo shot back.

"I'm not asking. You want to drink, you have to eat. I'll order us some wings and nachos."

Mirabel wrinkled her nose. "Please, no nachos. They'll give me dragon breath, and Nasir won't talk to me."

I gave her a look. "Who the fuck cares what Nasir or the guys think?"

"I do," Mirabel said, flipping her hair.

Cairo pushed back from the table. "I'm outta here as soon as they bring my drink."

"We just got here. Try to enjoy yourself for a little while."

She grumbled but didn't argue. "I'll try."

"You do that," I said, patting her arm. "Oh, and look. Our drinks are here."

Mirabel clinked her glass against mine. "They're about to treat us like queens up in this bitch!"

I laughed with her, though the words landed heavier than she knew. Malik already treated me like one. The problem was, I hadn't said the words back to prove I believed it.

Cairo rolled her eyes and slid off her stool. "I'm heading to the ladies' room."

I frowned, tracking her stiff shoulders as she disappeared into the crowd. Definitely still in a mood. Part of me wanted to follow, but Malik had a way of pulling me back in, even when my thoughts drifted elsewhere. He leaned down behind my stool, shouting over the music, "You want another lemon drop?"

I drained my glass, licking the tangy mix of sugar and sour from my lips. "Not yet. I'd better take it easy if I wanna last the night."

His lips brushed my ear, his voice dropping low enough to make my pulse quicken. "I don't plan on being here long."

My eyebrows shot up. "You don't?"

His eyes sparkled with mischief as he closed the distance between us. "Nope. I've got some business to handle."

Curiosity tugged at me. "What kind of business?"

He dipped his head, nuzzling my neck, whispering warm against my skin. "The kind of business best handled in private…with you."

A shiver darted down my spine. God help me, I loved this man. But the words sat heavy in my throat, unspoken.

"You're awfully sure of yourself tonight, Latimer."

His cocky smile was irresistible. "Just sure of what I want."

I tapped a fingernail against his chest, teasing. "And what if I'm not done partying yet?"

Malik leaned closer, his breath hot against my cheek. "Then I'll just have to convince you."

My heart skipped, the bass and chatter fading until there was only him. I bit my lip to hide my smile, but it was useless. "You'd better start working on your pitch, then. I'm going to look for CeeCee. She's been gone for a while."

"Challenge accepted," he murmured, pressing a quick, teasing kiss to the corner of my mouth. "Don't say I didn't warn you."

I weaved through the crowd to the restrooms tucked in the corner. Two women were at the sink, primping in the mirror. One wore a blonde wig—too brassy against her brown skin. Her friend had bright cherry-red braids hanging past her butt.

"Girl, did you see that fine motherfucker!" Blondie said, blotting her lipstick.

"Bitch, which one? All their asses fine, and they all got them eight figures!"

I assumed they meant Malik and the team. My ears pricked; the hair on my neck rose.

"Nah, I'm talking about that D-Cole. I used to do everything for that dick. Suck, ride, take it up the ass. Whatever he wanted."

My eyes grew wide when the blonde gazed wistfully in the mirror. She was talking about Desmond! Where the hell was Cairo?

A stall door swung open.

"Cee, you good?"

"Oh, I'm good," she said, leaning in to wash her hands.

Raggedy Ann kept running her mouth. "I know that's right. Ballers like him'll have your wrist iced and set you up in a crib. You better let him pipe that and get that bag."

Cee didn't blink as she flicked her hair over her shoulder. "They're off-limits."

Blondie had to jerk back to avoid it. Her face twisted. "Excuse you?"

Oh, hell. Cairo squared up, and I slid in fast. "She said D-Cole and Malik are off-limits. They're spoken for."

Blondie's top lip curled, a fang away from showing. She gave me a slow once-over, then cut her eyes at me and smirked. "Please. We saw y'all on the big screen. Think sittin' courtside makes you special? Bitch, you a seat filler."

"And you're a dirty skank fucking for tricks." I stepped closer, ready to dog-walk her.

"That's enough!" someone barked.

"Says who?"

"Says me." Mirabel stepped forward, hand at her waist, chin lifted. I hadn't seen her come in, but thank God for backup. Blondie could test it if she wanted; she and her friend were about to get molly-whopped all over this bathroom.

"Who the fuck are you?" Raggedy Ann snapped.

Mirabel didn't flinch. "I'm the smoke you don't want."

"Really?" Blondie scoffed. "You trying to tell me one of you basic chicks got D-Cole on lock?" She glanced at her friend. "You hear this?"

"I hear her talking wreck," the friend said. "She must have it twisted. Who you think you talking to?"

"I was talking to your Barbie-doll wannabe ass," Mirabel said evenly, "and your friend Skipper."

These broads were crazy. The first time I met Mirabel, I knew she wasn't one to test. I felt better stepping into the club without my heat because I knew she had my back.

I caught Cairo's eye—tight as a bowstring—then watched her jaw unclench as Mirabel's tone dropped.

"I'm gonna give y'all—and I use 'ladies' lightly—two seconds to disappear before you catch these hands." Mirabel planted her palms on her waist and patted it, just enough for them to get the message.

Barbie's eyes flashed. She opened her mouth, then shut it. "Let's go," she muttered, shoulder-checking Skipper on the way out.

I kept my eyes on the door until it closed. Only then did my pulse start to settle. "Mirabel, thanks—"

Her hand lifted, cutting me off. "I'm gonna need both of you to listen."

I glanced at Cairo—wide-eyed—then snapped back to Mirabel's glare.

"I know we're from the D, and you think you're some bad chicks. Maybe you figure nobody'll touch you 'cause you're moving with Latimer and Montague." She leaned in, voice like glass. "But there'll be plenty of thots out here wanting your man, claiming they had him, trying to stuff panties in his pockets. Some of it might be true, some of it pure bullshit."

Her chin ticked up. "You gonna throw hands with every last one? No. If you're not cut for this baller life, step. But if you're riding with DC and Malik, you act like these chicks don't matter. You hear me?"

All I could do was nod, because Cee and I had just gotten schooled in a Vegas bathroom.

The suite was hushed, the Strip glittering through the floor-to-ceiling windows like a million restless sparks. I stood at the glass in one of Malik's robes, the Vegas lights sketching shadows across my skin.

I felt him before I heard him—steady presence, warm arms sliding around my waist, drawing me back to his chest.

"You good, Bite-Size?" he murmured, lips at my temple.

I hesitated. The bathroom scene replayed—Blondie's seat filler remark, Mirabel's priceless advice: *Flex like these bitches don't matter.*

"I'm thinking about earlier," I said, low. I'd given him the Cliffs-Notes on the ride back.

He pressed closer, heartbeat even against my spine. No questions. No fix-it speech. Just his hold tightening, like he already knew.

We stayed there, breathing in sync while the city sprawled beneath us. Slowly, the knot in my shoulders unwound.

"I don't like the noise," I whispered, surprised to hear it out loud.

He kissed my crown, voice low and certain. "Then let it be noise."

Something in his tone settled me more than a dozen reassurances ever could. He wasn't asking me to ignore it—just reminding me it wasn't stronger than us.

I turned in his arms and looked up. He didn't press. He just waited.

And in that quiet, I knew: whatever came—whispers, rumors, ghosts of the past—it couldn't drown out this.

Just him. Just me.

Chapter Thirty-Seven

MALIK

The Pistons' practice facility was nearly empty when I walked out to the parking lot. Most of the guys had cleared an hour ago. I liked staying late—extra shots, extra treatment, whatever it took to keep my body tuned.

The early summer air was warm, not stifling—nothing like the Vegas heat that wrapped around you like a sauna. Here, the breeze carried just enough relief to keep it comfortable. I was fishing for my keys when I caught the unmistakable scent of cigarette smoke.

"Malik Latimer," a voice called, smooth as honey and sharp underneath.

I turned, jaw tightening. Tamara James leaned against a sedan like she was posing for a photo shoot, cigarette glowing between her fingers.

I shook my head. "Don't think I invited this."

She smiled like we were old friends. "Relax. I just wanted to say congratulations. Big win last night. Vegas looked good on you."

"Appreciate it." My tone was flat. I kept moving toward my SUV.

But she didn't budge. "Indira looked good on your arm, too.

Cameras caught all the right angles. Y'all looked like a headline out there."

My chest tightened, but I kept my face blank. "What's your point?"

Tamara flicked ash onto the pavement, lips curving. "Point is, I know things. Stories folks would eat up—especially about where Indira came from. Depending on how they're told, they could make y'all look picture-perfect... or messy as hell."

I froze, instincts sharp now.

"Sounds like a threat," I said evenly.

She lifted her hands in mock surrender. "Not a threat. Just... an opportunity. For both of us. All I'm saying is don't forget about me. A little help here, a little help there. Make it worth my while to keep quiet."

That was enough. I stepped in close, my voice low, steel in every word. "Stay out of Indy's life unless she asks you in. And stay the hell out of mine. You try selling stories, you won't like how I handle it."

Her eyes narrowed, smile faltering for just a second before snapping back into place. "You've got some fire, Malik. No wonder she can't get enough."

I didn't bite. Just unlocked my SUV, started the engine, and pulled out.

In the rearview, she was still standing there, smiling like she'd just set something in motion.

And I knew she wasn't finished.

I tried to shake off Tamara's ask, but it stuck to me like sweat that wouldn't dry. She wanted money. My teammates wanted a win. The city wanted a championship.

So, I did the only thing I knew—I locked in.

The arena pulsed the second I stepped onto the hardwood. Little

Caesars Arena was packed, the crowd draped in our colors, the roar vibrating through my chest. But it wasn't the fans that had my pulse jumping.

It was her.

Indy. Sitting low in the family section, tucked between Cairo and Zahara, her braids catching the arena lights. After the bathroom mess in Vegas, I half expected her to keep her distance. But here she was, chin high, letting the city see exactly who she was to me.

My chest tightened. I wasn't about to let her regret it.

The first quarter was all speed—trading buckets, fast breaks, scrapping for boards. My body hummed, sharp and alive.

Midway through the second, I drove the lane, planted hard off my left foot, and felt it—a tiny twinge in my knee. Nothing big, nothing that stopped me. Just a whisper, the kind you don't want to hear. I shook it off and finished the layup anyway.

Indy was on her feet, cheering, dimples flashing, and the ache faded.At least for now.

By halftime, we had a small lead. I grabbed a towel, chugged water, and let my eyes wander back to her. Reporters circled, fans shouted, but I only cared about her smile. I gave her a small wave. She shook her head like I was ridiculous, but she smiled wider, and the knot in my chest loosened.

The second half was grind time. Atlanta had been tough in the Conference Finals, but the Rattlers wanted to make us bleed on our home court before we returned toVegas.

I tightened my defense, dished out assists, and hit a couple of daggers from behind the arc. Every time my knee whispered, I ignored it. The scoreboard was louder.

When the final buzzer sounded, we walked out with a win and momentum. The crowd roared, and the city could smell a championship. I slapped hands with teammates, but my eyes went straight to Indy.

She was waiting near the tunnel, Cairo at her side. I jogged over, sweat dripping, adrenaline still pumping. "You came," I murmured when I reached her, low enough only she could hear.

"Of course I did," she said softly, eyes shining. "This is where I want to be."

That was it. Simple. But it felt bigger than any headline or highlight reel.

I pressed a quick kiss to her lips, ignoring the cameras flashing nearby. Let them see. She was mine.

When I finally made my way toward the locker room, I caught a flicker of movement in the shadows by the exit doors. A tall, thin woman in flashy colors hugged the wall, but even in the dim light, I knew who it was.

Tamara.

She didn't step forward. Just stood there, eyes locked, watching. My jaw tightened, but I kept walking. She didn't get to turn this moment into hers.

Chapter Thirty-Eight

INDIRA

Hours later, the noise was still in my head. I should've been thinking about the Fielding houses—demolition started that morning, and Asim had texted me progress photos—but all I could see was Malik on the hardwood, chest heaving, eyes locked on me in the stands like I was the only person in the arena.

I'd told myself basketball was *his* world, not mine. Yet somehow, I'd been in the stands consistently, carving hours out of my schedule, pushing showings and site visits back like it was nothing. Truth was, it mattered. I wasn't used to choosing anything over work.

But tonight? Watching him, feeling twenty thousand people chant for Detroit, seeing his smile when he found me in the crowd...I didn't regret a thing.

By the time we got back to his place, Malik suggested we cook. Spaghetti, of all things.

"You sure you know what you're doing?" I teased, watching him sauté ground beef like he was warming up for a free throw.

He smirked, dimples flashing. "Shortie, I run plays all night. I can handle meat sauce."

It felt good—the two of us shoulder-to-shoulder in the kitchen, steam climbing to the vent while the pot boiled.

Malik drained the pasta, steam rolling up around his face. I leaned

against the counter, glass of wine in hand, pretending not to admire the way his T-shirt clung to his back.

"You're taking this real serious," I said.

"Spaghetti is a classic. Can't mess it up." He plated the noodles, added sauce, and slid a dish my way with a proud grin. "Five-star dining, Bite-Size. No reservations required."

I arched a brow but took a bite. Rich, savory, balanced just right with Italian seasoning. "Okay, Latimer. Not bad."

"Not bad?" He clutched his chest like I'd wounded him. I laughed—the kind that loosened something in me.

We ate side-by-side at the island, shoulders brushing, conversation drifting from game stats to my Fielding project. He listened like every word mattered, nodding when I told him demolition had finally started.

"See? You're building neighborhoods. I'm chasing rings," he said.

"Same grind, just different courts."

It was simple, but the way he said it settled warmly in my chest. We could make this work, as long as we kept our perspective. Highlights were for the arena; beyond the arc, off the court, was where we were writing something real.

When I finished, Malik leaned over and swiped his thumb across my mouth. "Sauce," he murmured, though the grin tugging at his lips had nothing to do with marinara.

I caught his wrist before he could pull away, pulse tripping. The kiss started soft, still flavored with wine and garlic, but the second he slid his hand to the back of my neck, it deepened.

The plates were forgotten. So was everything else. He lifted me onto the counter in one motion, spreading my knees with his large body. My laugh turned into a gasp when his mouth moved to my jaw, then lower.

"Malik…" My fingers tangled in his shirt, pulling him closer.

"Hmm?" He kissed down my throat, his voice a low rumble against my skin. "Told you I could handle sauce."

We stayed tangled, skin slick, breaths ragged, his weight a comfort instead of a burden. He didn't pull away, didn't even shift—just held me like leaving wasn't an option.

Every time he breathed, I felt it—deep—like his rhythm had synced with mine.

When Malik finally lifted his head, brushing a strand of hair from my face, his eyes searched me, softer than I'd ever seen them. "You feel that, baby?"

I smiled, though my voice shook. "Yes."

His thumb skimmed my cheekbone, slow and reverent. "Good. 'Cause I'm not letting this go. Not ever." He pressed his forehead to mine. "I love you, Indy. "

Hearing the words didn't scare me anymore—but I was still working up the nerve to return them.

I pulled him down again, lips finding his, not because I needed more but because I couldn't stop myself. Moments later, as his body slid inside mine and his arms caged me in, the rest of the world fell away.

His heartbeat was steady against mine, and I realized how rare this was—feeling safe, feeling seen. Not just wanted. Chosen.

Chapter Thirty-Nine

MALIK

The night had been long—unrestrained, passionate, healing. Spaghetti plates pushed aside, we'd worked through more than just food. By the time sleep finally claimed us, I'd held her tighter than I ever had, like if I let go, all the progress we'd made would vanish.

When morning came, I wasn't surprised to find the bed empty. I heard the quiet hum of the oven, the faint clink of pans—she was already moving through the day. When I came out of the bedroom, she was tugging at the oven door, barefoot in one of my jerseys that swallowed her whole.

I couldn't help but pause. Braids in a messy bun, freckles fresh, and she was toasting garlic bread like we hadn't just faced my ghosts the night before.

"Smells good," I said, crossing to her.

"I didn't burn anything," she said with a shrug. "Small victories."

"I see, although it's a little early for that, don't you think?"

"Nope. My man put his foot in some spaghetti, and I'm gonna eat it around the clock."

I laughed, approaching her from behind and sliding my arms around her waist. When she leaned into me, I pressed a kiss to the crook of her neck. She smelled good, like lavender and honey, with no competition for the oregano and garlic aroma that floated throughout the kitchen.

"You good?" I asked, nuzzling her soft skin. I expected her to be sore after I'd spent hours invading every inch of her until we were both too exhausted to continue.

She paused before answering. "Not all the way. But better." I nodded against her shoulder. "That's enough for me." We ate in silence, both of us picking at the food more than really eating. Her eyes kept drifting to the time on the microwave. So did mine.

A short time after, when I grabbed my duffel bag, she walked me to the door. No drama. No tears. Just standing there like she was memorizing me again, like she knew what the stakes were and didn't want to waste a second.

"You ready for this?" she asked, her eyes studying mine, searching for truth.

"Yeah. More than ever. Almost there." I leaned down and kissed her slowly. The heat between us ignited the moment her soft lips pressed against mine. My hand slipped beneath the oversized jersey and slid up her back. I wanted to dig my fingers into her ass and press her against me so she knew just how much I wanted her.

This was the hardest part. Road trips were difficult enough with the time zone changes, sleep disruptions, and all that. However, I developed my strategy for dealing with those challenges years ago through meditation and breathing exercises.

But now, I had a whole woman I was leaving behind, who I wanted to be sleeping beside, and that wouldn't be possible. Not this time. I pulled away from her and leaned my forehead against hers.

"You're not letting anybody else take you to dinner while I'm gone, right?"

She rolled her eyes. "Really? You got two minutes to say bye to me, and instead of forcing your tongue down my throat or fingering me real quick, that's what you want to talk about?"

My eyes grew wide. Well damn. I could manage a quick finger-fuck if she wanted me to. Hell, I'd even eat her pussy again and risk missing my flight. I let my duffle bag slide to the floor and was prepared to put in work when she slapped me playfully on the chest.

"I'm not going anywhere but to check on the demos, and then I'm hopping my ass on the first flight heading your way."

"Handle your business, Shortie," I commanded. I kissed her again —this time deeper, longer. The kind of kiss you give when you don't want to leave, but you have to. I made love to her mouth with my lips, as my dick grew stiffer by the second.

I was barely holding on to my restraint, my heart beating so fast I thought it would explode. I had no choice but to pull back from her before I couldn't.

I felt her chest heaving against me when she whispered. "Keep your head clear out there. I want my MVP back in one piece."

"I got you," I said. "I love you."

She didn't say it back. Not out loud. But the way she looked at me —solid, grounded, hers—I felt it anyway.

I headed down the hallway, and she didn't call after me. She just accepted my truth. I walked out, but my heart didn't.

Chapter Forty

The sun was starting to dip, casting a honey-colored light across the kitchen counters. The windows were cracked, letting in a soft breeze that smelled like cut grass and fresh dirt. Detroit summer air was precious—it reminded you that you could make it through Midwest winter or any other troubling season.

Cairo knocked and let herself in. If we were at my place instead of the penthouse, she wouldn't have bothered with that courtesy. A pair of sunglasses perched on her wild curls spilling over her shoulders, and her strappy sandals clicked across the glossy floors. The fact that she wasn't in gym gear told me she had plans. That strapless slip dress gave her away before she even crossed the threshold.

"Hmph. You look cute or whatever," I teased.

"Thanks for your approval," she drawled.

"So, exactly what kind of trouble do you think you're getting into?"

"Oh, it's DC that'll be getting into me," she announced, sticking her hand out for a high five.

I slapped her palm, grinning. "Oh, snap! Talk your shit, CeeCee. I ain't mad at ya."

"You shouldn't be. I'm sure you're getting dicked down far more often than moi." She dropped her tote on the bench, kicked off her shoes, and claimed a seat at the kitchen island.

"I don't know what makes you say that, but…probably!" I stuck my tongue out, reaching for the wine. I didn't tell her how hard it had been to watch Malik walk out that morning with his duffel, leaving me with nothing but the taste of him—and the silence where my *I love you* should've been.

Cairo glanced at the steaming platter of food and licked her lips. "You made pasta and didn't call me? Rude."

"I didn't make it," I sassed, twisting the cap back on the bottle. "Malik did."

"Ah. Bae-chef strikes again." Cairo reached for a plate, piled it high, then showered it with parmesan.

"That's right. Malcolm's not the only one who can burn in the kitchen."

I followed her lead, moaning around the first forkful. "So damn good."

Cairo nodded. "It is. Real good. Might even put Aunt Millie to shame." She tilted her head, eyes sharp with that sister's intuition. "But how about you? You good?"

I sat across from her, legs dangling from the barstool, wine glass in hand. "Better than I should be. He left for Vegas today. Part of me is still at that door with him."

By nightfall, Detroit was behind me. The flight was short, but it felt like crossing worlds.

The suite was gorgeous—floor-to-ceiling windows overlooking the Strip, velvet blackout curtains I hadn't touched, and plush pillows on a bed I wasn't planning to sleep in much. I should've been unpacking or running a hot bath, maybe ordering room service. Instead, I was curled up in the corner of the couch, still in my travel clothes, phone in hand.

I'd already texted Malik to let him know I had landed. He'd be busy with team meetings and walkthroughs, but he still responded instantly.

MALIK: Good. Rest up. Luv you.

My chest pinched. I still hadn't said the words back, not out loud. But maybe he already knew. Maybe my showing up was its own kind of confession.

A knock at the door pulled me upright. I padded across the room and opened it to find hotel staff with a silver ice bucket and a sleek black box tied with a crimson ribbon. Inside: a chilled bottle of my favorite champagne and a note in Malik's messy scrawl.

Don't have too much fun without me, Bite-Size.

I smiled, my heart already lighter than before. Even when he wasn't beside me, he still knew how to show up.

Chapter Forty-One

MALIK

I was stretched out on the bed, headphones on, trying to get in the zone. Film review—done. Shootaround—done. Body stretched, mind clear. Except focus kept slipping.

Coach always said the hours before the game were for centering. Visualization. Locking in. I usually did that better than anyone. But today? It wouldn't hold. I should've known she'd be the reason.

My phone buzzed on the nightstand. I told myself I wouldn't check it. Could've been media. PR. My agent. Didn't matter. I looked anyway.

> BITE-SIZE: Enjoy your meditation, MVP. P.S.
> I only poured one glass. Maybe.

Attached was a mirror selfie from her suite. A cropped jersey, denim mini skirt hugging her thighs. Smooth, toned skin on display. Braids wild, flopping over one eye like she'd just tossed them without trying. A glass of champagne perched in her hand like she'd been born to hold it.

I blew out a breath through my nose, sat straighter. Heart less centered.

Damn.

If it weren't for the rules, I'd be across town with her already. But team rules were clear: players stayed with the team during The Finals. Mandatory. No exceptions. Didn't matter that she was five miles away in a luxury suite—I might as well have been on another planet.

And as much as I wanted to get lost in her, I worried about her. Tamara stayed in the back of my mind. Trouble. Circling already, hinting at selling stories if she didn't get paid off. Indira didn't deserve that kind of stress, not now. Not ever.

I stared at the photo longer than I should've, then typed back:

> ME: If you miss tip-off today, I'm blaming the champagne. And that outfit.

I tossed the phone face down and stood, pacing the room to shake her off—for now. She was like gravity, pulling me in even when I was supposed to be floating above it all.

I exhaled, rolled my shoulders, and forced myself back into the routine. Game time was coming.

I shook out my arms and took one last look in the mirror. Jersey on. Wrist taped. Eyes locked. Ready.

The hallway outside the locker room buzzed with pre-game electricity —squeaking sneakers, staff murmuring plays, cameras already rolling. I blocked it out. This was when everything narrowed. Through the tunnel with the team, nodding at the arena crew, fans screaming behind barricades, one image still lingered in my head.

Her.

Soft eyes. Glowing skin. Braids wild around her face. That blessed glass of champagne in her hand like she'd been born for the courtside throne. She wasn't just watching tonight. She was part of my game plan.

I pulled my earbud out and handed it to an attendant, cracked my knuckles, and stepped onto the hardwood as the lights dimmed and the announcer's voice thundered overhead. Roaring noise.

Blinding lights. A sea of bodies. It all faded once my Kobe 6s kissed the floor.

Then I saw them.

Desmond. Malcolm. My nephews and cousins. My brothers. My day ones. My tribe.

Desmond propped his phone like he was FaceTiming Cairo and Zahara. Malcolm looked ready to suit up himself.

And between them—my peace. Indira. Drop-dead gorgeous. Steady. Certain. The kind of presence that said, *You already won me. Now go finish this game.*

I cracked my neck, bounced twice on the balls of my feet, and let it settle in my chest.

I wasn't playing for the cameras tonight. I was playing for them.

INDIRA

The arena was loud, pulsing with pre-game hype, but I barely heard it. My focus stayed with the energy in our section. Desmond and Malcolm had flown in earlier, along with some of Malik's family. They were posted on each side of me, suited in team colors like honorary bench players. Desmond had Zahara on FaceTime for the warm-ups, while Malcolm was already jawing with a group of Rattler fans two rows up.

It felt good being surrounded. Like we weren't just spectators—we were witnesses. Part of something sacred. I only wished Cairo could've joined us, but she was still wrapping up things before flying east for her interview.

Then Malik emerged from the tunnel like he owned the air in the arena. Broad shoulders. Jaw set. Locked in. The lights hit him, and he didn't blink. Every step was battle-ready. The crowd roared as the announcer called his name, but I couldn't take my eyes off him long enough to cheer.

Just before he stepped fully into the spotlight, he looked up. At me. Not long—just a flicker, a heartbeat—but I felt it slam into my chest. That look said, *I see you; you ground me. Watch me work.*

I crossed my legs slowly, and a smirk tugged at my lips. No wave, no blown kiss. Just a moment held steady. Let him feel me—present, proud. He turned back like nothing had happened. But I knew better. And so did every man in this section who caught it.

"Damn," Desmond muttered, leaning in. "If he plays half as hard as he just looked at you, the Rattlers should call it early."

I rolled my eyes. "You're annoying."

Malcolm shook his head; a smirk ghosted across his mouth. "Man, spare us. At least until after the game."

We laughed, and the tension in my chest eased. Malik had his squad on the court, his tribe in the stands—and in that moment, we were all exactly where we were supposed to be.

I could barely stay seated.

Chapter Forty-Two

Ten minutes in, Malik had already drained two threes, dropped a no-look dime, and ripped down a rebound like it owed him money. He was everywhere—focused, fluid, possessed.

"He's in that zone," Desmond said beside me, eyes narrowed. "That scary one."

"He doesn't even blink," Malcolm added. "Swear it's not normal."

It wasn't. I knew the signs. The set jaw. The squint in his left eye. The way he never celebrated after a bucket—just reset like it was nothing. Like, *of course, it went in.*

I leaned forward, elbows braced on my knees. From here, I could see the way his muscles moved under his jersey—the slight limp he thought no one else noticed. But I did. He was playing through pain. I could feel it in my chest.

And still, he gave everything.

He drove the lane, absorbed a hit, and still finished with his left. The arena exploded. Fans screamed. I clapped with them, but the tightness in my stomach didn't ease.

He'd barely limped back on defense before Jarvis signaled for a timeout. Malik didn't sit. Just stood there, hands on his hips, eyes scanning the court like he was playing chess while the rest were still learning checkers.

"He should sit," I muttered.

Desmond glanced at me. "He won't. Not unless his body gives out first." That was what I was afraid of.

When play resumed, he went right back to slicing through defenders, picking passes, breaking ankles like it was personal. And every time he moved, I caught it: the hesitation, the softer plant on his right foot.

Malcolm leaned forward. "If he keeps pushing like this, it's only a matter of time. "I didn't want to believe it. I wanted to believe in grit. In adrenaline. In Malik Latimer, who always found a way. But even heroes have limits.

MALIK

I dropped onto the bench like I'd been hauling bricks. Sweat ran down my back, jersey clinging. The minute I peeled it off, the pain in my knee spiked, sharp and deep. Didn't let it show. Not more than a breath.

The trainer tossed me a towel and a Gatorade. I nodded, sipped, leaned forward. He gave me that look—the kind that asked without asking. Toradol. A quick shot and the fire would dull, pushed to the background.

I thought about it. Knew it could buy me the half. Knew it wouldn't fix a damn thing. And if I kept pushing, the joint could still give.

Didn't matter. I was finishing this game.

Coach talked plays. Jarvis chimed in. I heard them, but kept quiet.

Needed silence to calculate. My knee wasn't the only thing

screaming. My whole body was cashing every check I'd written all season. But this was legacy work. This was what I lived for.

"Yo." Nasir's voice cut in. "You good?"

I looked up. "I'm Gucci. Let's get it."

He squinted. "You lying."

I smirked. "A little."

He didn't press. Just nudged an extra wrap toward me. "Double it if you need to. Don't lose your handle."

The trainer crouched in front of me, tightening the band around my knee until it felt like armor.

My body was breaking—but my mind wasn't. Neither was my heart.

One more half. One more battle. A championship on the line. A legacy to protect.

And her—my anchor in the chaos. Indira's eyes on me made all of it sharper. She was why I had to finish.

Aomost thirty minutes later, my shot dropped and the building went wild—horns, thundersticks popping, strangers hugging strangers. We'd just sealed the championship. The scoreboard blazed and the noise hit like a bass drop.

Then my knee flared.

Heat flashed behind the kneecap, and my leg buckled. The floor tilted up and caught me. Confetti stuck to my sleeve. The place went up. I wasn't celebrating anymore; I was trying not to move while the world blurred around the pain.

Hands found me—JB first, then Nasir—before the trainers slid in and took over. "Stay still," one said, already talking about stabilizing my knee, and ordering X-rays like my season wasn't still echoing in the rafters.

I forced my breath even and looked past the cameras and the confetti for what—who—I actually needed.

My eyes went straight to her—hand to her chest, locked on me. I held her look and let it steady the shake in my gut. *I'm here. I see you.* I could almost hear her say it.

They cinched the wrap and cleared a path toward the tunnel. I
didn't take my eyes off the section where I'd seen her last.

Security rolled me through the noise that already felt distant.
They rolled the trophy out behind us. I kept my eyes forward. I kept
my focus narrowed—one hallway, one doorway, one person I needed
in the room when the rest of this hit.

"Tell Indy I'm asking for her," I said.

INDIRA

The arena exploded. Fans screamed. Confetti rained. Strangers
hugged like they'd won, too. Malik had just sealed the championship
with one impossible shot.

But something was wrong.

While everyone celebrated, I froze. Watching. Searching. I saw it
—the buckle of his leg, the grimace cutting across his face. He wasn't
celebrating. He was crumpling.

"No," I whispered, then louder. "No, no—Malik!" I shot up, heart
hammering, trying to see over the chaos. Security swarmed the
court. Jarvis ran first, then Nasir. They dropped to their knees beside
him while trainers rushed in.

From behind the barricade, I saw everything and nothing at
once.

Confetti fell. Fans screamed. Malik lay on the floor, pain etched
on his face.

The cameras turned to him.

Then to me.

I dug my nails into my clutch, feet locked, body leaning forward
like sheer will could carry me to him. And then—he searched. His
eyes combed the crowd until they found mine.

Time stopped.

I pressed my hand to my chest so he'd know: *I'm here. I see you.
I'm not going anywhere.*

The celebration blurred. One minute I was gripping the railing, the next I was in the tunnel—walking fast, then running, trying to reach the hallway outside the locker rooms.

Security recognized me. They didn't stop me this time. The crowd noise faded as I rounded the corner, but the pressure in my chest didn't.

I passed team staff, media, and a rep from the league. Everyone buzzed about the win, the shot, the comeback.

No one said what I needed to hear.

Outside the training room, Nasir paced, still in his jersey, sweat soaking his towel. He looked up when he saw me, expression unreadable.

"How bad?" I asked, barely a whisper.

"They're still looking," he said, rubbing his face. "But... it didn't look good."

My heart sank.

Before I could answer, Jarvis appeared with a trainer and a medical staffer, stride tight, eyes sharper than usual.

"Can I see him?" I asked, already bracing.

Jarvis nodded. "They're wrapping him and waiting on a mobile unit for imaging." He paused. "He's asking for you."

That was all I needed.

He led me through a side door the media wouldn't find. Malik was propped on the trainer's table, jersey cut, eyes a little glazed but fixed on the doorway—on me.

I crossed the room in three strides. His hand was already reaching. I grabbed it and held on like I could anchor him just by being there."I'm here," I said, low.

"I know," he murmured, grip tightening. "I saw you." His voice cracked, just barely, and something in me did, too.

"I couldn't get to you," I whispered.

"You did." His thumb brushed my knuckles. "You always do." We didn't say anything else. We didn't need to. There would be time for answers—headlines, questions, MRIs, maybe surgery.

For now? This moment was ours.

Chapter Forty-Three

The silence at home was louder than the crowd had ever been.

No cheers. No interviews. No Malik humming down the hallway or cracking jokes with JB.

Just the soft hum of the fridge, the quiet click of a heating pad cycling off... and the sound of him breathing beside me in fits and starts.

But outside? The world was on fire. Fans celebrated across the country. All eyes were on Detroit, and instead of joy, the headlines were brutal.

"Malik Latimer—fresh off a game-winning shot—has suffered what sources confirm is a torn ACL. The MVP is expected to miss most, if not all, of the next season."

The TV ran it on loop until I couldn't stand it anymore. *First Take* argued about his future. Twitter cut the highlight down to six seconds— Malik's fall on repeat, stripped of everything he'd fought through before it. Instagram had side-by-side photos: one of him crowned in confetti, the other curled on the hardwood. TikTok made it worse—clips spliced with captions like career over?

And the blogs? The whispers? Those cut deepest.

I stopped reading.

Because I already knew the truth. I wasn't leaving. Not when he needed someone to stay.

So I made soup. Microwaved heat pads. Sat beside him while he ignored calls, skipped meals, and stared at old games on his iPad with the sound off.

He hadn't said much since surgery. Slept most of the day. And when he was awake, he carried his silence like another kind of injury. Every time I looked at him, I wondered if he'd already checked out—mentally, emotionally—even though his body was still right there beside me.

A few days after surgery, during one of those long, hushed afternoons, I asked, "You okay?"

He nodded. Didn't look up.

I didn't believe him.

And still... I stayed.

Because I could see what the world couldn't.

The way he flinched when the therapist touched his knee.

The way he blinked at the ceiling like he wanted to disappear.

The way he avoided my touch—not from resentment, but shame.

I didn't know what to do.

But I knew what not to do.

I wouldn't walk away.

And I wouldn't be invisible, either.

Chapter Forty-Four

MALIK

The house was too quiet.

No cheers. No cameras. No hum of a locker room filled with life. Just the faint whir of the fridge, the muted tick of the clock, and the ache pulsing steadily in my knee.

Indira had finally gone to bed an hour ago. She'd spent the whole damn day making sure I had ice, soup, meds—someone to yell at when I needed to vent. But once she closed the bedroom door, the silence swallowed me.

I rolled off the bed and hobbled to the couch, leg propped the way the PT showed me. The cushions sagged like they were tired, too. I should've been exhausted, but sleep wouldn't come.

The pain was constant, but that wasn't the worst part. It was the shame. The image of me crumpling on the hardwood—projected across every screen in America. That was what stuck.

I'd hit the shot. Won the chip. Crowned the city. And instead of raising the trophy, I was carried off the floor like dead weight.

The calls kept buzzing in. Jarvis. Malcolm. Jackie. I ignored them all. Even Desmond. I couldn't face any of them.

Because what would I say? That my body betrayed me? That I

couldn't even walk to the bathroom without feeling like something was tearing inside me? That the guy they called MVP couldn't lift his own damn leg without help?

I tried to stretch. Tried to breathe through it. None of it worked. The shame sat heavier than the pain.

The only sound was the shift of the heating pad as it clicked off. I leaned forward, elbows on my thighs, palms pressed hard to my face. I couldn't look at the walls, couldn't look at my phone, couldn't look at the empty space where Indira usually sat—steady, watching me, keeping me upright when everything else fell sideways.

I wanted her near. Needed her near. But I couldn't stand the thought of her seeing me like this. Not the man who hit the shot. Just the man who fell after it.

I stayed like that until my back ached, the silence pressing down harder than the injury.

And that was the scariest part.

Not the pain.

Not the limp.

Not even the swelling.

It was the silence. The way it felt like a preview of what was waiting if I didn't find a way back.

I hated the sound of my name in her voice.

Soft. Hopeful. Patient. Everything I didn't feel.

Indira stepped into the room like she had every day since the surgery —quiet but certain, holding a plate I didn't want and a presence I didn't deserve.

"Brought you something," she said. "You haven't eaten today."

I nodded. Or maybe I didn't. Couldn't remember anymore.

She set the plate on the nightstand. Chicken stir fry. Warm and spicy. Her signature hint of ginger hit my nose before I even saw it.

"You need fuel if you're gonna handle PT ramping up this week," she said gently, settling into the chair across from the bed.

The air between us tightened. Not from anything she did—just from everything I hadn't.

I stared at the ceiling. "You don't have to keep showing up."

She raised a brow. "You want me to stop?"

"I didn't say that."

"Sounded like it."

I exhaled hard through my nose, jaw clenched. "I'm not who I was, Indy. You know that."

"I know you're healing."

I shook my head. "No. I mean I'm not that man anymore. The one you fell for. The one who carried teams and took the shot. The one who made you laugh and matched your fire. That guy? He died on the court."

She didn't flinch. Didn't look away.

"Then who are you now?"

"I don't know," I whispered. "But you don't want him."

Tears burned the back of my throat, but I swallowed them. I wouldn't cry. Not in front of her. Not when I already felt like a shell of the man she chose.

"I'm not strong right now," I admitted. "I feel… small. Weak. Useless. And the worst part? You're still here. Acting like you didn't notice I broke."

Indira stood slowly. Walked to the edge of the bed. Not angry. Not pitying. Just steady.

"You're right," she said quietly. "You're not the man I fell for."

My chest tightened.

"You're more."

I looked up. Met her eyes.

"Because now you're real," she said softly. "Now you know what it feels like to fall. And I'm still here, not because I didn't notice—but because I did. And because love doesn't clock out when things get ugly."

Heat rushed to my face. My fingers curled into fists, and when I shifted against the pillows, pain spiked sharply through my knee. I hissed under my breath, chest rising fast. I couldn't tell what burned worse—the knee or the way her words scraped at who I am.

"You love me?" My voice cracked, rougher than I intended.

She held my gaze, steady but with a flicker of nerves. "Yeah, Malik. I do."

She paused, swallowing. "And it scares the hell out of me. But it's true."

A laugh broke out of me—half disbelief, half something rawer. My hand shot out before I thought, finding hers, gripping like it was the only thing tethering me here.

"I get being scared," I rasped. "Hell, I'm terrified. Terrified that I can't be enough for you anymore."

"You don't have to carry this for me," she whispered. "We carry it together. That's the point." She stepped back, leaving the plate untouched on the nightstand. "When you're ready to talk like we're still us... I'll be in the study."

And she walked out.

No slammed doors. No tears. No begging.

Just quietly reminding me exactly what I stood to lose by pushing her away.

Chapter Forty-Five

INDIRA

I closed his door softly behind me, pulse still skittering from the words I hadn't planned to say out loud. *Yeah, Malik. I do.*

Not a sweeping confession. Not the way I'd pictured it if I ever let myself daydream. He asked; I answered. Simple. Too simple. He didn't even have to pull it out of me.

But it was still the truth. And now it was out there, heavy and irreversible, circling between us where neither of us could take it back.

I sank into the study chair, staring at the pile of contracts on my desk. Calls I hadn't returned. Clients I'd postponed. Deadlines I'd stretched thin. Normally, I didn't let anything slide. Hustle was my armor. Work was how I proved I'd never need saving.

But I'd slowed down. For him. For us.

The Fielding houses could wait. Commission checks could wait. My phone had been buzzing nonstop, but I let it. Because Malik needed me more than the grind ever had. And for once, I didn't feel guilty about easing off the gas. I felt... certain.

And yet—uneasy. Because the words hadn't spilled out of me in some grand, undeniable rush. They'd come in answer to him, to his breaking point, his need. Was it enough that he asked and I answered? Or would he wonder if I only said it because he cornered me with the question?

I didn't know if he believed me when I told him.

I'd carry his load with him.

But I meant every word.

Chapter Forty-Six

MALIK

It had been a week since Indy's confession.

A week where PT was supposed to ramp up—more pressure, more grind. Instead, I dodged more sessions than I finished. Told myself the knee needed rest. Truth was, I didn't want to face the mirrors, the trainers, the reminders of everything I wasn't anymore.

When Desmond rang the buzzer, the bottle was already half-empty. I saw his face on the camera and ignored it.

I poured two more fingers.

Then Jarvis called, followed by Malcolm. I let their calls go to voicemail. Same with Jackie, my nephews, and Nasir. My godson Jaelen even texted me—all of them in the span of an hour.

I answered none of them.

By the time the front door opened—thanks to the spare key Jarvis wasn't supposed to have—I was slouched on the couch, hoodie pulled low, my glass of whiskey sweating on the side table.

JB stormed in first. Malcolm was right behind him. Jackie trailing, quiet but watchful.

"What the hell is this?" Jarvis demanded, sweeping the bottle off the table.

My lip curled. "Give it back."

"No."

"I wasn't asking."

Malcolm stepped in. "Yo, relax."

"You relax," I snapped. "I didn't invite you."

"You stopped responding. You've skipped PT all week," Malcolm shot back. "You think we're just supposed to sit back and let you drown in here?"

"I said I'm fine."

"You're not fine," Jackie said quietly from the corner. "You haven't *been* fine."

I stood too fast. My leg buckled. Pain shot up my side like fire, forcing me to grip the couch for balance.

"I don't need a damn intervention," I growled. "I need space."

"You need help, Malik," Malcolm said. "You're spiraling."

"I won. I hit the game-winner. I brought this city a title. And what do I get? A blown ACL and pity parties from my family like I'm some damn charity case?"

"These aren't pity parties," Jackie offered.

Jarvis stepped closer. "We're here because we love you. Because we know what this is."

"No, you don't," I snapped. "You don't know what it's like to wake up and realize you're done. Washed. Forgotten."

"I do," Malcolm said. Quiet. Dangerous. "And I didn't burn everyone down on my way out."

That stung.

Malcolm's career ended before it started—drafted, then wrecked by injuries. He'd had to step away, find new purpose. Cooking. Building a different life.

I looked at him—my mirror, my blood—and hated how much truth lived in his eyes.

"Get out," I said.

No one moved.

"Get out!" Louder this time. "All of you!"

Jarvis stared at me like he wanted to say more. But Malcolm tugged his arm. "Let him sit in it," my brother muttered. "Sometimes pain needs silence to echo."

And they left.

The door clicked shut like a verdict.

I was alone—just me, the ache in my leg, the glass in my hand, and the crushing realization that I'd finally succeeded in pushing everyone away.

The first thing I noticed was the taste in my mouth. Bitter. Sour. Regret soaked in whiskey and the afterburn of pride.

The second was the silence. Not the good kind. Not the kind that lets you breathe. This was heavy—pressing down on my chest like punishment.

My tongue felt like sandpaper. My head pounded. My knee throbbed with every shallow breath. But none of it hit harder than the hollow ache in my chest.

I shifted upright slowly, every movement stiff and loud in the quiet. Pain shot through my knee like a warning: *You're not ready*.

But I moved anyway. Limped toward the kitchen on a single crutch. The coffee machine blinked at me—empty. Indira hadn't touched it. The house smelled empty, too.

I opened the fridge. Sports drinks. A half-eaten container of take-out. The soup she'd made three nights ago. I touched it like it might burn me.

I sat at the island, elbows on the counter, staring at the place she usually stood. Her mug was still in the sink. She hadn't left me. But she'd left the room. And kept her distance. That might've hurt more.

My phone was face down on the couch. I picked it up. Missed calls:

– Desmond (2)

– Malcolm (3)

– Cairo (1)

– Jarvis (1)

It wasn't the names listed that gutted me. It was the one missing. No texts. No "You okay?"

No "I'm outside."

No "Want company?"

I hadn't realized how much I'd counted on her quiet presence— until it wasn't there.

I dragged a hand down my face. *What the hell did I say last night?*

Bits and pieces floated back.

Jarvis growling.

Malcolm walking out.

Jackie's look of disappointment.

Me throwing words like knives at people who showed up when I didn't deserve them.

And Indira. I couldn't remember if she was even there… or if she'd said anything.

That scared me.

Because if she didn't say anything… she might be done saying everything.

The knock at the door was soft.

Not impatient. Not aggressive. Just… steady.

I knew it wasn't Indira. She had her own way of entering—like she belonged. This knock was permission-seeking.

I limped to the door, leaning heavily on my crutch before cracking it open.

Mama stood there in a flowing purple maxi dress, her hair pulled back neatly, with a chunky pearl necklace at her throat. She carried a straw tote in one hand and a Tupperware container in the other. Her eyes were calm but sharp, reading me the way only she could.

"Hi, baby."

I stepped aside without a word.

She walked in with the same quiet grace she always had. Not rushing. Not shrinking. Just present. She set the container on the counter, slipped her tote onto a stool, and let her gaze sweep the room.

It looked like hell.

Empty bottles. A forgotten ice pack. Crumpled takeout cartons.

Silence that had thickened into something ugly.

"I brought you some food," she said, opening the lid to let the scent roll out—smoky barbecue with onion and garlic. Her way of speaking, without saying much.

I sat at the island. Said nothing.

She poured water into a glass and slid it toward me. "Your daddy wanted to come," she added. "But I told him I needed a minute with my son."

I looked at her. Finally.

"I'm not dying," I muttered.

She arched a brow. "Didn't say you were."

"I'm just tired."

"You've always been tired after a long season. But this ain't that kind of tired."

I dropped my head into my hands. She waited. Just like she used to when I'd lie about being okay after a bad game in high school.

"I pushed everyone away last night," I said quietly. "Malcolm. Jarvis. Even Jackie."

"And Indira?"

I hesitated. "She must've stayed at her place. She didn't come home."

"That's worse," Mama said. "That's when a woman starts packing up her hope."

The words hit harder than I wanted to admit.

She circled the island and sat beside me, her hand warm and solid over mine.

"I watched the injury live," she said softly. "Watched you go down. And I knew—it wasn't just your body that would need healing."

Guilt clogged my throat.

"But I also know you, Malik," she pressed on. "And I know your strength isn't just in your legs. It's in your heart. And in the people who love you—if you let us in."

I nodded, barely.

She squeezed my hand once, firm. Then stood. "Call your brother," she said. "When you hurt, he hurts too. That's how it's always been."

I watched her grab her tote, the smell of barbecue lingering in the air.

"Don't wait too long, baby," she urged at the door. "You don't want to be alone when you remember how to feel again."

And like that—she was gone.

But her words stayed.

And for the first time in weeks, I wanted to feel something other than numb.

Chapter Forty-Seven

INDIRA

The days blurred after my confession.

I'd told him the words I'd never said to any man, and for a second, I thought they'd landed. That maybe we'd turned a corner. But since then? Silence. Nods instead of conversation. Shrugs instead of answers. Long hours where he let the TV glow against his face, but wouldn't look at me.

So, I eased off—fewer contractor calls, showings pushed. I'd never done that for anyone. Business has always been my armor. I laid it down to make room for us. When he didn't step into that room, the quiet hollowed out. And I went back to what has never failed me: work.

I stacked client calls back-to-back. Walked the Fielding site twice in one afternoon. Rewrote staging notes that didn't need revising. Answered midnight emails I could've ignored. Drove across town for a hardware run I didn't need. Color-corrected mood boards that were already fine. Let Cairo's call go to voicemail because I wasn't ready for the softness in her voice or the questions I couldn't answer. None of it fixed the ache, but the noise kept me upright.

And still—he slipped further away.

When I left the penthouse last night, I told myself it was just for space. Just one night in my own bed to remember who I was outside of being his shadow. But lying awake, I kept replaying the way his voice cracked when he said he wasn't the man I fell for.

The truth was, I believed him. And it scared me that I still loved him anyway.

This morning, I almost went back, plate in hand, words ready to coax him out of whatever dark cave he'd crawled into. Instead, I made myself stay put. Gave him the quiet he claimed to want. Gave myself the quiet I needed to breathe.

Because if I hovered too close, he'd never fight his way back. And if he didn't fight at all... I wasn't sure if love alone could save us.

Chapter Forty-Eight

MALIK

The walk from the parking deck felt like forever—every step a reminder of my injury. The whole way, I second-guessed meeting my brother, but I kept moving. Even with my hand on the doorknob, fear froze me mid-reach.

I took a breath. Then another. I'd come this far; I could see it through. I pushed the door open.

The office was quiet and warm—exposed brick, plants in the corners, a single ceramic mug on the table. I hated it. Not the space —what it meant to be here.

Malcolm was already in the chair, legs stretched out, arms loose like he had nothing to prove. He'd been here before. Not just this office—this aftermath. The identity crisis. The quiet war.

I couldn't meet his eyes.

The therapist, Dr. Esperanza Sanchez, looked about Jackie's age, a calm presence with a silver streak through her hair and cat-eye tortoiseshells. "Please, take a seat," she said, voice smooth as honey. I sat beside my brother.

She didn't rush it. Let the silence work. My gaze bounced from

Doc to Malcolm and back until she finally said, "I'm glad you're both here. Brothers. Athletes. Survivors."

I flinched at that last word. Malcolm didn't.

She turned to him. "Malcolm, do you want to start?"

He nodded, leaning forward. "When I tore my ACL and Achilles in college, I thought I'd bounce back. Even though it's almost unheard of to blow both at once. I was strong. Hungry. I refused to accept the consequences."

He glanced at me, then went on. "When my draft offer got pulled after surgery, therapy, rehab... I had to figure out who I was without the game. That part wasn't pretty."

My throat tightened.

"I spent two years pretending I didn't care," he said. "Told everyone I'd always wanted to coach. Truth? I hated the bench. Hated being the guy people used to talk about. And I hated watching you win while I sat still."

My head snapped up. "You hated me?"

"No," Malcolm said softly. "I envied you. Then I resented you. Then I had to forgive myself for not being you."

So much for twin telepathy. How did I miss that? All these years...

Dr. Sanchez cut in gently. "Malik, how do you feel hearing that?"

"Honestly? I had no idea Malcolm felt like this."

"About which part?"

I rubbed my scalp. "Okay—scratch that. Malc, I knew you hated not playing." I turned to him. "I didn't know you resented me for still being on the floor."

"I'm not trying to make you feel bad," he said, leaning in. "I learned to live with it."

"Then why tell me now? I've got enough on my plate."

"Because I relate more than you think," he said. "I wish I'd talked back then instead of bottling it."

"I know I can talk to you."

"But you don't," Malc said. "Doc can help."

Dr. Sanchez looked to me. "Malik, what are you carrying right now?"

"I feel like a ghost," I said. "Empty. Like everything that defined me got stolen—and I'm not even sure I want it back."

Malcolm nodded. "That's grief."

I let it land.

"I never mourned the game," I admitted. "I just won it. Over and over. Now I don't know how to exist without applause."

"That's the lie," Malcolm said, closer now. "Celebrity tells you your value is your stats. Seeing yourself without the lights? That's more."

"You survived without the lights," I said.

"I did," he said. "You will too. Just not alone. Don't make my mistake."

The room shrank—or maybe I was finally filling it out. "Think Indy's going to wait while I figure this out?"

"She already is," he said. "She just needs to see you trying."

"I'm tired, bruh."

"I know," he said. "Healing isn't reclaiming what you lost. It's deciding who you are now."

I stared at my phone for ten minutes before I picked it up. No script.

No speech. Just a need I couldn't name. I wanted to hear her voice—and I wasn't sure she'd answer.

I pressed her name.

One ring. Two. Three.

Voicemail. Professional Indy. "Hi, this is Indira James. Leave a message or send a text, and I'll respond at my earliest convenience. Thanks!"

I hung up. Thought about calling again. Didn't. Opened our thread instead—cold since the injury. We should've been to

Santorini and back by now, tans fading, memories soft around the edges. The post-championship dream trip—gone like the rest of my plans.

> ME: Hey Bite-Size

> BITE-SIZE: You need something?

> ME: Nope, Just checking in.

When she didn't respond, I knew I had more work to do. The next day, I texted again.

> ME: I'm sorry. For disappearing. For pushing. For not knowing how to ask you to stay.

I hovered, deleted. Typed:

> ME: You free to talk?

I watched the screen like it owed me something. Three dots. Gone. Three dots again. And then finally:

> BITE-SIZE: I'm listening.

Those two words were enough. It felt like air after drowning. I opened my notes app. Typed what I couldn't send and then settled on a more candid message.

> ME: I miss you. Feels empty without you.

No reply came. Not right away. But Indy showed up the next day, and I knew she'd heard me.

She didn't make it a thing. She just stepped back into my space like she'd never left. She didn't talk basketball. She whipped out a fresh pack of resistance bands, looped one around my foot, and counted reps in that low, steady voice she used when she didn't want me to hear her nervousness.

On the fifth stretch, I winced, swallowed a curse, and let my head fall back.

"You good?" she asked, dabbing my forehead with a cool cloth. "I'm trying."

"Okay," she said.

No pep talk. It somehow meant more.

She didn't hover. Didn't fix me. She folded laundry in the next room while I grunted through the rest. Filled the quiet with updates on her latest flip—a two-family brick with busted plumbing and seventies wallpaper.

"There's this green carpet," she said, laughing. "It smells like regrets and wet dog."

A small laugh escaped me—first real one in weeks. She didn't make it a moment. She kept folding.

That night, I hobbled into the living room for water, easing the crutch past the rug.

She didn't see me. Curled on the couch, one leg tucked under, tank top sliding off one shoulder. The TV cast a soft blue across her face. I started to speak—then saw what she was watching. Game 5. Me at my peak.

She wasn't watching like a fan. No wide-eyed gasps. Just a small, knowing half-smile. A beat before I jabbed left on screen, her chin tipped like she felt it.

When I rose for the pull-up three, her fingers tapped the cushion three times; when I whipped the no-look to Jarvis, she said his name a second early. "Jarvis."

At the line—sweat, chest heaving, eyes up—she leaned in, voice barely above the TV's hum. "The Malik I know wouldn't let an injury bench him for long. He'd grit his teeth, get up, and find a way back."

She didn't know I was there. I heard her anyway. And something in my chest cracked—not loud. A quiet splinter, the soft crack of thinning ice.

I didn't say anything then. Didn't let her know I'd heard. But I slept—for the first time in days.

In the morning, I showed up early. Asked my trainer to push the flexion. Took the extra set when he offered it. Let the tape bite a little while he wrapped me fresh.

When I stepped out of PT, day three of the heat wave hit me in the face. I just wanted to get in the SUV and let the A/C hit. Slade peeled off the wall and fell in a half step to my right, quiet as a shadow, eyes sweeping the lot.

"Ride's at the curb," he murmured. We headed that way. Before I answered, I spotted Tamara. Yellow dress bright as a highlighter, lipstick loud enough to make headlines—guaranteed I'd see her.

She smiled like we were old friends. "Congratulations on the championship, Mr. MVP."

I kept moving. I was sore, and it was too hot for her shenanigans. "You've been told not to approach me."

She stepped out of the shade, smile thinning. "You've been ignoring my messages." Her voice was sweet; the edge underneath was sharp enough to cut. "I told you: I've got stories about your little realtor. One call and your week's a shit show."

Slade shifted. I didn't stop until we were a couple of car lengths from the SUV. It idled at the curb, low and steady, heat shimmering off the asphalt. Then I faced her.

"You stood outside The Sisters' house. You made a scene at church. You popped up at games. That was your last shot, Tamara." I didn't raise my voice. I just squared to her, let the silence sit. "You're out of chances."

Her eyes flicked to the wrap under my shorts. "Shame if the wrong narrative got out. The Shade Room loves a bite. Pretty girl like Indira... people would eat the right story up."

My jaw set. "You don't care about headlines. You care about cash. You weren't there for her—you don't get to eat off her name now."

"I care about what I'm owed."

"I don't owe you shit. And Indy damn sure doesn't."

"No parking lot deals," I said. "You're on a dozen cameras; this is private property. You approach Indy or me again, I file. That's your notice."

She tilted her head. "Then where do we negotiate?"

"Blaise Harrington will contact you. He'll send an NDA. You sign, you get a one-time wire. You break it, you meet my attorneys in court. Don't sign, you get nothing—and still meet my attorneys. Different reason."

She stepped closer, perfume hitting sweet and loud. "Indira's not who you think," she said, testing for a flinch. "I could make people look at her different."

"Try it," I said evenly. "You will not make a career out of threatening her. Or me. And don't mistake manners for mercy. You drag me into the gutter, I don't wrestle—I end it."

We held our ground while the SUV idled at the curb, its hum the only thing moving in the tight, careful silence. Then her smile went all teeth. "Tell Blaise to find me."

"He already has your new number," I said. "And Tamara—don't come here again."

Slade opened my door. I got in. She watched me intensely. As the SUV rolled, I saw her in the side mirror—still, the heavy summer air closing back around her.

"Want me to sit on her for a few days?" Slade asked. "No. I want it on paper—NDA, the whole thing."

"A'ight. I'll loop Blaise."

Once Indy moved back into my space, our days fell into place. I worshiped her at night, slow and deep; at dawn, I woke her with my mouth and slid between those thighs like they were oxygen. Then I showered, made her latte, and headed to my trainer while she started her grind.

A few days later, I went straight from training to Blaise's office. I'd been to that building a dozen times this year, but since the championship, I'd been laying low—no fanfare, no autographs.

I wanted this Tamara mess dead so I could go home to Indy. That's why Slade routed us through the service entrance and the freight elevator.

After check-in, we hit the conference room, where Blaise had already had the pleasure of meeting the fashionable, yet conniving, Tamara Elle James.

Blaise slid the packet across the table, every tab flagged, every clause sharpened. "Mutual non-disparagement. Non-disclosure. No-contact. Liquidated damages on breach. Injunctive relief pre-agreed. Wire queued upon signature. Last page certifies she understands without counsel."

Tamara sat across from me in a watermelon-pink sundress, sunglasses on indoors. "How much?" she asked, already reaching for the pen.

"Enough to make this the last time we speak," I said. "Not a penny more."

No attorney at her side. She skimmed—badly—then signed with a flourish. Blaise checked each line, nodded to the paralegal. Keys clicked. "Wire sent," the paralegal said.

Tamara leaned back, syrupy smile. "You're very generous when you want to be."

"I'm very clear," I said. "You contact me, Indy, or anyone in my family again—you violate paragraph six. You say our names into a microphone—paragraph three. You sell a rumor or make one up— paragraph four. We will enforce every line."

Something flickered behind the glasses—annoyance, maybe respect.

She stood, chair legs whispering against the carpet. "Heal up, Mr. MVP."

"I plan to," I said. "Without you in my way."

Blaise walked her out, then handed me the countersigned copy in a tidy folder.

"One and done," he said.

"Make sure security has her photo," I told him, tucking the folder under my arm. "If she gets cute, I want it logged before she hits the sidewalk."

"Already done." He paused. "You good?"

I thought of Indy's laugh in my kitchen, the way her eyes go soft when she isn't bracing for impact. "Yeah," I said. "I'm good."

On the ride home, the weight lifted. Boundaries set. Noise handled.

And the only story I planned to feed was ours.

Chapter Forty-Nine

INDIRA

I found him in the kitchen after midnight.

One sock on, one off. Sweatpants slung low on his hips. A beard was starting to shadow his jaw. His T-shirt pulled tight across his shoulders.

He poured a glass of milk with both hands, as if precision mattered. I leaned against the doorway, arms crossed, heart steady but soft. "I thought you were asleep," he said.

He set the glass down. "I saw Blaise today."

My arms folded tighter. "And?"

"She signed. Mutual NDA. No-contact. The paralegal pushed the button—wire's sent. It's done."

Something in me unclenched. "Thanks for having my back."

"Always," he said, eyes steady.

I pushed off the doorframe and crossed the cool tile until I was in his space. I set my palm to his chest. "And I'm glad I have you back." I rose onto my toes and kissed his chin. "You've been hiding from me," I whispered.

Malik paused. He didn't argue. The silence between us wasn't sharp anymore. It had softened these last few days, but it still carried weight.

I stepped back, padded to the island, and sat across from him.

"I see you, Malik. You've been letting me in again," I said. "Little by little."

He looked up—eyes tired, but clearer than before.

"I didn't know how to say it," he said.

"Say what?"

"That I was scared you'd stop loving me when I stopped winning."

I swallowed. "Malik..."

He lifted a hand—not to stop me, just to get through it.

"I know that's not who you are. I know you didn't fall for the MVP, or the stats, or the name on my back. But I did."

"I don't understand."

"I needed him. That version of me. Because I didn't know who I was without him. When he got taken away, I panicked. I treated you like an audience I didn't want to disappoint. Or worse—like a mirror I couldn't face."

I let that sit.

"Do you know why I stayed?" I asked.

He shook his head slowly.

"Because you broke in front of me," I said. "And that takes more courage than pretending you're fine."

His jaw flexed.

"I never needed perfect," I continued. "I needed honesty. I needed presence. I needed you. And I'm finally starting to see him again."

He leaned on the counter, pressing a palm to his chest. "I want to be better for you," he whispered.

"No," I said, circling the island to stand in front of him. "Be better for *you*. I'll meet you there."

He pulled me in—slow, unsure, as if asking, "Is it still okay to hold you like this?"

I answered by melting into him. And for the first time since the injury, he kissed my forehead. Not out of habit or to prove anything. Just because it was real again.

I nudged my sunglasses into place—indoors or not, I needed them. Between the flashing cameras, blinding reflector panels, and the stage lights, the studio felt hotter than any arena I'd ever stepped foot in.

But it wasn't the heat that had me breathless.

It was him.

Malik stood in the center of the set wearing a slate gray tracksuit with VALET x MALICE stitched across the chest in metallic embroidery. Clean. Bold. Powerful. The pants were tapered, hitting right above his high-top sneakers, and just beneath the fabric, the outline of his compression brace was still faintly visible on his left knee.

He wasn't hiding it anymore. And that alone nearly brought tears to my eyes.

He moved like he'd never been broken. Chin high. Shoulders back. Legs steady. Every frame snapped by the photographer told the story he'd worked so hard to reclaim—that he was still that guy. Still the one people watched. Followed. Believed in.

"Let's get a crouch pose near the wall," the creative director called out. Malik dipped low, bracing himself against the edge of the set. It wasn't the full squat he used to drop into with ease, but it was solid. Controlled. His gaze locked into the camera like he had something to prove. And he did.

He caught my eye between takes and smirked, subtle and smooth. I felt it all the way down to my ankles.

The same man who couldn't get out of bed a month ago now stood in front of a room full of creatives, stylists, and corporate execs like he owned the damn place. Because he did. Valet wasn't just cutting him a check— they were naming a capsule after him. A full line built around recovery, resilience, and rise.

"He's a natural," Desmond said, coming up beside me, arms folded across his chest.

"I know," I said, not looking away.

Desmond chuckled. "I remember when we pitched the collab. Told Malik I wanted someone who could represent more than just game stats. Somebody who could show people what perseverance looked like."

"And you got him."

Desmond nodded. "Yeah, I did."

The cameras kept clicking, and Malik shifted into another pose— this time standing, one leg slightly turned to show the brace detail beneath the fabric, chin tilted like he was daring the world to challenge his comeback.

He wasn't just showing off for the brand. He was showing up for himself.

And I'd never been prouder to witness it.

Sunlight poured through the blinds, warming the edge of the comforter and tracing a golden path across Malik's skin.

He was still asleep, sprawled across disheveled sheets with one arm flung over my waist, his carved chest rising and falling in that slow, deep rhythm I'd come to love. Finally, peaceful and unbothered.

I rested my tiny hand over his larger one, taking a moment to soak it in.

Not just the quiet, but everything it meant.

Yesterday's Valet shoot had left him glowing. Not from the camera
flashes or the buzz around the capsule line—but from something

more profound. From proving to himself that he hadn't lost every-thing. That he could still show up for himself and command a room even if his game was on pause.

He'd been walking taller when we left the studio. And not just because of the brace hidden under his pants.

Last night, he came home, wrapped his arms around me, and said,

"Thank you." No fanfare. No performative moment. Just a quiet, heartfelt whisper while we stood in the kitchen barefoot and exhausted.

"Thank you for not giving up on me, Shortie." Not only did he not give up on me, but he also went to bat for me. I didn't cry. But it was close—the good kind, the I-made-it-through kind.

Chapter Fifty

INDIRA

The street outside flared white-hot as we pulled in. The Dolby Theatre burned like a star, and Malik's hand on my thigh was the only thing grounding me. He sat beside me in silence, his fingers tracing slow circles as if he could draw confidence into me.

"You breathing?" he asked softly.

"Barely," I whispered, watching the barricades slide by. The Dolby loomed—massive, glowing, ringed by a sea of photographers and screaming fans.

He adjusted his cufflink. "You don't have to prove anything to them, Indy."

"I know."

"You just have to show up."

He'd done carpets before, but hosting the ESPYs was new. He was steady for me; I was steady for him.

The SUV door opened. Malik stepped out first, and the crowd reacted like he was the main event—which, in a lot of ways, he was. A wave of noise rolled toward us. Cheers. Applause. Flashbulbs exploded like fireworks—like royalty had just arrived.

I hadn't pictured it like this. So many cameras. This many lights. Thousands of eyes.

Then it was my turn. My stomach dipped—then steadied. *Showtime.*

I gripped his hand like it was the only solid thing in the world. And when I stepped out, the volume rose again.

I used to dream of red carpets. Not like this, though. There's the red carpet, and then there's *the red carpet at the ESPYs.* The difference? This one shimmered under the spotlights, like it had been dusted with diamonds. Or maybe that was just my heart pounding in my ears, insisting this wasn't a dream.

Malik squeezed my hand gently. A silent reminder: *You got this.*

I glanced at him beneath my dramatic lashes, and damn, he looked obscenely sexy. A cropped black blazer hit just above his waist, razor-tailored. Clean, structured shoulders hugged his frame. Black silk lapels contrasted against a crisp white shirt open at the collar. No tie. His trousers were tapered just enough at the ankle to show off his high-shine patent loafers. The walk was still smooth, the limp barely a whisper.

He owned the moment—but somehow, he looked at me like I owned it, too. My stylist vetoed white; I trusted her. I'd spent weeks working the fit, the details, the moment.

We landed on a shimmery crimson silk—liquid, with sheer mesh cutouts and a thigh-high slit that meant business. Gold straps kissed my shoulders; my pixie cut showed off the David Yurman drop earrings Malik surprised me with that morning.

The fabric twinkled with every step— like a quiet blaze in silk.

"You good?" he asked low, almost like a secret, as we took our first step forward.

I nodded, swallowing the lump in my throat. "You?"

"Always," he flashed a charming smile. "But tonight... we're gonna break the internet."

My gold stilettos gave me four inches of confidence I didn't know I needed. The carpet under my heels was softer than expected, plush and surreal—like walking on a velvet wire. Spotlights tracked our every move, the heat from them kissing my shoulders.

I could smell perfume in the air—expensive, aggressive. Something powdery and floral swept past as a woman in a gold Elie Saab gown glided by, trailing paparazzi like a royal procession.

I clocked every look as we passed—silver chainmail Versace, sculpted metallic Balmain, liquid lamé in rose gold. It felt like living inside a fashion editorial.

But people were looking *at us.*

"Malik! Indira!" someone from *Entertainment Tonight* called. "You look incredible—can we get a few words?"

We paused. Malik glanced at me like, "You want this?"

I nodded. "Let's do it."

The interviewer beamed. "Malik—welcome back! How does it feel to be hosting tonight?"

"It's an honor," he said smoothly. "I've been on this stage for other reasons, but this time, I'm here with a new perspective."

"And Indira, you are stunning tonight. Who are you wearing?"

"Custom from a Detroit designer named Paige Bryce," I reported, voice steady. "Styled by Tori. And David Yurman, of course."

Cameras flashed again. The next interviewer's smile was sharper.

"Malik, some critics wondered if you'd step away from the spotlight permanently after the injury. Was tonight your way of shutting that down?"

His jaw flexed just slightly. "I took time off to heal—physically and emotionally," he answered evenly. "Tonight isn't about shutting anyone down. It's about showing up fully."

He glanced at me again. "For the people who never left."

My throat went tight. I gripped his hand harder.

We moved along the red carpet buzzing with glamour and history. Celebrities, athletes, actors, influencers—I saw them all—or I thought I did, until I realized half of then were looking back at us. Not the *who's she with him* kind of look, but the *she belongs here* kind.

I straightened my shoulders and let them look.

"Malik and Indira!" someone shouted. "Power couple!"

I blinked under the lights. This was the moment.

We climbed the final steps toward the Dolby doors. Just before we went inside, I looked back—cameras still flashing, names still being called. Dresses. Suits. Sequins. Energy.

I reached for his hand again. Not for balance. Not out of nerves. Just because I could.

"Indira!" I heard again. I turned. Serena Williams waved us over — flawless in black velvet with a high slit, diamond cuffs sparking like strobe lights. "Good to see you again," Serena said, like the quick intro during the Finals had been enough to remember me.

"I've been rooting for y'all," she said, pulling me into a quick hug. "And Malik, glad to see you back out here. Y'all are giving legacy. Can I get a selfie?"

"Only if you tag me," I said, grinning.

She laughed, raised her phone, and we leaned in. Click. Click. My head spun.

Afterward, Malik bent to my ear. "You handled that like a pro."

"Serena Williams just asked me for a selfie," I whispered. "What world am I living in?"

"Mine," he said. "Now yours, too."

The applause was thunderous—almost too loud. I stayed seated, spine straight, hands folded in my lap, trying not to fidget. The lights bathed Malik in gold, and for a moment he just stood there—still, steady—letting it wash over him.

The crowd was on its feet—players, coaches, analysts, celebrities. I spotted Blaise, Desmond, Cairo, Jarvis, and Twinna in the front row. But Malik wasn't looking at them.

He was looking at me.

I felt it before I saw it—that pull, that focus, like I was the only person in the room. Under the lights, his eyes settled on me, and the noise fell away. I was steady. Ready.

He exhaled.

"I appreciate the love," he said into the mic. His voice was smooth. "Hosting tonight is a huge honor, but let's be real—I didn't want to be here."

Laughter rippled. Cameras zoomed in.

"I spent a long time thinking the game was all I had. That if I wasn't on the court, I wasn't anybody. I let my identity live and die by the box score. So when my body gave out—when the season ended and the noise stopped—I didn't know what to do with myself."

My chest tightened.

"I thought I let my fans down. And worse, I thought she deserved someone whole. But I learned that healing doesn't mean hiding the broken parts. It means letting someone help you carry them."

He found me again.

I didn't move. I didn't need to. My eyes told him everything. "She stayed," he said. "Even when I gave her every excuse to walk.

She stayed. And that changed everything."

The room went silent.

I could hear my heartbeat. One beat. Two.

"I may not know what my future looks like in basketball," he said, "but I know who I want beside me."

He stepped down from the stage. My hand flew to my mouth.Was this happening? Was this now?

"Indira Lynn James," he said, voice steady, eyes locked on mine, "you're the best thing that ever happened to me. I don't want another season, another headline, another anything if it doesn't include you.

"Malik..." I whispered.

The entire room held its breath.

"Will you marry me?"

I laughed through a sob, eyes blurred, lips trembling. "Of course I will."

He slid the ring onto my finger and pulled me in. I kissed him like the world wasn't watching. If it was, I didn't care.

Until now, he'd thought the world needed to see him win. Turns out, he just needed me to see him. Beyond the arc, off the court, beyond the noise—the rest would be ours to build.

Afterword

I hope you enjoyed reading ***Beyond the Arc.*** Please consider leaving a review on Amazon or Goodreads.

I would love to hear from you. Join my squad to receive my newsletter, bonus content, sneak peeks, and giveaways.

Website:
https://www.monetsimone.com
Like me on Facebook:
https://www.facebook.com/monet.simone.2025/
Follow me on Instagram:
https://www.instagram.com/monetsimone.writes